HYDE PLACE

A NOVEL BY

Virginia Coffman

ARBOR HOUSE

NEW YORK

For my sister Donnie,
who was also born at old 379,
and for my brother-in-law, Johnny Micciche,
San Franciscan by adoption

ONE

FEW PLACES IN LIFE seem to improve over one's childhood memory of them. But San Francisco was an exception. As I carried my carpetbag from the transcontinental train to the ferryboat's open deck, I found myself behind a dozen homecoming soldiers still in their khaki puttees and trench caps. Beyond them I glimpsed the skyline of the city across the Bay, looking like a fantasy silhouette, and I was sure things would be better this time.

Thirteen years had passed since that other April day in 1906 when Father and I passed through the rubble-strewn Ferry Building and leaped onto a great, flat gangplank which was already rising beneath our feet. As the Oakland ferryboat carried us across the Bay to safety, our much-loved, much-feared port, which seafaring men all over the world called *THE CITY*, began to burn.

Now, on the afternoon of my return four months after the Armistice, I had a moment's shocked sensation that history was repeating itself. San Francisco seemed again on fire. But the train had arrived late and that gaudy, burning light behind the Golden Gate proved to be the sunset. I suspected my uneasiness was due to my conscience, which troubled me because I was here less than a month after Father's funeral. His last advice to me had been to avoid San Francisco and let his lawyers sell the old Hyde Place property where I was born. Yet I had chosen the excuse of this small property sale to make the San Francisco trip for a reason he would never have approved, and I badly needed the enthusiasm provided by this first distant sight of my native city in thirteen years.

I assured myself that the modern streets of 1919 would be different from those alleys I had seen upon occasion when I was a child. Poverty-stricken and depressing by day, foggy and sinister by night, they were the streets that swallowed up my mother long ago, those streets plus the whiskey and dancehall lights she could not resist.

At the rail of the ferryboat's open deck I studied that hilly skyline and remembered the dream which had haunted me as a child: a dream of my mother—just beyond my reach in one of those strange, shadowed streets, calling to me.

"Mery! Merideth, honey? Wait for me."

I used to wake up in tears and if Father was not at his work, singing popular songs in the small Opera House of Virginia City, Nevada, he would hurry into my bedroom and joke and tease with me until the haunting sadness of the dream faded. To the very last day of his life Father insisted Mother was dead, although he did not really know this to be true. But such a dreamy, romantic man would prefer to think of her as dead in the earthquake or its aftermath, the fire, so that Polly Hyde's pert, unforgettable face could not show him what those years had done to it.

With the passing of time the nightmare dream had vanished. But not the memory. Was she still over there in San Francisco, somewhere in those canyon streets, calling to me in her misery: "Mery . . . wait for me?"

"And you call *me* sentimental!" Father complained to me once when I described the dream in detail. I know he remembered her quite differently, the way her pretty face seemed to swell up and her mouth get ugly and her language with it when she'd gotten hold of a bottle of whiskey. She even drank gin. Anything with alcohol. But not all the time, only now and then after she and Father had quarreled. Other times she was a delightful, gay and amusing companion. People couldn't help loving Polly Hyde.

My mother, who had left us just after my fifth birthday, was the only subject on which Father had been implacable. He possessed the qualities of charm, good looks and manners, but gumption had been left out of him, so he went through life making people happy for the moment but never really putting his mark on the world as he had expected to. When he died of tuberculosis in March of 1919, while the rest of the world was threatened by the dreaded Spanish Influenza, it was amazing how many Nevadans appeared at the funeral of the man whose only claim to fame was that he had sung the old Illustrated Song Slides during the boom day of Goldfield and Tonopah.

As the white, plump-sided ferryboat headed out into the Bay, I tried not to think of that wide expanse of choppy water around us. All my life I had known that fear of certain confined waters —in pools or tanks. Now I felt that the Bay was something quite different, not hideous and terrifying, but vast, splendid and free. I had more immediate worries, anyway. I realized I would be arriving in San Francisco an hour or so after Father's lawyers, Cafferetto and Brubick, had closed their offices. It was the one problem I hadn't considered. I'd counted on them to advise me about a respectable cheap hotel or rooming house in which I could stay for the next few nights.

All my old childhood fears came briefly to the fore. I saw myself wandering the same alleys Father had wandered before the Fire, when he trailed Polly Hyde to Spider Kelly's or the Thalia or some other Barbary Coast dive, never quite catching up with her. But everyone said San Francisco was very different, very modern, these days. The Barbary Coast, the frightful if fascinating old Chinatown alleys full of misery, the opium dens—all that part of the city had been wiped out in the fire, and whatever replaced it was probably more respectable than our own main street in Virginia City. I was eighteen years old now and grown up. It was absurd to connect that beautiful city across the Bay with the painful memories of a child.

Led by tantalizing glimpses that I caught before we rounded the white-chalked rocks at the base of Yerba Buena Island, I decided to watch our approach from the forward end of the boat. Someone had left the nearest door open a foot or two and I squeezed through with my carpetbag, smoothing my tangled, windblown hair with my free hand.

I felt self-conscious about my long, unfashionable light-chestnut hair, seeing that almost every woman on the train had bobbed hers. I should at least have worn mine done up in buns over my ears, like the girls I saw when I caught the train at Reno. But my clothes were out of fashion too. Father loathed mourning clothes, so today I was wearing his favorite outfit instead of black. I had worn this shirtwaist or one like it, as well as the too-long blue skirt and matching blue coat to college at Reno more than a year ago. Though blue was my best color, my dream was to look sophisticated like my favorite movie star, Elsie Ferguson. It seemed a forlorn hope, though. The Reno station agent this very morning had said I looked "sweet." Ugh! No Elsie Ferguson about that!

In the boat's sheltered interior, sailors, Marines, Red Cross nurses, men in all the uniforms of the American Expeditionary Forces filled the long, varnished benches. Most of them joked among themselves. They paid little attention to us civilians, but as I passed along the wide right aisle, feeling the throb of the engines under my feet, I noticed that some of the soldiers began to stand up on the benches, turning and looking west through the forward windows, pointing out various familiar landmarks on the San Francisco skyline, such as the Ferry Building and Coit Tower.

I passed a nurse whose smile was a warm contradiction to her nunlike headdress with its small red cross on the forehead, and I thought of Father, who would never know whether the much-disputed Armistice in Europe was going to be broken. Every day until a week before he died I had read to him about the progress of the peace talks. Only this morning the newspapers had claimed that "the Allies would advance farther into Germany if the foe spurned the peace terms." And the Armistice had been signed five months ago! I wondered what these khaki-clad men thought about the possible renewal of fighting on the Western Front. With what bitterness they must read those headlines!

A little flushed as I passed them, and conscious of their eyes following my movements, I went directly to the forward door. I was just trying to slide the heavy door open when I got a terrific shock. Peering in at me through the glass was a creature with no face below the staring eyes.

The door was pushed open and I realized the faceless thing was a stout man wearing a white gauze flu mask over the lower half of his face. His presence reminded me that the Spanish Influenza had been literally far more deadly than the war itself. I slipped out past him onto the forward deck and leaned against the rail, tasting the salt air as I concentrated on what actions I should take once I reached San Francisco.

I was particularly pleased to find I was not afraid of the Bay spread out before me. I could never recall any disaster connected with a swimming tank that had involved me, and Father had claimed not to know of one. Perhaps if I studied the much more dangerous waters of the Bay I would rid myself of the other fear once and for all.

Meanwhile, there was this late arrival to account for. I must find the offices of Cafferetto and Brubick in the hope that at least one of the partners was working late. Even more important, they might have received some replies to the advertisement they had run at my instruction. I shivered in the brisk wind sweeping in from the Golden Gate. And at the prospect of hearing about my mother?

I could see her now in my mind's eye. Polly Hyde's face with its crinkling eyes when she smiled. And her wide-mouthed smile itself. . . . The perfume she used that reminded me of a morning when we hiked up the hill beyond the Hyde Place house and picked blue lupine and the wind made the grass all slant in one direction. Even today whenever I caught a whiff of the same light, flowery perfume, I remembered Mother and that day on the hill. And yet she had left us, with these few cold words in a hastily scrawled note:

15

"I wasn't meant to be a mama, much less the wife of a second-rate singer. I've my own life to live and without being forever nagged about my drinking. I do love the kid. Take care of her."

In my handbag was the clipping I had torn out of a three-day-old copy of the San Francisco *Examiner*. It was my own advertisement that I had dictated over the telephone to Mr. Brubick. I took it out and reread it, holding it tight as the torn paper fluttered in the breeze.

"ANYONE WITH PROOF OF THE WHEREABOUTS OF PATRICIA (POLLY) HYDE, BORN APRIL 5, 1877, IN VIRGINIA CITY, NEVADA, TO JETHROW AND ARABEL MERIDETH, NOW DECEASED, PLEASE CONTACT THE FIRM OF CAFFERETTO AND BRUBICK AT THE MONARCH BUILDING, MARKET STREET, DOUGLAS 5340."

The strain of uncertainty I was now under, added to those last hopeless days of my father's life, seemed to have finally caught up with me. My head ached as though a hot thread had been sewn across my forehead, and it was difficult to concentrate on even the few words in the ad. I folded the clipping between my finger and thumb and slipped it into my open handbag, but the wind whirled around the deck and carried the clipping off into the evening sky. It floated out over the churning waters and dropped into the trough of a wave. Seconds later a seagull dove down to the paper, stabbed at it with its powerful beak, then flew away, screeching protest at the swindle.

The wind felt comforting on my cheeks, which were unexpectedly hot. I had wanted to save the clipping and was disappointed to lose it, though no doubt I could get a copy from Mr. Brubick. Then I realized it wasn't the loss of the torn bit of paper I regretted so much as the depressing thought that this was a sign, an omen that I had perhaps lost my last hope of finding my mother, or at the least of finding out what had happened to her.

One day while I was going to college in Reno I had looked up the lists of the known dead from the earthquake and fire in the very old Bay area papers. I hadn't found the name Polly

Hyde, but thirteen years had gone by since those papers were printed. How easily she might have died during that period without my knowing it. I couldn't very well look through the daily death notices of thirteen years. The only hint that she wasn't dead came in answer to a letter I secretly wrote to the hall of records in San Francisco when I was fifteen. They said their only record of anyone by that name was the birth of a daughter Merideth in 1901 to Jeffrey and Patricia Julanne Hyde of 379 Hyde Place. That there was no death notice was a negative kind of hope at best, but I felt I must make this one final effort, especially since I was coming to San Francisco anyway.

The doors behind me had slid open. Passengers poured out onto the deck, hoping to be first off when the wide gangplank went crashing down and the rope barrier was removed. Every time someone in the crowd pushed against me my bones hurt. I decided I really must be catching cold. As soon as I found a room for the next few nights I would have to buy some of those foul-tasting quinine cold tablets. That would settle any cold germs. It was unusual for me to be sick, and I didn't like it at all.

Shadowed by the Ferry Building, we were in darkness as the ferryboat groped its way into a slip, bumping against the piles with hideous screeching sounds. Swept along with the other passengers, including the eager soldiers, I hurried into the Ferry Building, searching for a telephone. A small tidal wave of people, some wearing frightening homemade flu masks, poured toward us and I could hear the excitement as mothers, wives, fathers and sweethearts embraced this group of returning doughboys. I forgot all the newspaper talk of armistice problems. What I heard around me made me blink back tears. It was a beautiful moment and I envied these people their ties to loved ones.

The brightly lighted main concourse smelled deliciously of roasting peanuts and reminded me that I had not eaten since breakfast in Reno. When I could not immediately find a public telephone and saw the streetcars circling on the tracks outside before they headed up Market Street, I decided to save my nickel for the streetcar. At any other time, if money had been a little more plentiful and I had felt better, I would love to have bought a bag of those peanuts, shelled and eaten them right in the waiting room.

Now there were more important things to do. No doubt after I had gone to the offices of Cafferetto and Brubick I would lose this maddening headache. It was the suspense, the effort to behave like the mature lady they were used to dealing with that made me feel so tired, so anxious to get to bed and sleep.

A scattering of people, mostly men alone, jumped off each streetcar and rushed into the Ferry Building. They were probably commuters going home to the cities across the Bay. An hour earlier there would have been hundreds rushing past me. I hadn't realized it was so late. The Embarcadero was still wet and slick after a recent rain and I stood there for a long minute or two, trying to decide which car to take. Market Street spread out before me like a fabulous pathway lined with electric lights clear to the darkened Twin Peaks in the far distance. I had forgotten that a street could be so unbelievably wide, or that there were four car tracks.

Suddenly an old memory flashed into my mind, and I wanted to be certain I took a car that ran on the outside track. One day long ago, I had stood with Mother, waiting for a car that ran on the inside tracks. As it approached, another car rattled by behind us on the outer tracks and we were trapped in the narrow space between the two. For me it was a terrifying moment before we climbed aboard our own car.

A loud clang in front of me made me jump. I stepped into the car and it started the long run up Market Street. I was not alone. Several uniformed men with their families watched me from across the aisle, together with a lean, light-haired man in a black overcoat. At first I thought he was staring through me, his mind elsewhere, but when I glanced at him again, one of his eyebrows went up as if he found me amusing, and I decided he was only trying to flirt with me. In other circumstances I might have thought him good looking, but I was a little uneasy about his eyes. Green and lively, they gave the impression of missing nothing.

I glanced out the window behind me but I couldn't remember any of the buildings. All this area had burned thirteen years ago and been rebuilt, of course. Only the side streets running into

Market at angles, like fishbones to a spine, looked at all familiar, and even they had been entirely gutted years ago. I gave the woman beside me a glance. She was wearing a slightly soiled flu mask, and it was hard to make out her features, except that dark hair curled around the green velvet brim of her sailor-style hat. She was busy reading the newspaper she held between her gloved hands and seemed fairly young, under thirty—I wondered why I thought so. Nobody else in the car was wearing a flu mask, and I took this for a good sign. As the Eastern papers were predicting, the horrible disease seemed to have run its course.

"Excuse me," I began tentatively, "could you tell me when we get to the Monarch Building?"

The young woman raised her head. She took a breath and the mask seemed to flutter around her mouth before being sucked in slightly, making her look like a statue with all its features flattened out. But the good-looking man across the aisle who had been watching me leaned forward and said, "Watch for the Palace Hotel. You see it up ahead? Get off a block this side of it."

Surprised at his helpfulness, I thanked him, huddled into my coat and pulled the collar up around my cheeks. My face was hot but the rest of me was chilled. The sooner I got through with this interview—if there was anyone in Cafferetto and Brubick's offices to interview—the better.

Prominent as the legendary Palace Hotel might be, I almost missed it. I didn't like to be caught looking again at the man across the aisle, and by avoiding him I unfortunately also avoided seeing my stop. Then suddenly I saw the great white Palace building was behind him. I was startled but grateful when an elderly lady leaned around the girl next to me and said, "Oh, Miss . . . we've passed your stop."

I thanked her and rushed to the door in a panic. The man across the aisle obligingly pulled the cord. I got off with two or three other people a block beyond my stop, and after crossing the endless width of the street, dodging more automobiles than I had ever seen before, I found the sidewalk unexpectedly dark and deserted. Everyone was going home; people—nice people—didn't remain downtown after six o'clock when there were so many good restaurants and theaters to attend and so many fine saloons to visit before Prohibition took effect in the coming summer.

As I reached the building I began to realize that I should have eaten something on the train despite the expense. It would have helped me now. I could walk rapidly for a good distance and I shouldn't have been as tired as I was. It wasn't natural for me to get headaches. Nevertheless, I was forced to slow down and even to stop in the entrance of the solid-gray Monarch Building to recover from a dizzy spell. It was infuriating.

I started through the vestibule to the elevator, wondering what I would do if the operator had left for the night. To my relief a gnome of a man, hearing me walking across the floor, stuck his head out of the elevator.

"Looking for somebody in the building, Miss? Most offices closed now, you know."

In spite of my effort to act businesslike, my voice gave me away when I said, "Cafferetto and Brubick, please. Do you know their room number?"

The little man was pleasantly soothing. "Sure-mike. Suite 520. Miss Falassi hasn't come down yet. That's Mr. Brubick's lady clerk."

I stepped into the elevator and briefly pressed my cheek against the wall. It was cool, soothing to my heated face. The operator looked out toward the street and waited. Anxious to get my visit over and done, I asked, "Are we waiting for someone?"

He was still standing there. Over his shoulder he made the casual explanation, "Uh—waiting? Just waiting for your—" He shrugged and stepped back beside me. "Guessed wrong. I thought she was with you, Miss."

"I am alone." Then I tensed up as I began to understand him. "You thought *who* was with me?"

The doors of the elevator closed. We started up.

"That lady—thought she was coming in."

"What did she look like?"

"Couldn't say. Might've been a man. I just got a glimpse. Right behind you when you come in. Somebody in a big coat. And a hat. Sort of a small brim hat. Couldn't see the face. Pretty dark out there between streetlights, you know." He was watching the register of floors as we moved up slowly. "Don't worry, Miss. When you come out, I'll walk you to the sidewalk. If we see anybody, I'll keep 'em talking 'til you get on your way."

"Thank you. You've been awfully kind."

He was normal and reassuring, but I couldn't put out of my mind the picture of some shadowy man or woman following me down Market Street without my being aware of their presence behind me.

"It wasn't anyone following me," I said. "No one even knows I am in town except my lawyers and they surely wouldn't dog my footsteps."

He said, smiling at me, "Nope. Guess not, then. Here's your floor, Miss. End of the hall and turn right. First three doors."

Stepping out into the dimly lit hall and hearing the elevator doors close behind me, I suddenly felt bereft of my only friend.

TWO

THE MARKET STREET TRAFFIC NOISES intruded only faintly up here on the deserted fifth floor. My own footsteps in my best new high-button shoes sounded far too loud, augmented by the embarrassment of a faint squeak. I changed my pace, took longer steps and tried to smooth down my hair, but I could not shake the feeling that, to Miss Falassi, I would look exactly like what I was—an out-of-date country girl facing a sleek, sophisticated San Franciscan.

I reached the end of the hall, having passed several dark offices, and turning to my right as directed read the names of Cafferetto and Brubick on three doors in a row. The word "ENTER" had been stenciled on the first door and I could see a light through the glass. After moistening my lips and inhaling deeply, I walked in.

A gloomy business office lined with file cabinets and a whole wall of fat legal books in red or brown bindings confronted me. A woman wearing a green eyeshade was sitting at a desk under a hanging light bulb. One sleeve of her shirtwaist was protected from soiling dust and ink by a celluloid cuff. Miss Falassi had a long face with a high-bridged, haughty nose and close-set gray eyes. I expected to be properly snubbed and hardly knew what to say when she saw me and immediately reached across the desk to shake my hand. Her smile may have been toothy, but it was as enthusiastic as it was wide.

"Merideth Hyde! I'd know you anywhere." She pulled a straight-backed, cane-bottomed chair away from the wall and with a forceful click set it on the bare floor beside her desk. She waved me toward it and I sat down in a gingerly way on the edge of the chair. I had been wishing for a friend in San Francisco and was so surprised to find one I scarcely knew how to behave. She went on, "What a shame Mr. Brubick didn't know you were coming today! He could have taken you with him. He and Mister C are at City Hall. A reception for our heroes. They've been arriving all week. Their ship got into New York from St. Nazaire —that's in France, you know—only last week. Think of it! All the way from France!"

"Excuse me. You are Miss Falassi?"

She nodded.

"How did you know me?" I continued. "Did you guess I'd be here tonight?"

She shook her head and a pencil fell out of her pompadour as she reached under her big green blotter and pulled out a section of newspaper. "I saw your picture. Your little advertisement about your mother seems to have stirred up wide interest. This is Monday night's paper. It may help our search."

I looked at the short article, but it was the picture above the column that annoyed me. I recognized myself in that fifteen-year-old girl. My face had been cut out of a picture of my grammar-school graduating class and enlarged. Above my picture was the caption "FILIAL LOVE." The column below, written by someone called "The Passerby," was loathesome. The second paragraph, especially:

"And so it is that lush, golden-haired little Merideth, bereft of her father's parental cloak of protection, seeks now that long-lost mother, the mother who once surrendered a beloved daughter because she believed herself unworthy to rear this innocent child. Will young Meredith, now an heiress, find this tragic Magdalene and provide the cloak of protection once denied her by that same mother?"

I hardly wanted to touch the page as I handed it back to Miss Falassi.

"How can anyone write such awful stuff? And full of lies. Mother was not a—a Magdalene. She simply wanted to return to the dance halls and places where she had a dancing and singing act. She was quite popular before she married Father. She was on the stage in other cities, too, you know. Magdalene! Fallen woman! How dare they print such trash. And where did they get my name? It wasn't in the advertisement."

Miss Falassi fluttered her long hands. "The Passerby has a way with words. Quite a terrible man, Neil Burnham. Absolutely fatal charm when he wants something, but otherwise—" She shuddered pleasurably. "Anyway, his column may bring out the very information Mister C and Mister B were looking for. The picture—well, I'm afraid I sneaked that out of Mister B's files. Your daddy sent it the month you graduated. He was so proud of you!" She had the decency to look a trifle apologetic.

"But it's all lies. My hair isn't golden, to begin with. And I am not 'little Merideth.' " All this sounded petty, so I added, with better cause for indignation, "I'm not an heiress, either. Don't you realize all kinds of greedy people will be swarming around trying to fool us because of that lie about an 'heiress'?"

"Ah!" She was triumphant and slapped the desk top so hard that the echo seemed to resound through the empty building. "But there is the Hyde Place block, and the acreage somewhat west of that. Didn't your daddy tell you it was getting more valuable every day? The city is moving right out to the county line. We've been after your daddy to sell that property for ages, but he was so stubborn about not wanting to come back to San Francisco again. It's ridiculous for you to have to live on the rent of the Hyde Place house when that whole area is booming now. Just booming."

I didn't believe her. Father and I existed for years on that monthly rent check along with what he earned now and then as a singer. Lately I had helped out by waiting on table. It was silly to talk about heiresses.

"I came to sell the Hyde Place property, Miss Falassi. Didn't Mr. Brubick explain? I don't really expect to find my mother. I just want to know where she is buried. Very likely she was killed in the quake, or the fire." Was I finally telling myself the truth? Did I know in my own heart that Polly Hyde had died in some rooming house in the Tenderloin District, forgotten by everyone who had once thought she was such an enchanting creature on stage? Father was the dreamer, not I. I mustn't go on thinking she would pop up somewhere alive, well and young as ever. But I couldn't seem to kill that dream. Maybe I was more like Father than I thought, the only difference being that he never wanted to see his wife again after that last failure to locate her on the eve of the fire.

I looked around the office. It was very quiet now that we had stopped talking. What did I know about this Falassi woman, really? She had gotten me into trouble. People might recognize me by the newspaper picture and put that together with exaggerated talk of heiresses. Anybody could claim anything, hoping to get money out of me. And that was funny, because I hardly had enough for a week's lodging and a minimum of meals until the April rent check was paid to me.

Hoping she wouldn't notice, I tried to move my chair back an inch or two, away from this exuberant and almost too friendly stranger.

"Have the people in the Hyde Place house paid this month's rent yet? I think it is twenty dollars." I knew perfectly well it was twenty. It was humiliating to have to ask. But worse was to come.

"No, no. We didn't renew their lease, of course. Except for some of the old furniture, the house is empty. You are lucky there."

Lucky!

Her talkative, waving hands knocked against the light bulb overhead and it swayed back and forth, casting her features into shadows, sometimes weirdly attenuated, sometimes short and jolly. Her teeth sparkled, but her gums were a peculiar shade of dull orange and I realized I was looking at a set of false teeth. Like her hands, they seemed to have a life all their own. I wondered if she had ever bitten anyone.

"You mean it is lucky because the house can be sold? It's not old, really. It was completed just before I was born, in 1901, on the property that belonged to Grandpa, my father's father." I still couldn't seem to admit that the money was needed, that I had figured on the April rent from the Hyde house to pay my own food and rent in Nevada while I made plans—I thought I might go back and finish college and support myself by waiting on table again in the evenings until I at least learned how to typewrite.

"My dear child"—she saw my expression and corrected herself— "my dear young lady, it doesn't in the least matter what the house brings at sale. It is the property! Including the acreage about a mile west of Hyde Place, it will bring about one hundred thousand dollars, Mr. Brubick says. Mister C thinks he may be a bit optimistic on that, but I heard the developers in this very office discussing it. One hundred thousand all told, is how they put it. It's going to be a nice neighborhood as the houses move in farther south and west. We should give a party for you, introduce you to your neighbors. You are a celebrity now."

Parties, when I had just buried Father! Still, it was a long time since I had gone to a party, much less had one in my honor.

She tapped the indelible pencil on my picture and the column below it. "Isn't that nice? So you see, Mr. Burnham—I mean the Passerby—wasn't lying when he called you an heiress. With a hundred thousand dollars, you will be rich, if all goes well. It isn't quite what it was before the war, but believe me, it would keep whole families in luxury for a lifetime! Oooooh, la-la!" She rolled her eyes as she must have seen the girls in France do in the newsreels. Her fingers played with the indelible pencil, flipping it unconsciously so that the points at either end took turns tapping holes in my picture. It occurred to me that she was uneasy, as if holding something back. I caught one crucial phrase.

"You said, 'if all goes well.' Then something may go wrong? The property isn't worth what they think it is?"

She laughed. "A figure of speech. Legal jargon. The property is worth every cent they're willing to offer. Some pretty fancy homes are going up a little farther out. It will only require a legal document in which you swear before witnesses that you are Merideth Hyde, heir of Mr. Andrew Hyde, your grandfather. Your poor father was never interested in the property, no matter how often we wrote him about it. But one can see why. To be completely overlooked by one's own parent who leaves everything to a grandchild—well, at any rate, you were to receive the property on your eighteenth birthday."

"I just know that nothing I own could be worth a hundred thousand dollars. It's silly! They'll find some way to prove I'm not me, or that it isn't worth that much. Miss Falassi, can we talk about this tomorrow? I am dead tired."

She was sympathetic and agreed at once. "Don't you worry. Everything's going to be fine. It's only a formality. Mr. Cafferetto is the thorough kind, you know. We'll get the thing signed, witnessed, and that's all there is to it. . . . Where will you be staying?"

"I thought maybe you could suggest a place. I've got a headache and I am really not feeling so well."

With a bouncy cheerfulness that made me more tired to watch, she walked with me to the door. "You do look a bit flushed, but a good night's sleep will make you fit as a fiddle. You don't want to go too far, being alone and all. Better go to the Palace. I can telephone and recommend you. It's just up the street. . . . Well, I needn't tell anyone where the Palace is."

I laughed. I hadn't laughed so hard since long before father became sick. "Me? At the Palace Hotel? I don't have one hundred thousand dollars yet, Miss Falassi."

She tried to think of an alternative but it was clear that anything below the elite was also below her sphere of knowledge. We ended by looking through the morning *Chronicle*'s ad section, where we found a rooming house off California Street "with furnished sunny rooms for light housekeeping at $2.00 per week. Lights and electric included." She wasn't too sure just where this was and suggested I take a taxicab or—as she saw my expression—a jitney.

"They charge a dime. Private cars licensed to carry passengers.

Very convenient if you are going in their direction. Calvin, the elevator operator, will see if he can get one for you."

She walked with me to the elevator and waited until Calvin arrived. "Remember tomorrow, Merideth. Mr. Brubick will be so happy to see you all grown up, as it were. And maybe we will have word about your mother by that time. I am hopeful the article by the Passerby will bring results. Just everyone reads him. Now, don't you worry."

Easier said than done, as they say.

Calvin and his cage came along silently and he was his own friendly self. After I had said goodbye to Miss Falassi and we were descending at a sedate pace, Calvin said, "Most of the jitneys will be heading uptown at this hour. What you need is the California Street cable car. Just walk over a couple of blocks. You can't miss it. Or if I find a jitney—"

I wasn't anxious to ride in a private automobile with several strangers, but neither did I feel like walking a long distance in this dark, masked city. When the doors opened onto the street vestibule, we saw a man waiting there for the elevator.

I went out past him, then looked back. I recognized the good-looking, rather amused man on the streetcar, the man in the black overcoat.

"Five," he instructed Calvin, without appearing to notice me. He stepped into the elevator. Calvin excused himself and came over to me.

"Be right down, Miss. You wait here. I'll get you a jitney in a shake."

I whispered, "Is he the one you saw following me a while ago?"

"Nothing like it! That was a bundled up old woman. I think it was, and wearing a hat. . . . Don't you worry. Probably a beggar. Won't hang around here."

He ducked into the elevator and as the doors closed I heard him apologize to the man going to the fifth floor. Since Calvin didn't seem to know the man, it wasn't likely he had an office in the building. And Miss Falassi was the only person still working on that floor. She must have been waiting for this man when I found her in the office after hours.

It might all be a colossal coincidence that the light-haired man

in the black coat had been on the streetcar with me, that someone then apparently followed me to this building, and that this
man now visited the fifth floor just after I had left it. It might
be, but I strongly doubted it.

I waited, too nervous, too impatient to stay in one spot, and
walked toward the sidewalk and back a couple of times. Two
men passed. I could hear them discussing street robberies.

"Crime everywhere you look, and you know perfectly well what
is back of it all," one of them said.

"Clean out City Hall. That's the only answer."

They had walked beyond my hearing. As I looked after them
I saw that they had passed an old woman who shuffled along
close to the building. She stopped to blow her nose, whipping a
large handkerchief back under the man's coat that she wore,
and came on unsteadily in my direction. The elevator operator
was right, after all. She was exactly like his description of the
person who had followed me.

I started to retreat, taking a step back nearer the elevator, but
too late. The old creature shuffled on inexorably and now she
called to me, waving a hand I could barely make out inside a
coat sleeve that was inches too long.

"Mery, honey! Don't run away. It's damn cold waiting out
here in the fog. Come a little nearer. I can't walk fast as I could
before I broke my hip. That's the dearie."

This chilling, slobbery insistence suggested to me that the
Passerby's article may already have brought out its lying claim-
ants, but there was a part of me that twisted painfully at the
possibility the woman really did know me.

THREE

I BACKED INTO THE VESTIBULE of the building. I hadn't been try-ing to run away from her. I knew I was stronger than this sad woman but I wanted to get a good look at her by the high, dim electric-light fixture over our heads.

To judge from her face and the straggly gray hair under that hat, which did have a kind of shabby grandeur, I would say she was an old woman, fifty at least. So she couldn't be my mother, which was considerable relief. At the same time I became aware of some feeling for her. Her faded, rheumy eyes and her wrinkled mouth working together tried hard to give her face a coquettish smile.

"Mind if I step inside here, out of the fog? Just creeps into your bones. . . . Well, not yours, maybe—not at your age, child. . . ."

I moved backward again, to give her room, but I tried not to let her notice how I was avoiding her breath, which exuded alco-hol. Even her clothes seemed to be saturated with it. She was certainly on her best behavior, though, careful not even to touch me. I wished I had some money to give her but every one of the three silver dollars I had brought with me was already earmarked. I also had one ten-dollar gold piece that would pay my San Francisco rent and help me get home to Nevada when the property was sold. Of course I had counted on receiving the April rent from the Hyde Place house. Now, with all the idiotic talk about a hundred-thousand-dollar sale, I couldn't even get hold of that twenty dollars rent that I so badly needed for the future.

"Miss," I began, and then corrected when it sounded absurd in the circumstances. "Ma'am, have you been waiting for me?" I don't know why I expected her to deny it. She had already admitted as much.

"Well, sure! What else would I be doing down here practically South-of-the-Slot at this hour? Things may not be good for me, but I've never had to go South-of-Market to keep alive. Even Egon wouldn't get me to do that."

"Who is Egon?" I asked quickly, hoping she would answer before she had time to think of a lie.

"Why, the guy I bundle with, naturally. I'm not the type to live alone, you know. Off and on, he takes an interest in me. Look, honey, can't we go somewhere and talk? Where you staying?"

Drunk or not, the woman looked concerned, anxious. Her hands, which were short and sturdy like Mama's, crumpled up so that her ragged, not-too-clean fingernails cut into her palms. I was ashamed that I had built up a picture of this woman as some deformed, monstrous thing. She was small and did have vestiges of the good looks she must have had when she was young. Except for the hideous male clothing, the smell of whiskey, and what appeared to be her age, she might conceivably be Polly Hyde.

I felt terribly guilty because I hoped so much that she was just some poor drunken woman who had read the Passerby's column and decided to take advantage of a possible opportunity.

"You know me? Did you know my mother?" I prompted her gently.

"Know her! Well, of course I knew her! Mery, don't you rec'nize me at all? Honey! Take a good square look."

She had a habit of giving her chapped lips a quick swipe with her tongue, a habit I did not associate with my pretty mother, whom I had heard described as pert and sassy. This unfortunate woman had a bloated, round face with sagging jowls. Did pert and pretty women actually come to this?

No! This could not be Polly Hyde. Why not a friend of hers, someone who had known my mother, had heard about her past? If she had been genuine, she would have gone to see Cafferetto and Brubick instead of skulking around darkened buildings. Still, I wondered what she would look like if she had a bath and decent clothes. The man's coat she wore was actually rather dandyish in cut, but ludicrous and of course much too big for her.

While I stared at her, she straightened her hat. It was made of braid and black silk, with a high rolling brim. Long ago, the crown had been tucked with chiffon. It belonged to a period in my childhood when such hats were still called bonnets. The silk was now rotting, half the chiffon tucks were ripped out. Somehow I felt that this woman would never have worn dull black, not with those hazel eyes. And if you looked beyond their watery condition, and the wrinkled eyelids, they were hazel, like mine, like Polly Hyde's.

Calvin had come up behind us. "Back as promised, Miss." His head tilted toward the old woman. "Any trouble here?"

"No. We were just talking." I didn't dare to take her into one of those jitney automobiles with me. She would smell to high heaven of liquor, and while many people seemed to be drinking enough alcohol these days to see them through a lifetime of the coming Prohibition, I didn't expect that other passengers would exactly welcome her among them. Besides, I was feeling too sentimental tonight. It would be better to talk to her tomorrow in the office upstairs, with other witnesses.

I said to her, "Maybe you could meet me here tomorrow, say at ten o'clock in the morning, and we could go up and see my lawyers. Or Miss Falassi. You'll like her, she's very nice . . ."

"Miss—" began Calvin, but I gave him a look and he shrugged and was silent.

I picked up my carpetbag and saw her eyes following my movements. There was a longing, almost a greed in her eyes that seemed to remind me of my mother and the way she had looked once when Father brought her a gorgeous new wide-brimmed green silk bonnet with aigrettes. This woman, too, wanted something so badly she seemed to almost taste the very pleasure of it. So much like Polly Hyde.

While she stood there looking down at the contents, I opened my carpetbag and took out my old brown serge jacket.

"Try it on."

She glanced hastily at Calvin, who raised his eyes heavenward, then ripped off the out-sized man's coat and wriggled her arms into the worn but neat brown jacket. It was a suit jacket and came down well below her hips. This, with her long skirts, would be warm enough, and it certainly made her look more presentable. I had always disliked it. Now I kept telling myself, "soon they may give you some of that hundred thousand they are bragging about and you can get another jacket."

"I'll borrow it," she said with a slight toss of her head. "I only wore Egon's coat because it was coming on foggy." She smoothed the brown sleeves with each small hand. "Nice quality. You can tell. I know good quality."

Was she Polly Hyde? I had to talk to her, question her, pin her down to facts and old memories that only she and I could know.

Common sense said let it be tomorrow, by daylight.

She patted me on the hand, gave me a little smile that curled her mouth up at either end with a poignant hint of old enchantment. "Tomorrow then, honey. I understand. Meanwhile, tootle-loo."

She shuffled out of the building. I went after her to see if she had some definite place to go. I couldn't bear to think of her wandering the streets all night.

Calvin called after me, "You shouldn't have given her the coat, miss. You'll never see that again."

"Don't be silly," I said, feeling too bad for politeness. I watched her step out onto the sidewalk. Carrying the man's coat in her left hand, somewhat away from her body as if with disdain, she leveled her shoulders and started down the street. It seemed clear to me that each step was taken with care, avoiding the now-familiar shuffle, as if trying to live up to the old brown jacket.

Suddenly I called to her. I couldn't bring myself to say "Mother" or "Polly," and so I compromised on "Ma'am? Wait a minute. Please."

She stopped. Her body seemed to stiffen, or maybe it was just that she hadn't immediately realized I was speaking to her. She peered over her shoulder, her neck stretched to see me more clearly in the fog.

"Mery? You call me?"

I took several hurried steps after her, increasingly aware with every movement that I seemed to be coming down with my worst cold in years. Still, by the time I reached her I had made up my mind. She could have no idea where I was going. She couldn't have friends who might waylay me if she didn't have my address. I could and would take her with me and learn more about her. Perhaps learn about my real mother, in case this woman actually had known her.

"Do you want to go along with me for a few minutes and have a talk?" I said.

Her wrinkled eyelids twitched. I wondered if it was just possible she didn't trust me. That would be ironic.

"Sure. Where to?"

I motioned northward. "That way first."

Satisfied, she stepped carefully along beside me. "Why not? I live that direction."

We crossed Market Street in quick, running spurts. The many white, gleaming electric signs that illuminated the city were missing from the empty, silent financial district where we found ourselves, and it became darker and darker, like a dead city. Suddenly there was brightness and a noise I welcomed, the hum and the slapping sound of the street cables as a cable car clattered along, preparing to start the breathtaking climb to the crest of Nob Hill. We had reached California Street.

Surprised, my companion murmured, "You live in this district, with your money?"

"I have no money."

She was disappointed. No mistake about that, but she came along nimbly behind me. We squeezed onto the outside rear bench, and I got out a dime and paid our fare. I felt it safe to say now, "We get off at Baudry Lane."

She was puzzled at first, though she appeared to know the place well enough.

"Funny place for an heiress to stay."

"I'm *not* an—"

"I know. I know. You just hop off when I do, honey. No problem."

It may have been no problem but there was something wrong about it, and I began to guess what it was. Among others, our fellow riders at this hour were a few well-dressed men from the financial district, long hours after the closing of the New York Stock Exchange, which governed their affairs here on Montgomery Street. These men, in their expensive-looking clothes, sat inside. They had farther to go—Nob Hill and beyond. There were also a number of hard-faced tough seamen and longshoremen up from the Embarcadero, and most of all Orientals of all ages. Calm and impassive, in many cases far better-dressed than we were, their presence indicated even before I saw the pagoda roofs on the hill ahead that our car cut crossways through Chinatown.

I glanced at my companion. She seemed perfectly at home, but I was very much aware that several of the young Chinese found us as interesting, and perhaps as mysterious, as we found them. Still thinking about my companion, I knew that if I had let the woman go off alone tonight without speaking to her, and then never saw her again, I couldn't have forgiven myself. She might know *something* about mother, and any information would be worth hearing. After all, the advertisement in the newspaper had specified that it was "information" about Polly Hyde we wanted. We didn't demand that she be produced.

"You're doing more for me than I've got coming," she said unexpectedly. As I looked at her in surprise, she showed a wry, gamine grin. "I know why you're pretending you don't remember. You think I don't deserve better. You almost getting killed and all, just because of a careless mother. Drunk I was. Don't forget. And more than once it happened." It was true my mother had been drinking at times when I wandered away on the hillside, or Golden Gate Park, or the beach. But there was hardly danger of getting killed, as she had said. She went on, "Maybe I don't deserve you should know me. The way I walked out on you and Jeff. But you see, I shouldn't have married Jeff in the first place. He had no gumption, no get-up-and-go."

I remembered uneasily that I had thought the same thing about Father any number of times.

She tried to study my face as we passed a lighted corner, and I had the feeling she guessed my thoughts.

"Yes," she went on with a complacency I found extraordinary in the circumstances, "that was beautiful Jeff. I guess that's why I married him. All the girls in the show were crazy about him. The Perfect Gent. But I won him. Lucky me!" She laughed. I might have expected a grating, bitter laugh, but what troubled and hurt was the light, airy quality of her amusement. I found myself thinking of her as the real Polly Hyde, and this was exactly the reaction I had been afraid of—a quick decision based on the shrewd manipulation of my feelings. Anyone who had done no more than read the Passerby's column could have talked as this woman did. Thanks to Miss Falassi's chatter, people now knew all about the backgrounds of Jeffrey and Polly Hyde.

"I always thought I was lucky to be Jeffrey Hyde's daughter."

Still lightly, she asked, "But not to be Polly Hyde's girl?"

"I don't know Polly Hyde."

She sat back against the bench, stroking the sleeves of the old brown jacket. "I had that coming." She gave me a side-glance. "You want the truth? I can tell you now. My head's clear. Had to have a drop or two before I got up the nerve to hang around waiting for you, but I'm all right now. Want to ask me some questions? Long ago and far away? The color of your first party dress? Pink, wasn't it? All baby girls had pink, didn't they? Or the dining-room wallpaper? No, best not ask me that. I'm not sure I remember. Been so many wallpapers."

One of her hands moved away from her sleeve and along to my hand and squeezed my fingers briefly before retreating. I had responded to her pressure too late. I hoped she didn't notice that. She said, "I thought I'd glom onto you just long enough to get a few dollars, then hightail it out of your life. Maybe I'll do that anyway." She caught my tired smile. "You think it's funny? You're not going to turn me out penniless like in *East Lynne*, I hope."

"Even if you are Polly Hyde, I'm afraid I can't give you any money."

She looked out at our surroundings before she shrugged and said, "Well, I thought I'd try. It was nice to see you. I got to give old Jeff credit. He did a good job raising you, except I guess—knowing Jeff—you kind of raised him."

Our cable car clanged and rattled past the first of the pagoda roofs. There was nothing romantic here. Narrow, dingy rooming houses put up in a hurry after the fire to bring their absentee owners quick, if small, profits, they were separated by alleys so narrow only a cat seemed able to navigate their length. A Chinese woman in black trousers and padded jacket jumped off the car and shuffled away on thick-soled slippers. Darkness swallowed her up.

I felt my companion's muscles tense and hoped she wouldn't get off here. The next stop was brightly lighted Dupont Street, now called Grant Avenue, which bisected the district. When I was a child my father had taken me along this street and I was fascinated by the foreignness of it. The long, stiff queues were gone from the dark male heads now, but the busy reserve, the faintly shuffling gait remained, as did the habit of putting one's hands into each sleeve in a practical way to avoid the cold fog.

"Here we are," my companion said suddenly and, just as I had feared, jumped off in the middle of the steep block. I jumped after her, trying not to twist my ankle as I landed on the cobblestones. We could have been in the middle of the Orient. I scrambled to catch up with this woman who pretended to be Polly Hyde. She passed a two-story wooden building with a Chinese meat-and-vegetable store on the ground floor. The shop was closed, but under the dim light from a lamp in the window I caught glimpses of stiff, dried creatures that I guessed were fish and thick, unfamiliar fibrous objects that might be vegetables.

"Baudry Lane. This way," the old woman told me, and then disappeared around the corner of the store. The lane proved to be a narrow alley ending at the back wall of a three-story brick building. A single, microscopic light on the ground floor of the brick building showed us the vague outline of a staircase. I hung back. Something wet streaked by my ankle and I screamed.

Polly, who had reached the brick building and that dimly lighted staircase, swung around.

"What happened?"

"Something awful and damp. It brushed right by me."

"Just a rat. Come on, honey, this is your Baudry Lane. There's a sign here. Says 'Rooms to let.' "

Unfortunately, there was no mistake. I joined Polly and we started up the stairs. On the second floor, which smelled strongly of boiled potatoes, we found the landlady's two-room apartment. My companion stayed out in the hall and tried to smooth the snakelocks of hair below her hat while I talked briefly to the landlady, a jolly red-haired woman named Angel Ybarra, whose husband lay stretched out, snoring, on a davenport in the parlor, below windows that looked out over the alley we had just come through. She was willing to take me for three days at a time, in case all my business affairs, as she put it, were settled soon.

"I must say, I'm kind of surprised to see you here, Miss Hyde. Not that it ain't clean and decent. Because it is. You can ask the city inspectors. None of your hourly trade here. Strictly room to let, for decent folk."

I said I was sure that was true, "but how do you know me, Mrs. Ybarra?"

"We read about you in the Passerby's column. Wouldn't miss that column for worlds. He's so good looking. I took his picture from a newspaper clipping and pasted it over my sink. A skunk, I'll bet. But aren't they all! You'll be using the bedsheets and the rest, I expect. They're on the bed now. Fresh. That's going to be two bits a week extra. We don't give a rate on linen less'n a week." She started puffily up the stairs, but stopped to ask me in a stage whisper, "The—ah—female behind us, she isn't staying?"

"I think she may have known my mother. Maybe she can tell me about her."

"Polly Hyde, your mother!" my landlady cried ecstatically. "You want her to tell you about darling Polly?"

I was finding it hard to climb the stairs—it must have been the full day's train ride that made my body stiff as a poker—but her comment naturally aroused my curiosity. "You knew my mother? You saw her on the stage?"

"My old man says we saw her on the Orpheum Circuit."

Behind us, my stand-in Polly Hyde said, "You couldn't have. She never played the Orpheum, worse luck. She topped the bill at the Poodle Dog here in San Francisco, though. That was before the fire. On the other hand, you might've seen her swimming out at the beach, or indoors at—you sure you never saw her at the Poodle Dog?" She had hoisted her skirts and appeared to be having much less trouble than I in mounting the stairs. I noted that all the information this Polly Hyde offered was public, that she hadn't said a single thing that she and I alone could know.

She left us in the large, barny back room with its tulip-shaped light fixture in the ceiling. I have foggy memories about the furnishings: a rocking chair—I dropped into it abruptly—a round table and two chairs that stood by the window that she said gave her a bird's-eye view between rooftops. The brass bed with its lumpy mattress is more vivid in my memory.

"If you can spare about two bits or thirty-five cents," she suggested, taking her hat off and fluffing up her thin hair, "I'll see what I can get for supper. You mind Chinese food? After I get you settled, I'll be on my way." She gave me a quick look, too proud to ask to be invited to the supper she promised to make for me.

"During supper you can talk to me about the old days," I said mockingly, since by now I was almost sure she knew nothing that would prove her claim. I wondered if I dared trust her with the money. "All I feel like is soup. And coffee, maybe. I've got a frightful cold coming on."

"You're not looking too good," she agreed, studying my flushed face. "Why are you shivering? Look here, you're not coming down with that damned flu, are you? I've never had it and I don't want it, neither."

"It's a cold. Haven't you ever heard of a plain cold? I don't need you. Please leave me alone."

She stuck her hat back on, dropped the stained man's coat on one of the chairs, and reached for my purse. I sat up straight. She took three dimes and two pennies, holding out the palm of her hand so I could see its contents. Then, with her hand folded into a fist, she went out the door. I wondered if I had seen the last of her.

Moving my head was painful, but with an effort I looked over at the high brass bed in the corner. It seemed to me that nothing on earth would feel better than those patched, white sheets and the much-used brown comforter. I got up and started toward the bed. It was an unaccountably long distance.

I must have caught my shoe in the threadbare carpet because I fell against the mattress. I managed to get one knee onto the bed and then the other. I turned with an effort and lay back on the bed. The room misted over, filled with fog, or seemed to. The light bulb was miles above my head, and even its glow seen through fog—or was it my own half-conscious state?—hurt my eyes.

What was wrong with me? A flu-type cold? The grippe? Or that other, that deadly thing, that had been taking lives twice as fast as the deaths on the Western Front during the last bloody months of war.

I had the Spanish Influenza.

I knew I must call someone but I had enough sense to realize the jolly landlady would run for her life if she suspected anything. And worse, she might order me out on the street as I was. My alleged Polly Hyde had already expressed herself on that subject.

I was thirsty, but I found it impossible to sit up. I pictured myself lying there without food or water, going through all the torments of my disease with the whole world afraid to touch me. I always imagined such horrors when I saw the terrible red signs go up on the houses of friends and knew that someone in them had scarlet fever. Blue signs for diphtheria . . . yellow, black and white . . .

I felt too hot and feverish to shed any tears of panic. Besides, I didn't dare give way. If I could expect no help, I would have to rely on myself. I tried again to get up. My best bet would be to hire a taxicab and have myself taken to a hospital. I could surely find a taxi on Grant Avenue, where the tourists came, if I could just get down there. It shouldn't be far. I turned, tried to use my elbows for leverage. Heat rose in waves around me.

Every inch of my body felt excruciatingly painful. And I had difficulty breathing. Consciousness came and went. Hours—or minutes—later my imitation Polly Hyde knocked and shuffled in without waiting for my voice. She joked about the containers she brought, set them down on the table.

"Your landlady gave me a bottle of hot potato soup. That'll fix you up. . . . Say, honey, you got anybody liable to be following you?"

"No . . . nobody who knows me." Was she trying to frighten me? I couldn't concentrate on what she said.

She nodded. "Thought as much. It's probably me, not you. Say! You do look terrible!"

"Get—doctor . . . It's flu!"

She jerked back in mid-step. I tried to say something else. I have a recollection now that I asked her to find a taxicab, but the worlds all jumbled up and came out in nonsense. The room whirled around and around for an eternity.

Later, blessed darkness.

FOUR

"TELL MISS FALASSI I WILL BE LATE . . . I have a cold. Bad cold."

I heard my voice repeating this several times during the night, but whether it was that night or a later time I have no idea. A quiet, soothing male voice ordered me not to worry, the matter was being attended to.

For a long time I could not straighten out in my own mind the truth from the eerie dreams I lived through during the days that followed. My greatest confusion occurred in the earliest stage of my recovery when a folding white screen still separated me from the other critically ill hospital patients and the only world I could make out was through a window at the far end of a long sterile white corridor. That world told me the time of day. Foggy in the morning. Incredibly blue sky at midday, brisk in the afternoon when wind-driven pigeons fluttered past the window. Then, rain at night.

At that time the only other human beings we saw wore masks. Each doctor and every nurse looked more sinister than the one before. On one occasion I saw the mother I remembered from my childhood. Polly Hyde was here, her crinkling hazel eyes staring at me above the dehumanizing flu mask she wore as a privileged visitor. I could not tell whether this was just another dream or the real Polly Hyde. But when did I ever know the answers to that enigma, even in my normal hours? In any case, she certainly didn't look like my drunken old reprobate who called herself Polly Hyde.

During the worst times, in my frantic efforts to breathe, I was brought back to painful life by Dr. Demos, who looked after our ward. It was this kind, attractive young doctor who told me, when I questioned him, that my bills were being paid by Cafferetto and Brubick and I wasn't to worry. But of course I did. I would have to repay them out of whatever I got for the sale of the Hyde Place property. Providing I finally received the property. I remember once when I felt especially overwrought I took hold of the doctor's hand and asked him, "My *real* mother, where is she?"

He said quietly, "She has seen you. She loves you. Polly Hyde is your real mother."

But how could that old woman be accepted as Polly Hyde . . . except her eyes did look younger and even tender, the eyes of the mother I liked to remember?

Dr. Demos tried to explain to me later why I dreamed of my mother and myself when I was a child, and of broken conversations with her when I didn't even know if she were alive or dead. I had *wished* for it to happen, he said, "and then, at last, like a miracle—"

"When you are feeling better," he promised me, breaking off in the middle of that most interesting sentence. "You can best recuperate in your own surroundings, which are being made easy and familiar for you at this very minute. You will get over this doubt about your mother, I promise you, as soon as you are home again."

By this time I had been removed to a ward with women in various stages of recovery from the Spanish Influenza. We were interested in each other's cases and in each other's lives. They all listened now, almost as anxious as I was to unravel this mystery.

"I haven't any familiar surroundings," I insisted.

Dr. Demos smiled. He had very dark eyes, deep set and compassionate, and he reminded me, "You have Hyde Place, the

43

home where you were born. And better than that, you have—but I can't tell you about that yet." He popped a thermometer into my mouth to shut off further questions.

The women in the ward adored Dr. Anthony Demos, and referred to him fondly as "Dr. Tony." My first would-be visitor after I had been removed to this friendly, gossipy ward was a certain Neil Burnham, who wanted to interview me. When I flatly refused to see him because I couldn't imagine what this stranger wanted of a dreadful pallid scarecrow named Merideth Hyde, the ladies in the ward enlightened me. They were thrilled to death—you would have thought they were talking about someone as handsome and graceful as Douglas Fairbanks or John Barrymore, the good-looking new actor.

"Neil Burnham is the Passerby. He has that newspaper column. Fascinating man. A heartbreaker, they say. Very independent."

If there was one thing I didn't need besides the Passerby, who had caused me so much trouble, it was a heart-breaking male. And all in one package! I was sure when Dr. Demos refused to let him see me that Mr. Burnham would not be able to write another sickening column like the one I had read. I might have known nothing stops such men.

He talked to one of the women who had shared our ward and since left. As a result I was treated in print to such intimacies as my very dreams during the worst time of my illness.

One of my ward companions had received a copy of the new column and read parts of it aloud that evening when Dr. Demos was making his rounds elsewhere.

> " 'Lying on her bed of pain, little golden-haired Meredith Hyde moans her departed mother's name, little knowing that this one-time Belle of the Barbary Coast, now a respectable wife and matron, waits to take her suffering child to her bosom when young Merideth is released from City and County Hospital's Contagious Ward.' "

"But it's all a lie," I assured my companions as they propped up on their elbows to hear this garbage "The woman who called herself Polly Hyde was a dear funny old soul who just wanted to get money. Which I don't have."

The women exchanged glances. They probably thought I was a terrible miser, but I couldn't help that. Romantic Mrs. Rivarol was puzzled.

"She didn't seem that way to my husband. He met her this morning in Administration."

We all felt as deeply involved in the cure and affairs of our fellow victims as the doctors themselves, having shared the common disaster and what seemed the miracle of our own cure. We were also closely involved in anything that involved each other. The remark of Mrs. Rivarol's husband stirred my curiosity.

"You mean Mr. Rivarol met that woman who called herself Polly Hyde? Was she sober?"

Mrs. Rivarol said she couldn't imagine her husband thinking a lady charming and attractive when she was drunk. "He definitely said she was pretty and charming. . . . He doesn't like females who drink, so I don't see how Mrs. Hyde could possibly have been drunk when he met her."

The Polly Hyde of my childhood had been pretty, charming, possessing all the other qualities Mrs. Rivarol's picture conjured up. The other side of her I had seldom considered, and tried hard not to remember. I wondered again what the woman I had met would look like if she bathed, sobered up, took care of her hair and dressed decently. I thought she would still probably look older than my mother's age. But then, if the real Polly Hyde had lived the life of the woman I met the night I arrived in San Francisco, she certainly would have looked older than her years. Whether she was genuine or not, and I was sure she wasn't, I had taken a real interest in her. Did she run away when she found out I had the flu? Or had she gotten a doctor for me? Now she was apparently waiting to go home with me, and that might be a serious problem. Besides, where could she be taking me? Not to my own half-furnished Hyde Place house, surely. . . .

As Dr. Demos came in, one of the girls whispered to me that she intended to go out to the Demos Baths every Sunday she got off from her job, in hopes of catching sight of him there now and then. I hadn't connected our Anthony Demos with the world's largest indoor bathhouse out on the point facing the

45

Pacific. It was only a hundred feet below Demos Heights, the home of what must be Dr. Demos' distinguished pioneer family. He didn't seem like the child of rich and famous parents, spending as he did his working hours taking care of the contagious wards where most of the patients were even poorer than I was.

We watched Dr. Tony's tall shadow against the wall as he came to us from the next ward. The girls all spruced up. I felt about for the old black comb one of the nurses had taken out of my carpetbag and left for my use. While I combed the snarls out of my hair, wishing I had a mirror, I tried to think of something special to say to this being we all regarded as superior to the rest of mankind, this man who had saved our lives.

While he was visiting the young woman at the end of the ward I tried out several subjects: Did he think the Armistice would hold, or were we going back to war? Not too happy a subject, considering Dr. Demos had spent almost a year treating those invalids home from France before he went into the Spanish Influenza wards. There was always the matter of how our returning doughboys would be absorbed into industry. Or what about Prohibition? All bad.

When Dr. Demos reached my bed, showing his warm smile that I also found rather touchingly somber, I forgot all the intellectual talk and asked with unsophisticated eagerness, "Did anyone come to the hospital and ask about me today?"

"Someone who saw you the other day when you were very sick. You don't remember, do you? Who would you rather see than anyone else?"

I knew this must be the woman who went with me to the Chinatown rooming house, and so I could not be as surprised as he wanted me to be. "Polly Hyde?"

"Polly Hyde, your *mother*."

I tried to explain and still keep the false eagerness in my voice. "I always think of her the way she used to be billed: Pert Polly Hyde. Or Pert, Pretty Polly Hyde."

"*That* is a tongue-twister. I'm not sure I could say it more than once."

"I may owe that woman my life," I said, still thinking of the impostor Polly. "Did she get me to the hospital? How did she manage? She was so afraid of catching the flu, but all the same she helped me."

Dr. Demos had my wrist between his strong thumb and fore-finger. He looked at me intently. "No, Merideth. It wasn't quite like that. Someone from the rooming house, your landlady prob-ably, went down to a restaurant a block or so away and used their telephone to call the hospital."

"But you said—"

"Your mother tells me that the first time she saw you in thir-teen years was the other night here in the hospital when you were so ill. She was brought here by your lawyer, Mr. Lawrence Brubick. She says she knew your father would not let you see her while he was alive."

Why would my false Polly Hyde lie about that? Much smarter to tell everyone that we met early on the evening I took sick, which was true enough as far as it went.

"She must have sobered up when she came here."

He looked exasperated, as if he couldn't believe what he heard. "She was quite sober. Polly Hyde, as you call her, is a lovely woman. Very much a lady. I don't really think you should talk any more about her drinking. It isn't very attractive of you, and it's not true. Not true at all."

She certainly has you fooled, I thought, but didn't want to hurt his feelings or be scolded like a schoolgirl for describing her as she was. Apparently even normally wise and good men could be rather pig-headed and bossy on subjects they knew nothing whatever about.

Yet in an odd sort of way it pleased me to think my drunken Polly Hyde had so clearly pulled the wool over Dr. Demos' innocent dark eyes. At the same time I made up my mind she wasn't going to fool me as she apparently fooled the others.

The doctor patted the bed briskly. "You are to get your sleep now. Tomorrow is going to be exciting and you don't want to tire." He looked down at me, studying my face for signs of fa-tigue. "You do want to see your mother . . . don't you?"

I nodded, but my reaction obviously wasn't fast enough to satisfy him so I tried to backtrack, to put on more enthusiasm. I wanted very much to see those I knew, even the old drunken woman, but I had not supposed I would be paroled into the custody of someone I had to mistrust. "I want to see her very much," I said, "but I don't know that I want to live with—"

"Yes?"

"Nothing. I'm very happy to be well again. That's the main thing."

He was disappointed, no question about it. I tried to show my gratitude, gave him my biggest smile. I thanked him. I really liked him and thought him the most romantic man I had ever seen, at least off the movie screen. But he *was* a little stupid about human nature. When he left us that night he still couldn't understand why I wasn't overcome by joy. The truth was, I had a haunting fear of this future being planned for me without my having anything to say about it, and with people I instinctively was afraid of.

FIVE

I WAS TO GO "HOME" the next day. The sensible thing would be to tell everyone what I knew about this so-called mother, but I hesitated to do that. Not yet, at least. She may have helped me before I got to the hospital and it was likely this was her first piece of decent luck in years. I would let things ride for the moment, see how I felt after I got out of the hospital.

The night nurse gave me some powders to make me rest, sleep, or *something*. Taking the powders was an act I loathed. Poured almost forcibly from a creased paper into my mouth, they were followed by a glass of water, and in a few minutes, with the lights dimmed, I found myself dozing off. But though I slept, I awoke often and remembered that this time tomorrow I would be going to bed in a strange house, with what sort of strange people?

I'm not anybody's property. I'm my own boss, I reminded myself. I don't have to stay in San Francisco. Let Mr. Brubick sell the Hyde Place property. I'll go back to Nevada.

At one point in the blue, predawn hours, I felt for my purse, which shared the handy little utility stand with Mrs. Rivarol's satchel. Opening the coin purse, I tried to guess by the feel of them how many coins remained. My ten-dollar gold piece was gone.

The fake Polly Hyde . . . that light-fingered old harridan had robbed me!

But as I counted up in the darkness I found I had six silver dollars and three paper ones. Like most westerners, I disliked paper dollars. Somehow they never seemed like real money.

If my Sherlock Holmesian deductions were accurate, it appeared that someone had changed my gold piece. Was it possible my Polly Hyde had changed the gold piece and used the money to get me to the hospital? Was it possible someone in the hospital had taken the money? But why not take it all? Why leave the silver and paper money?

I suspected this was wishful thinking . . . I just didn't want to believe Polly Hyde was as bad as she represented herself. Anyway, I'd know more in the morning. I sighed, yawned, bent the pillow around my ears, and went to sleep.

I had taken a bit of walking exercise the previous afternoon and now after breakfast I spent an hour and a half walking through what appeared to be miles of corridors and around other convalescent wards. Returning to my own world I got ready for the exciting moment of departure. My new friends helped me to dress and look halfway presentable. We all decided that since father had ordered it made for me on my birthday in January, it was appropriate to wear my new spring dress, a lilac voile, even this soon after his death. It had the fashionable V-neck that the magazines still referred to as "daring," with a self-belt made like a sash. The dress was the new, shorter length, above my ankles—altogether the modern look.

Mrs. Rivarol curled my hair and Bertha Hohenfelt, whose bed was on the other side, powdered my face, carefully dusting a little rouge on my cheeks. "Lipstick, dearie?" she asked.

A trifle uneasy, I agreed. My lips certainly needed something, and I must say I liked the result. I also realized how much these women had meant to me during what could have been a nightmare imprisonment. I hugged everyone in the ward and we all swore, impossibly, to keep in contact with each other.

Then Dr. Demos came in and took my hand, and I had to try

extra hard not to show how nervous I was. "Am I all right?" I asked anxiously, smoothing first my hair and then my dress.

"You'll be fine, Merideth, as soon as you get home and put on some weight. A little good home cooking should do that. I wish my mother had you to work on. My father spent a lifetime making enough money to keep mother out of the kitchen, and now, every Thursday on cook's night out, mother can't wait to get at the pots and pans. Her cooking would do wonders for you."

I was thrilled at that hint, but then he ruined it by adding, "You're lucky to have a strong, healthy constitution."

My constitution was not what I had in mind when I spoke to him. He made me feel about six years old when he took my hand and walked me out of the ward past my waving, well-wishing friends. By the time we reached the corridor after these farewells I was blinking my eyes.

"Come on now," he urged, looking down at me and shaking my hand in his. "You don't want your mother to see you all red-eyed."

"She is not my—" I began, and broke off. Why argue? Mr. Brubick, or more likely the eagle-eyed Mr. Cafferetto, would find out the truth soon enough.

Dr. Demos took my blue coat off his arm and draped it about my shoulders. "You mustn't catch cold. You will find it is a trifle windy in spite of the beautiful blue sky."

"It will look marvelous to me. It's freedom after prison." I caught his expression and wished he didn't take things so seriously. It kept me forever apologizing. "I didn't mean prison exactly, I just meant that there is no privacy. I did like my friends here, only now that I am free I don't especially want to be with a woman I hardly know. I mean—" But I could see that he didn't understand. "I'm so sorry," I said to Dr. Demos. "I guess I am a little afraid of meeting Polly Hyde again."

"Perfectly understandable, but you mustn't worry about that. She is prepared to be understanding and patient."

I tried to hide my feelings from him. I very much wanted to retain his good opinion. Nevertheless, it was odd, I thought, that he could not understand my uncertainty and fear of this future that other people were so busy arranging for me. Then I reminded myself that he couldn't know of my recent experience with "Polly Hyde," and so how could he realize my doubts and fears? Well, when I saw her, if it seemed necessary, I would tell him the whole story.

Just before we reached the end of the corridor he lowered his head and kissed me gently, not quite on my lips but near enough for me to wish his aim were a little better—or worse . . . He seemed a bit embarrassed, which was as charming as it was unnecessary. "Here we are," he said as we reached the visitors' room which, unnervingly, seemed full of people. When he pushed open the door I felt a dozen pairs of eyes staring at me. Some of these people, of course, were visiting other patients, but the moment we entered everyone seemed to look up at the doorway.

There was a hush as I saw two men—one middle-aged and thin, with a pince-nez. That was Mr. Brubick, considerably older than when he had visited us at the Hyde Place house when I was a child. His smile was prim but seemed genuine. The other man was stout with a small mustache that accentuated fleshy lips and had a big bald spot on the crown of his head—the sharp-eyed Frank Cafferetto. I smiled at them and waved in response to exuberant Miss Falassi behind them, though I did wonder who was tending the office.

Polly Hyde stood between the two lawyers. Her small, sturdy hands were outstretched but unmoving. Her hair, still red-gold but with threads of gray, was as I remembered it except that it had been bobbed in the popular new style. Crinkling hazel eyes . . . I had seen those eyes during my illness. A few fine lines there, fanned out from the corners of the eyes. The dainty nose and the mouth with a slight, petulant fullness . . . The compact little figure that had spread only slightly in thirteen years. She was certainly not the old harridan I had met the first night I arrived in San Francisco. Was she, then, my *real* mother?

I went into her arms at once. Mr. Brubick had to remove his pince-nez while he blew his nose. Somebody snapped a picture from a large camera on a tripod. I figured it was for a newspaper but didn't care.

"Honey . . ." she said, her head against my ear. "Don't cry."

I was aware that I was laughing and crying all at once and behaving in too emotional a fashion but I couldn't seem to stop. "It's you, really you this time. I couldn't really believe it, but I was afraid the other one was Polly Hyde."

"What other one?" Mr. Cafferetto asked in a scratchy voice.

"Nothing, just a dream." I decided there was no need to get the would-be Polly Hyde in trouble. She would have enough of that just surviving after Prohibition.

It was easy to see how pleased Dr. Demos was, though he didn't make his feeling as evident as Miss Falassi and Mr. Brubick. They nodded to each other, assuring the world they had known all the time that they would bring us together.

But there was Mr. Cafferetto's legal disclaimer: "It would appear that all questions of identity are answered. However—"

No one but me seemed to pay any attention to him, and I pretended not to. This warm, pretty Polly Hyde was so exactly the way I remembered—or imagined—her in my childhood that it was as though the thirteen and a half years had never happened. She had hardly grown old at all. Only a line here and there. Nothing unbecoming. And the drinking that father hated and feared, what had happened to that? Obviously he had exaggerated.

"Let's go home, honey," she said.

It was strange to have someone else making the decisions. I looked at Dr. Demos, who nodded. With Polly's arm around my waist I told myself this was my first completely happy moment since father's illness first turned serious. I repeated this thought because I wanted very much to believe it.

"All right," I said. "Let's go home." One day soon I would ask what had happened in my mother's life after she left that long-ago note for father and myself. Then I remembered—"But where is your home?"

I seemed either to have shaken or embarrassed everyone by this perfectly natural question. Mr. Brubick, nudged from behind by either Polly Hyde or Miss Falassi, cleared his throat and explained carefully, "You are going home to recover from your illness, Merideth. To the house where you were born. You and your family. Going home for a little while. Until you decide

53

what you want to do about your property. Isn't that nice?" After a slight pause, he asked nervously, "You do remember 379 Hyde Place?"

"Naturally I remember where I was born and where mother left father and me." Polly's arm tightened around me and then relaxed. I smiled at her and she responded, weakly. I told the men, "I just supposed it would be hard to move into my house right now, what with no furniture and all. However, I guess it's been fixed up for . . . us." I tried not to put emphasis on my ownership of the Hyde Place house, but realized it might have been in their minds. That didn't discourage me from feeling guilty of bad manners.

Dr. Demos turned and started out again without saying good-bye to me. That hurt. But he stopped in the doorway.

"Good luck, Miss Hyde. We are all happy for you."

I broke from Polly's confining arm. "Doctor, thank you for everything."

This time he rewarded me with a smile, which made me feel much better. "Merideth . . . I'll call on you one day and see how you are doing."

I felt suddenly that I had lost my last friend. I tried not to show this because everyone now crowded around me. Mr. Brubick was at great pains to whisper to me in a voice audible to Polly and the others, "My dear, someday we must show you the accumulation of evidence by which your lovely mother identified herself. Including the furnishing of the Hyde Place house. I visited you there, you know, back in the old days, and your mother very nearly duplicated certain objects that I myself remember. There could be no doubt of her identity. You must be very happy at this quick response to our efforts."

I did wonder what this evidence was. Half the house's original furniture still remained, as I understood it, and I was curious to learn what the other evidence might be, though I couldn't very well do so at the moment. Mr. Brubick picked up my carpet-bag and Mr. Cafferetto said, "I'm late to a luncheon of the Downtown Association. Shall we be on our way?"

We took that as more than a hint and left the hospital, I with Polly Hyde and the wildly enthusiastic Miss Falassi, along with one of the young nurses, stiff in her starchy uniform but smiling at me like the dear old friend she had become.

One breath of fresh spring air blowing in off the Pacific was enough to cheer me up, and once we were beyond the hospital's shadow I found that everyone improved immensely and my stupid resentment of them all but disappeared. Mr. Cafferetto having departed in his chauffeur-driven Pierce Arrow, Mr. Brubick and his lady clerk shook hands all around and Miss Falassi made me promise to call and let them know how I succeeded in my new life. "Your mother has had a telephone installed, just in case you have a relapse or anything, which is most unlikely. But, as she points out, one never knows about these things."

I promised to call her and Polly Hyde drew me away. I still found it difficult to call her "mother." I had thought of her so long as "Pert Polly Hyde," the charmer, the entertainer, but maybe after I got to know her better I could forget the public name and feel natural with the private one.

I took big, delicious gulps of air and thought how wonderful it was to be healthy. I had never appreciated good health before.

Now that we were free of all the talkative, interfering acquaintances, Polly appeared to be relieved. She squeezed my arm in a sudden impulse of tenderness that made me feel wanted and loved for the first time since I had kissed father's quiet face good-bye.

"Thank the Lord!" she said. "We have you all to ourselves now and we can begin to get acquainted. Reacquainted, I should say. We have been allowed to get an Overland Touring Car, isn't that nice? We're leaving the top down. You can see everything as we drive. We can take you for nice drives down the Peninsula and just everywhere so you can get back your lovely healthy complexion. It was dreadful when we found out where you were, in that awful contagious ward."

"Anyway, it's all wonderful now. And I'm surely proud to know anyone with an Overland Touring Car! We never—I mean, father and I never needed a car in Nevada. We hired a buckboard. They still use horses and mules in the desert country." Besides, though I didn't tell her, we had never had enough money to buy a Ford, much less an Overland Touring Car. "You must have done awfully well with your life," I added. "I'm sure father would have been so proud of you. You look simply lovely."

Staring up and down the street and standing on tiptoe, she said in an absent manner, "Yes, I suppose I am lucky. Howard has been a great help, of course."

"Howard?" I shouldn't have been surprised. A pretty woman who still possessed the aura of her stage days, she must have had male admirers. It would be astonishing if she did not. But I couldn't bring myself to think of her as the other Polly Hyde —a woman with lovers, paying or otherwise.

"Howard MacPherson. My husband. Hasn't Mr. Brubick told you about him? Actually he's your stepfather. You'll love him . . . where on earth is he with that car?"

"But—father—"

Polly squeezed my ribs in what I seemed to recall as a joking little gesture from the old days.

"Honey, don't worry. I'm not a bigamist. I divorced your father years ago. Before the war. Didn't he tell you? He was served with papers. Anyway, I've been married to Howard Mac-Pherson for ages. He was in France, you know. Went over with the YMCA contingent. Food, cigarettes to the boys, snuff, and candy. Writing home for our heroes. He was a hero himself. He received a nasty head wound when he and some others were caught at St. Mihiel . . . Ah, here he comes now. Isn't it a handsome car . . . I'm really in love with it . . ."

They must have bought the car recently, she was still so impressed by it. I wondered what Howard MacPherson's profession was that he could afford expensive cars and furnishing the Hyde Place house and all.

SIX

THE AUTOMOBILE ROLLING ALONG beside the curb made me think of a great ocean liner in the movies floating serenely up to the dock. I half expected to see Douglas Fairbanks make one of his graceful leaps to shore, all dressed up in natty plus-fours and a straw hat. It was not the darkly handsome, swarthy star who moved across the front seat of the open car and got out, but a big blond man about forty-five with a curious flat expression in his pale-blue eyes. He did have an expansive elegance about him, though. I could see what Polly meant about Howard MacPherson's war wound. There was a livid scar more than an inch long running back from his left temple to his slightly receding hairline. His smile was a little overblown as he greeted us, brushing Polly's cheek with his lips and shaking my hand in his own big powerful fingers. He started to kiss me, but I moved, pretending I hadn't noticed. All the same he was not unpleasant. If only he didn't have that actorish, sweeping quality, as if he were too overpowering for the small stage on which he performed.

Speaking quickly, Polly said, "Merideth . . . *Mery,* dear, as you must have guessed, this is your stepfather, Howard. Please like each other. For my sake."

Under orders, Mr. MacPherson and I smiled at each other. He was about to help me into the back seat of the car when Polly stepped up on the running board, evidently intending to give over the front seat beside her husband to me. Then I got a surprise. Howard MacPherson's calm voice, empty of emotion, still managed to chill me a little as he ordered Polly into the front seat "where you belong, as you very well know, my dear."

Polly's nervous obedience without the least argument showed me who was the ruler of that marriage. Quite unlike my memories of Father and my—and Polly. She and I got into the big car according to my stepfather's orders, I in the back seat, regally isolated.

In spite of the wind I was delighted to be in a car with its top down. Howard MacPherson closed the car door after Polly took the front seat, then went around and got behind the wheel. Neither he nor Polly looked at each other. It was almost as though they were strangers. I wondered what marriage problem had come between them and hoped very much it wasn't me. Finally I settled back to let the wind make a tangled thicket out of my hair and watch the City by daylight. It was far more beautiful than it had been to me the April night I had arrived, though with all the automobiles racing back and forth on both sides of the street it looked just as exciting and dangerous. For the last dozen years I had thought of Reno as the typical western city. The three-story buildings there seemed tall, nothing like the skyscrapers I saw in the movies, but reasonable signs of a city. Now I saw real skyscrapers everywhere, ten, twelve stories, heaven knew how much higher. It was as if they had never heard of 1906.

After we passed the viaduct over a deep ravine, which Mr. MacPherson pointed out to me along with a few other landmarks, the buildings and scenery began to look more natural. Small and lean, some of the houses were perched high, with garages below, but most of the wooden buildings had little shops on the street floor and rooms above with bay windows extending over the sidewalk.

I had felt like a visitor from the moon, but now the world possessed several familiar points by which I could get my bearings. No matter where I looked, in any direction, I could see green hilltops, bald peaks, and sometimes slopes onto which rows of houses had already begun to encroach, all exactly alike. Maybe Mr. Brubick was right in thinking the property I had inherited from Grandpa Hyde could be worth a great deal of money.

There was so much to see here by the time we passed Geneva Avenue, which was beyond the built-up area when I was a child, I began to find myself ever so slightly tired. I sat up, flexed my fingers, stretched my arms and legs, and again made a point of inhaling the good clear air. But as we swung off Mission Street onto Hyde Place, that dream street created by Grandpa when there was nothing out in this tract except grassy hills, I felt like jelly inside. It was ridiculous, because I had no sentimental attachment to the area. I had lost my mother here, and even now, in spite of everyone's efforts, including hers, I felt as if the lost years between could never be made up. So why was I feeling all shivery and emotional as we rolled along toward my birthplace?

It took me a full minute or two, a long time when you are shivering, to realize it was not so much anticipation as fear that made my shiver, and that it was not so much fear of my birthplace as of my mother and stepfather and, especially, the way I had been snatched up and placed in their . . . well, power. I told myself not to be foolish, and that I no doubt was indulging my familiar and rather overgrown resentment at not being always in charge of what happened to me.

"Does the tract look at all familiar?" Polly asked me, glancing over her shoulder.

"In a way. I remember the street we are crossing. That big spreading house on the corner, the little park where the ground is dug up. Ready for spring flowers, I'd guess. And the pillars of the pergola running down the middle of Pompeii Street, I remember those."

My stepfather said ,"You must feel very happy, coming home."

"Awfully," I lied, and as he was clearly on the watch for it, I gave him a big false smile. Indeed, I felt a falseness in my attitude and my manner I'd never noticed before. I didn't like it.

But ever since I'd arrived at the office of Cafferetto and Brubick that first night, already, if unknowingly, sick with the flu, my life seemed to have been manipulated, as if it were not my own. It was all so contrary to my life since the day Father and I had escaped from burning San Francisco. I surely wasn't used to strong parents dictating my movements, people like the lawyers and my mother, her new husband, and even Dr. Demos.

Now we were riding up the block that had been Grandfather's property and now was mine. Halfway along that block, perched high on top of its big garage-basement, was the Hyde Place house, enthroned in imperious solitude. It had been untouched by the earthquake thirteen years before and was, of course, far beyond the fire line. All around the district and across the street almost every lot twenty-five by a hundred feet had been built upon. Only Grandfather's block was weed-grown, empty, full of muddy chuckholes and, to me, splendidly untouched by developers. But then, I had become used to the wide-open spaces. I knew my ideas were something less than modern, at least in this respect.

"Do you remember everything, dear?" my mother asked me in an anxious, breathy way that I didn't recall to have been her habit when we lived together.

As I examined my own reactions, trying to choose words which would not offend or upset her, I noted that Mr. McPherson had stiffened to attention and was listening very carefully, which made me even more tense, more anxious . . . I didn't want Polly to find herself in trouble with her husband. For all his appearance of languid indifference to the world, this big, powerful man was beginning to strike me as far less indifferent than he pretended to be.

As we reached the house I began to revise my opinion, to think it looked lonely perched there on the east side of the street, completely surrounded by vacant space in this crowded city. The west side of the street was built up wall-to-wall every twenty-five feet, and all those bay windows seemed to stare across at this faintly shabby building that considered itself so aloof.

"It needs painting," I said. The dark-brown painted wood was weathered and fading after all these years of desultory occupation by renters.

Polly said excitedly, "She knows our house, all right," and her husband remarked with unmistakable sarcasm, "This strikes you as odd, my dear? Naturally she recognizes the only house on this side of the street. She was born here, after all."

At this rebuke Polly shut up most uncharacteristically and the big car turned into the driveway. Howard MacPherson got out, unlocked and opened the basement doors. I could see a cavernous interior and at the same time noticed that outside the doors there must have been at least twenty wooden stairs running steeply up to the porch and the main floor. There was only a large half-attic above that. I liked the three bay windows in the front room, high over the basement garage below, remembering how the Christmas tree always stood in that alcove surrounded by a low white fence to keep me, as a child, from clutching and breaking the new-style spun-glass ornaments.

We had used candles on the tree in those days and during my fourth Christmas here, Polly, celebrating on wine made by some friends across Geneva Street, fell into me while I was playing inside the fence and set my flannel nightgown afire. Father put it out in a few seconds with no harm done except a small burn or two, but it was the beginning of the end for Father and Mother.

Polly looked back at me warmly. "Thinking about the old days, dear? Things will go better this time."

"I was just remembering the Christmas when I was four." The second I blurted it out I wished I hadn't and hurried to change the subject, but before I could do so Polly nodded. Her smile was surprisingly happy in the circumstances.

"We'll have more. We've only begun to enjoy life together again. That wasn't the last happy Christmas for us, you know."

I was momentarily stunned. I had learned in the mining country that people who drink don't always remember what happens to them in those hours, and I should not have been surprised. She might well have blotted such a thing from her mind because it was so painful to remember. Howard interrupted my thoughts as he opened the car door for me and I got out.

"Home again," he announced with a jovial wave, indicating the spacious emptiness of the combined garage and basement.

The small windows, one on either side, filtered through heavy cobwebs a handsome view of empty lots in both directions.

I began to see items I had forgotten since my childhood. At the far end of the basement in the shadowy recesses beside the door into the backyard was a mound of coal, just as in the old days when it was used for the pot-bellied black stove in the dining room and sometimes in the fireplace in the front room. Not far from the right bumper of the car was the door to a narrow flight of stairs leading up to a closet in the dining room, and from there it remained enclosed as it ran up to the attic. Father and Mother used it when I was a child to get supplies from the basement on rainy days. I had used it to reach the wide, spacious attic, where I had made myself a playhouse. . . . I wondered now if it was still there in the attic, the roofless little nest of rooms made out of old crates and boxes.

"Looking at the secret passage you used in the old days?" Howard MacPherson said lightly as he took my arm and ushered —or hustled?—me out of the basement. Polly came on behind us, happily pointing out the improvements that had been made. The greatest change was in the use of the basement. Father had never owned an automobile in the old days, but Grandpa Hyde, who was right up to the minute on everything, had talked of using the center of the basement as a garage for a new Hupmobile. Then he died, along with his small Civil War pension, and there was never enough money afterward for such luxuries.

"Don't be nervous, dear," Polly told me anxiously. "You'll soon feel right at home."

For sentimental reasons I hoped she would not guess how I really felt, but then, I hoped Mr. MacPherson could not guess for quite different reasons. I suppose I was somewhat afraid of him, of his power. I tried to give the impression I was only excited, thrilled. But as we climbed the high steps to the front door with its three narrow glass panels, I found myself almost missing the safe, familiar hospital ward I had only left an hour ago.

"You'll go straight to bed," Polly informed me as her husband unlocked the door and gave me a key as well. Locks: basement doors, now the front door. I must ask Mr. Brubick how many people had keys to this house, along with a growing list of other questions.

Meanwhile, I had to admit, Howard MacPherson was being kind without being obtrusive about it. He led me inside the wide front hall where the afternoon sun cut a thick trail through the dust from the south wall to the archway leading into the front room.

"Don't bother looking around yet," Polly advised. "You just lie down, slip off your shoes and I'll bring you some hot—" She caught her husband's eye, coughed, and finished, "hot cocoa."

I held back a smile. That was like the old Polly. Undoubtedly she had been about to say hot schnapps, which was what she used to call her drinks when father caught her with a bottle of whiskey.

Mr. MacPherson tried to veto the hot cocoa, saying, "Leave the child alone. She'll feel more like eating later. Something substantial, the doctor advised. Tell Eve."

Eve?

Polly hurried through the dining room past the spare room to the kitchen beyond. She called, "Eve? We're home." Seeing the way I looked around, she came back into the hall and explained. "That nice Mr. Brubick felt we needed a girl to help us out with the cooking. He also suggested we get somebody in each week to do the heavy work, cleaning and washing. As long as we—as you—choose to hold this property."

"But I've always done my own cleaning and washing. Cooking, too. Between us, we could manage." In fact, as I recollected with a touch of irony, I had been earning my college tuition by just such work. It seemed absurd that two able-bodied women couldn't take care of a house of only six rooms, a bath and attic.

My stepfather patted me on the shoulder. "Now, really, your doctor wouldn't even release you into our care without assurance of this help."

I managed a glimpse of the front room, furnished so exactly like the one I had last seen in early 1906 that I wondered if they had somehow resurrected every bit of the old furniture from some place arrested in time. There was the upright piano in the front room, against the wall bordering the master bedroom where mother and father had slept, and the little settee in the window alcove. It had been re-covered in old rose, which somewhat relieved me. Not that I didn't want to see things as they were, but it would have been so unlikely, almost as if it were a stage set. At any rate, it should put to rest my last doubts about Polly's identity. No one but my mother could possibly remember every piece of furniture as it existed in the house that long ago. In fact it was an astonishing feat even for her. She must have thought about it a great deal during the eventful years that followed in order to have it so fixed in her mind. A woman who had suffered poverty and degradation in that intervening time might well have dreamed about this house, reliving the lost years, but that hardly seemed the case with Polly Hyde. Obviously life had not been so hard on her during the time father and I lived from hand to mouth, and yet she remembered so many details. . . .

I didn't need to ask which was my room. It had been called the nursery and I assumed I would find it quite changed now. I took up the carpetbag Howard had dropped and when Polly nudged him he said, wisely I thought, "No. I'm sure she prefers to find it herself."

It was at the back of the house, opposite the kitchen and laundry annex, and I was glad to be going here alone. On the other hand, had it occurred to Howard that he really had no legal right whatever to dole out the rooms and be in charge of all their keys?

I always loved my room, partly because it had two exposures— a window facing north, and the entire east wall made up of windows looking out over the yard far below and creating a sunroom out of an ordinary boxy little nursery. I found changes. The wallpaper, chosen by some previous tenant, was faded, but I liked the pale yellow and white-and-green daffodil design, and the bed itself of bird's-eye maple, a light creamy color.

There was a matching chair, a chiffonier and French dresser with three mirrors I'd never had before in my life. The room pleased me more than all the rest of the house. What I saw reflected in the mirrors, however, did not please me. I had just decided I'd be reduced to buying some of Miss Hohenfelt's cosmetics in order to look human when I caught a darkish streak of movement in one of the side mirrors.

A young woman came into my view from the closet with a beautifully tucked and embroidered tunic blouse and sash over her arm. She was dark, with huge, soft brown eyes and dark hair in ringlets. Her voice was as soft as her looks.

"I'm sorry. I meant to be finished in here before you arrived. I'm Eve Carpe. Mr. MacPherson hired me to help out for a while."

I smiled, expressed suitable pleasure at her presence and the hope that she would like it here. She was certainly a surprise. With her babyish voice and those sensuous brown eyes she was the most harmless-looking person in the world. Somehow, and for some inexplicable reason, I had been expecting an Amazon, a powerful bad-tempered maid of all work. Instead, here was an enchanting soubrette right out of those French farces I'd read about.

I didn't want to remonstrate with her at our first meeting, especially as she seemed so extraordinarily sweet-natured, but I had to mention the obvious fact that the tunic blouse wasn't mine.

"Oh—excuse me, Miss Merideth, but it is. All the clothes in here are yours. They were purchased or made at Mr. Brubick's express order."

"But the sizes?"

She smiled. "We went by the size of the clothes you brought with you to San Francisco. Miss Falassi thought you would need a different kind of wardrobe here. Cooler climate, you know."

She turned and hung up the exquisite blouse, tilted her head in a subtle gesture of deference, and left the room.

I went to the row of windows that looked out over the muddy weed-covered backyard below. Near the eastern boundary somebody had left a big double swing with the two full-backed seats facing each other swinging back and forth an inch or two above the platform on which the uprights were fastened. I stared beyond to the built-up, hilly district behind big busy Geneva Avenue, the east boundary of the Hyde block that like the rest of San Francisco seemed to be awash with automobiles. I had never seen so many in my whole life as I had seen in the short time I had been in the city.

To the south, beyond the wood fence enclosing the yard, was a man with what appeared to be a camera. Probably not. More likely a surveyor. He looked familiar, thin and fairly young, and he was wearing a black overcoat. I turned to glance at something more immediately exciting, my closet full of wonderful new clothes.

Everything was as it should be if one dreamed of perfection. But I was like Cinderella. It all seemed too perfect. When did it turn back into a pumpkin?

SEVEN

THINGS WERE HAPPENING TOO FAST around me and no one seemed to feel I was ready for explanations. I wondered what they thought I had been doing with my life up to the night I arrived in San Francisco. Certainly they couldn't believe I had been raised with no experience in managing things, but now I was not allowed to make a single decision. They might blame my health, that would be their excuse, but except for a slight, normal tiredness I felt fine.

Following Polly's advice, I took off my coat and shoes, turned back the comforter and lay down on the attractive maple bed. I hadn't felt sleepy earlier. I had been too keyed up and tense for that, and so I surprised myself when I went straight off to sleep. I aroused to a kind of semiconsciousness when someone knocked lightly on the door and looked in at me during the afternoon. Then I went back to sleep, and when I did awaken it was sunset and I felt infinitely better, much like my old self.

I lay there a few minutes studying the various objects in the room and trying to get used to the idea that they were mine. If there weren't so many uncertainties, so many questions to be answered, I felt I could be happy here. It was a far cry from the partially empty house Miss Falassi had described. I got up and again looked at the clothes in my closet. They looked expensive, especially an exquisite silk evening dress the color of flame, and with its very own train. And another was the color I imagined sapphires might be, all frothy blue and romantic. Would I ever have occasion to wear such gowns? The sapphire one would be flattering, but the flame-colored dress would make me exciting. I thought I would rather be exciting. Besides, I needed every embellishment possible after my sick spell. There were also several daytime dresses, a green and white muslin, a cheerful yellow challis.

I tried on a pair of new-style pumps of black suede that seemed too elegant for ordinary daytime wear, but surely I could wear them tonight, just to break them in. They were a shade too long but otherwise perfect. I felt very grand in them and strolled to the window with a side glance at my reflection in the dressing-table mirrors.

All my doubts and fears seemed to have faded. I felt like a great lady, a Nob Hill heiress. I had a right to wear these elegant shoes. Enjoying this absurd self-justifying conversation with myself, I looked out the east windows, reminding my other nervous, uneasy self that I owned this whole block in every direction, clear to—

A total stranger was sitting in the big, wood-framed double swing at the foot of my back-yard. He was doing something, writing or drawing on a small flat object in his lap—the back of a notebook, I thought. His feet were propped up on the swing seat across from him and as he wrote or sketched he swung gently with the swing. What nerve!

I recognized that black overcoat and the way he wore it, with the collar turned up jauntily. The last vermilion sunlight gleamed on his hair, which was a light brown. Or it might even be gray, I thought cattily. And he was making himself at home in *my* yard. He was also the man I'd twice seen the night I arrived in San Francisco—once on the streetcar, once entering the Monarch Building.

"I'll put a spoke in his wheel," I assured myself, and went running out of my room past the kitchen opposite. The door was closed but I could hear the murmur of voices—Eve Carpe talking to someone while she prepared dinner.

In passing I felt guilty about that girl doing all the work. As soon as I routed this interloper I would have to go in and help her. I reached the top of the steep back-yard stairs. They had one landing halfway to the ground where the stairs changed their direction. I had reached this level when I thought the intruder must have seen me. He moved, recrossing his legs, but he did not look up. The huge double swing went rocking forward and backward.

I think if I had calmed down I wouldn't have found myself so ridiculously angry, but I had a strong sense of property in those days, perhaps due to the fact that my experience with my own property was so limited. I started walking the length of the yard toward the swing and had gone about a third of the way in such a hurry I found out too late that every footstep was sinking my precious new pumps into an inch of mud. It was a sickening discovery. It would probably ruin the suede, and I was not a woman given to buying· extra pairs of black suede pumps. Money had been too scarce for such foolishness.

"It's all that man's fault," I told myself, and by the time I reached the swing I was not only angry at the intruder for these reasons but had also begun to suspect his real identity. I should have before . . . wasn't he Miss Falassi's confederate, and hadn't I seen him entering the building to visit her? She said he was invincible, or irresistible, or some such idiocy.

I cleared my throat as silently as possible to give myself more confidence before demanding, "Are you by chance Mr. Neil Burnham?"

He looked up. "Probably by chance, knowing my father."

For a moment my annoyance obscured his intended humor, but I could hardly miss that eyebrow of his that skyrocketed as he gave forth with this witticism. It also made me want to laugh, which of course was what he intended. I tried to keep as cool as possible.

"Among your aliases, I take it you will admit to being the Passerby?"

The beginnings of that sardonic smile widened. "I take it that if I admit to being the Passerby I am barely one step above admitting to being Jesse James."

"As far as I'm concerned, I prefer Jesse James."

"The railroads wouldn't agree with you. Now, look here, Miss Hyde"—he sat his feet down on the floor of the swing so abruptly I jumped backward—"I think you owe me a little common courtesy."

"Me?"

"In repayment for having located that saintly Magdalene, your mother, you ought, at the least, to give me an interview."

I groped for some brilliant, cutting rejoinder. What I came up with was, "How did you get in here? This is private property. As a matter of fact, this is *my* property."

"I wondered when that would occur to you. They seem to be using it as if it belonged to anybody but you. All this redecorating, refurnishing . . . As you may have guessed, I'm a sometime drinking acquaintance of your stepfather . . . thought you intended to sell Hyde Place. The time surely seems right . . . The acreage farther out near the county line is worth considerably more. Fact is, several construction companies would like to build some pretty elaborate homes."

"Never mind that. It has nothing to do with you."

He looked at me a moment, then got up from the swing, brushed off imaginary threads, and asked with all politeness, "In that case, shall I leave?"

He didn't wait for my predictable answer but began to pick up his drawing materials. He had been doing a charcoal sketch that appeared to be the rear view of the house with a woman looking out one of the nursery windows. I glanced at it over his arm.

"It doesn't look the least bit like me."

"Why should it? It is meant to be that beautiful maid of yours. Eve what's-her-name."

I decided my best—my only—answer was to turn and walk back to the house without giving him further ammunition. He called after me, "Let me sketch those ankles of yours and I'll see that Passerby describes you without the Mary Pickford curls and the saintly Magdalene label."

I had to stop myself from looking down at my ankles, force myself to walk on, and found him beside me.

"I really meant it, Miss Hyde. I'll recant if you'll give me an interview. I'll even describe you as you are, which really isn't bad at all."

"And I really suggest you go interview Miss Carpe."

"Jealous?"

I ignored that and started up the steep back stairs. When he gave every sign of following me, I said, "You go out the way you came in."

He shrugged, turned slowly in the general direction of the south fence, and said as if to himself. . . . "Delicate, golden-haired little Merideth, the innocent pawn in a million-dollar inheritance—"

It worked. "I am not delicate," I said. "I am not little, and does this look like golden hair? Try reporting the facts."

Neil Burnham looked up the stairs at me, his smile in place. "From this viewpoint I consider the facts admirable. Why *won't* you give me an interview?"

"Because I don't admire your style, Mr. Burnham. It's silly in person and quite sickening in print."

"It is," he agreed, "but it also sells." Then, lowering his voice and suddenly without any apparent humor, he said, "Be careful, Miss Hyde."

I heard Eve Carpe, above, come out on the top landing and bang a colander of potato peelings against the inside of a large trash can. When I looked back at the newspaperman he was his old self as he flippantly saluted me and began to cross the yard. I leaned over the banister.

"And just what do you mean by that?"

"Another time, Miss Hyde. And don't forget."

"Don't forget *what,* Mr. Burnham?"

"Just read the Passerby, where truth is, as they say, laid bare."

I leaned far over the banister watching him go, thinking of his odd remark, but Eve Carpe was waiting for me on the landing, and so I went on up to her.

"I do believe he is going to climb over that fence," she said. "He's awfully attractive, don't you think?"

"Who?" I asked, wondering now much she knew of our conversation.

"Neil Burnham, naturally."

"You know him?"

"Mr. MacPherson does. And everyone's seen his picture."

"A very difficult man, you're lucky you don't know him"—except had she actually said she didn't know him, or just that Mr. MacPherson did?

As for Neil Burnham, he was probably lying when he said he had drawn Miss Carpe's picture. Still, he had known her name, and she was in my room when I first saw her. He could have seen her there and sketched her at the window. Anyway, why did it matter to me?

I went in with Eve, and while I set the big round dining-room table for dinner I tried to find out what, if anything, Eve knew about the background of the Passerby. She was more interested in the stiff new linen tablecloth and napkins but mentioned she had seen Mr. Burnham vault over the fence "just like Doug Fairbanks. . . . What did he say to you, Miss? He seemed awfully interested in you. Miss, you haven't gone and believed all his blarney, have you? They say he's a terrible liar." That innocent, wide-eyed look of hers saw more than one would suspect.

"Don't worry," I said. "I've met men like that before." Which wasn't strictly true. Though he was handy with the blarney, as Eve said, he was not a man one could easily forget. After I changed and cleaned my suede shoes, I kept looking down at my ankles and wondering . . . had it all been blarney when he mentioned them? . . . How did Dr. Demos think of my ankles? . . . No doubt professionally, as useful appendages. Nothing more? . . .

"Be careful, Miss Hyde." Be careful of what? Of whom? I shouldn't have been so bullheaded. I would have accomplished more if I'd pretended friendship and questioned him.

At dinner over delicious fried round steak and raw fried potatoes I learned that Howard MacPherson had returned to his stage career very recently and would soon be in a thriller at the small Giralda Theatre downtown, famed for its excellent melodrama stock company.

I tried hard to make conversation, all the while not liking the sight of Howard MacPherson in father's seat, with Polly and me on either side. I knew I was being unfair so I pretended a less than real interest in his career to make up for my ungenerous thoughts.

"It must be very exciting, acting on the stage. Is that how you met my—met Polly?"

I thought his big, broad, handsome face winced or was momentarily shadowed, but I simply found it impossible to speak of her as mother after all these years. He made a gracious enough recovery, though.

"No, I was lucky enough to catch a performance of your mother's in Chicago some years before the War started. Nineteen-ten, wasn't it?" He reached across the table for her hand, which seemed to move uneasily in his grasp, I thought, and then warned myself I had better stop making up fantasies about a man who had so far been only kind and polite to me.

"It was Nineteen-nine, I think," Polly corrected him gently, apologetically? The old Polly would have thought nothing of correcting her husband.

He agreed quickly with her date, presumably yielding to the better memory of a romantic female. "But our Merideth can't possibly be interested in those old days."

"Oh, but I am! Really, I'd like to know all about the years when we were separated."

I could see tears in her eyes and I looked away, touched and embarrassed.

Howard cleared his throat. "Now, Polly, what Merideth is really interested in is how we happened to read that fellow's column and find out our girl really wanted to communicate with her mother. A glorious feeling, I can tell you. Polly here almost drowned me in tears, she was so happy. 'She wants me back. She's forgiven me.' That's what your mother said, didn't you, Polly?"

"Yes." She looked at me. "Yes, that's what I said, dear. I said . . . 'Mery has forgiven me. I must go and see her right away.' I said—"

"You repeat yourself, honey," Howard cut in with the superior manner I already detested. "To make a long story short, Polly paid a call on Mister—it was Cafferetto first, wasn't it? And that

73

was when we learned you had been taken to the hospital the night before and were critically ill. It was a shock, I can tell you."

"A shock," Polly said. She toyed with the remains of her raisin-and-rice pudding. She had eaten the baked frosting and left the pudding, just as she used to do. This new proof of her identity delighted me so much I realized even more how troubled I had been about the Polly Hyde I remembered and her subdued self I was just coming to know.

I considered what they had told me. "I wonder how I got to the hospital. Can you believe it, I don't remember a thing about it? I just woke staring up into Dr. Demos' very nice dark eyes."

"You like dark eyes?" Polly asked. "I thought you preferred blue eyes, like your father's."

"Laughing eyes," I said. "Unfortunately, Father didn't laugh much. I like laughing eyes, and when I get to know Dr. Demos better, I'm going to teach him how to make those sad eyes of his smile. Or crinkle like yours, Polly."

"Mother?" she corrected me somewhat wistfully.

I begged her pardon, promised to do better next time, but I knew it was going to be a struggle. So many years had gone by. . . .

"Anyway"—I changed the subject—"I never did find out who saved my life. Somebody got me to the hospital, after all."

Howard understood. "I should imagine it was your landlady. By the time your mother was allowed to see you, no one seemed to know who had called the hospital and arranged for the ambulance to come and pick you up. But they knew your name from something in your purse, I believe, and the hospital called the office of Cafferetto and Brubick. After that—but you know the rest."

"I really don't know. . . . Why did you and Mr. Brubick furnish this house? And so quickly. Miss Falassi said they were just waiting for my arrival in order to sell it."

Except in the desert outside Goldfield, I had never heard such a profound silence. The dining-room door swung open from the hall after a few seconds and Eve Carpe came in to clear away the table. Howard surprised me and especially Polly by calling Miss Carpe down for interrupting us.

"That's what the bell is for, at Mrs. MacPherson's right hand. Please remember after this, Eve."

"Excuse me, sir."

All the same, I thought she was feeling less servile than her words suggested. She went right on removing dishes.

"If I may resume," Howard said, "there was the obvious fact that you needed some pleasant, healthy place in which to recover your strength. And, of course, it was helpful when Polly could show Brubick she remembered those details about the old homestead—"

"If that isn't just like Jeffrey to die and let you wander about with the flu," Polly said crisply, and got up to help Eve with the dishes.

"I'm afraid your father was a rather improvident man," Howard remarked, tucking his napkin into his napkin ring and likewise getting up from the table.

I wouldn't stand for that. "It is through Father's providence that I grew up at all." I expected a blunt or sarcastic answer. None came. He went into the front room, took a roll out of the piano stool and fastened it into the brackets above the music rack. While I remained at the dining-room table, wondering about him, the house was suddenly treated to the music of "Madame Sherry," and I heard my stepfather humming in accompaniment to the popular old hit, "Every Little Movement."

It was and it wasn't like something that might have happened long ago with Father. He had never owned a player piano but he often sang to Polly's playing on our old piano. It seemed a mockery, though, when this actor, this Howard MacPherson, played mechanical music and hummed along with it. . . . But after a few minutes I decided I was once again behaving like a spoiled child. I got up and went into the kitchen where Polly was washing and Eve Carpe drying the dishes. I tried to move mother away from the sink but she refused.

She had apparently been reduced to very different habits in the years since she left us. She had never volunteered for kitchen service beyond making an occasional slumgullion, or other delicious stew, the recipe for which she had obtained from an odd

75

but savory source. Eve found an extra flour sack for me to use as a towel and I helped her dry the silver and then the big skillet and the cake pan in which the pudding had been baked.

I was only killing time. I really wanted to go to bed. Not that I was sleepy, but because I wasn't accustomed to being in close company with comparative strangers for so long a time. I made the excuse that I was tired, and then felt guilty when Polly fussed over me. I could hardly wait to go into my room and be free of all pretenses, just to be myself.

I walked back to my room and then, silently as possible, tucked my chair under the doorknob. I now felt secure from interruption. I wasn't afraid of my own mother, or even of her husband. But I remembered that someone had opened the door while I was half-asleep that afternoon and couldn't bear to have one of these strangers peer in at me again during my sleep.

I had already undressed and was standing before the back windows brushing my hair and looking at the amazing collection of little city lights appearing over hill and dale in the distance when somewhere in the house a telephone rang, shrill and clanging. The noise stopped and a minute later Eve Carpe knocked on my door, then turned the knob. When nothing happened, she called, "Gentleman for you on the telephone, Miss Merideth."

I dressed, removed the chair and went out through the hall to the dining room where the telephone had been installed on the south wall. I was not accustomed to operating these mechanical contrivanves, having called only once to tell Mr. Brubick of Father's death, but after a few seconds I got up the nerve to take the receiver down and put it to my ear. For some reason I expected to hear Neil Burnham's voice pestering me about that interview and was ready with several choice and, I hoped, snappish answers. Mr. Burnham was a challenge, though not an unpleasant one, this Passerby who was much too sure of himself.

It came as a shock to hear Dr. Anthony Demos' voice.

"I just called to find out how you were coming along, Miss Hyde."

Somehow, I did not feel I was at my best with him, and I certainly proved it now. "Fine, just fine. It's good to hear from a friend." I was about to ask how *he* was getting along, which

76

seemed ridiculous. The conversation was moving nowhere. I wondered how I could get onto some subject that would interest him.

He said abruptly, "I mentioned you to my mother. About your needing good food. She suggested I bring you to dinner Thursday night."

"I'd love to." Merideth Hyde a guest at Demos Heights? He had not asked my family, for which I was grateful, though it wasn't quite proper. What would I wear? What would I say?

"Good. I hope you will continue to be well and happy. You must be sure and tell me if any symptoms return." And he hung up.

I heard much roaring and squawking on the line and then I put the receiver back up onto its hook. I didn't even know where I would meet him, or at what time. Now, if only he could learn to be a trifle more lighthearted, make a few jokes—be what he was not?

I must have been worrying about something that night, probably the nerve-racking remark of Mr. Burnham's, because I had what I supposed to be a very unsettling dream after that first hour or two of deep sleep. Two people were arguing somewhere not too far away, in darkness. Or maybe it was only that my room was in darkness and the voices vague, unintelligible. A light voice first intruded on my consciousness; even in my sleep I realized I was hearing only part of a conversation, but I didn't make out what was said until I heard Howard MacPherson's angry reply:

"Yes, patience. Every step has got to build up . . . I promised you, didn't I? My motto is make things seem natural . . . It won't be long, I tell you—"

The distant closing of a door woke me up. I already felt myself losing the precise details of what I had heard. I sat straight up in bed, so quickly and straight I was dizzy for a minute or two and held my head until things cleared up.

If I had heard a real conversation while I slept, would I know the difference now between that and a dream? And could I prove it?

EIGHT

Sitting up in bed, hugging myself against the chill, foggy night that seemed to claw at the many windows of my room, I repeated to myself what I had heard in my dream. I may have missed one side of the conversation but I was fairly certain about Howard's end of it. Whether I imagined the meaning or not, time would tell.

I looked across the room at the windows overlooking the backyard and remembered Mr. Burnham's cryptic warning. Even if what I had heard was a senseless dream, I did not quite trust my stepfather, or this newly furnished house, or the attention of mother. I suspected it was Howard MacPherson who had been responsible for pushing the Polly Hyde I knew from the past into this uncustomary behavior. Mr. MacPherson had an eye on this property and the other acreage bought by Grandpa Hyde. I understood his greed—I'd known plenty of greed in the gold and silver country. It was the false smile I hated, the hypocrisy.

. . . But if that conversation had been just part of my rambling dream?

I looked around the room. I hadn't unpacked my carpetbag. Good. I would keep that handy at the back of the closet and be ready to return to Nevada at a moment's notice. And I would not stay in this town any longer than was required for me to be certain Mother didn't need me.

As I lay down again I tried to understand Polly Hyde who had deserted her daughter and a man like Father yet had allowed herself to be captured by the easy charm of a Howard MacPherson. It was a reminder to me when I listened to charmers like the Passerby. Still, he *may* have been right to warn me. Anybody could be right once in a while. . . .

I had expected to toss and turn and go through other bad dreams the rest of my first night in this house where I had spent so many bittersweet days of my childhood. But though the mattress was too soft and not at all like the hard lumpy one I remembered, I had become myself again—watchful, in command of myself, or so I tried to believe. At any rate, I slept peacefully until after dawn.

I woke up early and met Eve Carpe in the hall. We talked in whispers because the door of the big bedroom that had once belonged to my parents was still tightly closed. Eve wore a pink nightgown of some thin, silky material with a low neck. Her bathrobe wasn't a robe at all but a Japanese kimono of pink with black flowers. I must say I envied that outfit.

"She won't be up for a while. She's a little—you know," Eve whispered, pointing to the master bedroom.

I suspected what she was talking about but wouldn't give her the satisfaction of saying so.

"No," I said, "I don't know."

"Soused." The word sounded especially coarse on her sweetly turned lips.

"And is he too?"

"Heavens, no! He has to be at rehearsal by eleven. He never drinks anymore. If you will give me a minute, miss, I'll get your breakfast." She seemed to know her employer's habits and condition tolerably well after only a few days on her job.

I said, "Never mind. I am used to getting my own breakfast."

"Oh, I can't let you. That handsome doctor of yours was very strict. Good, wholesome meals, he said."

I wished Dr. Demos would stop thinking of me as a case and

that his romantic looks were more in tune with his thoughts. I would be sure to wear my marvelous new pumps when I went to dinner with him—I wondered if he would notice my ankles at all.

During my prescribed breakfast of richly buttered milk toast I kept reminding myself that I was going to dine with the great Demos family on the Heights. I had never quite pictured myself involved in such a splendid adventure. It wouldn't take place for two days, which gave me time to make myself presentable and also to decide what I was going to do about these people at 379 Hyde Place.

Once I knew Anthony Demos better, maybe it would turn out that he had a keen sense of humor, that his conversation was lively. I hoped it was just that one had to know him, or perhaps be intelligent enough to talk to this man who did so much good in the world. I certainly wouldn't make any precipitous decision about my departure from San Francisco until I had mentioned it to Dr. Demos.

As Eve Carpe had foreseen, Howard MacPherson was ready at ten-thirty, neatly shaven and smelling of a somewhat overwhelming shaving cream, on his way to rehearsal downtown. I was anxious to see Mr. Brubick but I didn't want Howard to know my every move—and so when he offered in his jovial manner to take me downtown for some shopping, I told him I was a little tired and thought I might look about the house instead. "Find out whether I really want to sell or not. Maybe I should keep the property for the future," I said casually, imagining the anger he must have been hiding.

"That doesn't seem too practical," Howard said, not unexpectedly. "Sooner or later there are depressions after wars, and prices tend to go down. The sooner the better is my motto." He had a lot of mottoes. "I am a believer in getting right to things."

Last night his motto—dream or real—had been step by step, be natural. . . .

"By the way," he added, "I'm afraid we do need you to sign for a refund of forty dollars on the lease."

This was news. "You mean the people who lived here didn't

run out their lease?"

Howard shrugged. "Just the deposit, which hasn't been returned. While you were ill, we were permitted to handle things for you but now it's all yours. Once you sign, it will be sent to Brubick and he'll send through the refund."

Miss Carpe, at Howard's request, brought out a long white sheaf of papers in blue covers and set them on the dining-room table. While she went back to the drawer of the china closet to get a pen and bottle of ink, I looked over the papers very carefully, word for word. I even read the copies. Howard didn't seem very interested. Miss Carpe didn't do so well with the pen and ink. The old black pen had a split nib, and after I stuck it into the bottle, it splattered so much Miss Carpe said abruptly, "Let me. I'll clean it."

Between us we managed to drop the pen. As I knelt to recover it under the table, she rescued the bottle, which threatened to overturn on my head. This time the pen worked more smoothly and I quickly signed paper and copies. Howard rolled them up in the original blue legal cover.

"This ought to satisfy those legal fellows, all tidy and normal," he said pleasantly, waving the roll.

Normal . . . as I thought I'd heard his voice say last night. I was now almost sure of it.

Howard excused himself, passed me and took the stairs down to the basement-garage. Eve went back to her room just behind the dining room and I was left alone, to wonder which of the women my stepfather had been talking to last night.

I got hold of myself and went exploring. The attic intrigued me, and I took the inside staircase up to the place that had been my haven in the old days. When Mother and Father quarreled Father would retreat to the spare room Eve Carpe now occupied and I would have the marvelous, sunny attic to myself. It tended to lose some of its magic when Mother came stumbling up to find me with the complaint that everyone avoided her. The truth was, she needed an audience. And I think she knew it.

I rather expected to find the attic stairs dusty and unused, but I saw that they had been worn down by many feet and that initials had been carved on the enclosing unfinished wooden wall. I turned on an electric light plugged into a wall socket near the dining-room entrance to the staircase, but it was hardly necessary. Sunlight poured in overhead from a distant attic window. The steps ended at the floor of the attic. There had originally been a trap door to keep drafts from traveling down the stairs, but now there was no way of sealing off the attic. Father had taken off the trap door long ago because it had once closed on Polly's fumbling, unsteady fingers. You merely climbed the stairs, stepped out on the attic floor and there you were.

A window under the sloping roof at the east end of the long, nearly empty room let in a surprising amount of light. The glass had been broken. Another tiny window helped to illuminate the room from the west. My old playhouse of wooden crates must have been removed or broken up long ago. Instead, I found a box of toy furniture made of gold-painted lead. Almost every piece had its legs broken off, but I felt warmly for the owner. I was certain some child had played with them long after they were broken. What good was a broken toy chair with only one leg missing? You had to break off all the legs, so it sat evenly and then it was as good as ever.

I found a child's little red automobile, the pedals gone and one wheel off. There were a few pieces of old furniture, a chair with the cushion split and shredded—nothing I remembered. I felt terribly sad. It all came over me suddenly, the longing for loved ones, for my gentle father, and for my mother—my drinking, devil-may-care Polly Hyde who had walked with me on the hill above Hyde Place long ago, who put that strong but effective vinegar on my temple when I fell down the stairs and cracked my forehead—

"Don't cry, Mery . . . please don't cry. . . ."

For a second I thought that a ghost had floated into the attic behind me. I jumped and turned around. Polly Hyde stood there in a pretty, frilly wool nightgown with red ribbons threaded around neck and wrists. Was she drunk? She did not seem so. Nor did she look as if she had been drinking all night, as Eve had implied. But there was something not quite right about her, something vague. Perhaps she was sleepwalking, or frightened, cold and frightened?

"Are you all right?" I asked her when I could get my voice.

"Of course I'm all right, dear. Why wouldn't I be? Did anybody tell you otherwise?"

I looked at her. "Tell me about Eve."

She didn't seem surprised at my question. "I thought Howard might have told you by now. She was in France with one of those helping-out units, serving coffee and that sort of thing to the troops. Such a nice child! She might almost have been Howard's daughter. Then he lost track of her until recently when she looked him up and asked for a job. And here she is. Very efficient, don't you agree, dear?" She seemed surprisingly anxious for me to accept Eve Carpe. "You aren't angry about anything, are you? Please don't be."

I put my arms around her and hugged her.

"How could I be angry with my own Polly Hyde? You shouldn't have come up here without a robe, though. Do you want to catch the flu as I did?"

She lifted her head, seemed somehow almost childlike and defenseless. "Merideth . . . I know this sounds strange, but, please, perhaps you should ask yourself if you really do recognize some of these things you had as a child, but if you do, at least don't mention it just now . . . not for a while, anyway. . . ."

I could feel the tension, the unease, coming back over me again. "I suppose," I said, "but that would mean I couldn't sell my property—I mean if I didn't clearly establish my identity—and then I'd have to stay here longer . . ."

"Well, dear, something may turn up, people can be impatient, or you may even find you can get more for your property in years to come. . . ." Then she straightened, shook her head as if to compose herself, and said, "Well, Mery, have you found any of your old toys up here?"

"You just suggested I shouldn't."

She shook her head again. "So I did. . . . Mery, I must be losing what few brains I have. Now, do forgive me, I've got to go and dress."

"I'll go down with you." She did not smell of liquor but of a pleasant perfume. Eve Carpe had certainly misled me about her drinking, or Polly was being clever in disguising it. She looked back at me, worry in her face.

"I wouldn't want you to think I was talking about Howard or anybody else when I said that about people being impatient . . . not at all . . . it's just that I honestly think you *might* do better if you wait a while, but please"—she smiled again nervously—"don't say I said so. . . ."

I nodded and started after her. She held out one hand. "No, I'll go first. Give me a minute or two ahead of you, that's all."

It made me furious to see her fussing like a frightened hen over something, undoubtedly her husband.

"All right, Mother. Just tell me what you want, but for heaven's sake, don't cringe!"

"Yes, dear. And thank you for not asking questions about—you know," and she went scrambling down the steps.

I took a deep breath, waited several minutes and went down after her. So her husband, despite her denial, wanted my inheritance. Certainly not a surprise to me. And she couldn't have it both ways—at least she couldn't very well expect me to continue to trust the man. As I was opening the door into the dining room the telephone rang. I waited, expecting Eve Carpe to hurry in for some personal message, but I heard nothing throughout the house except the piercing clang of the telephone bell. It was within arm's reach and I pushed aside a chair and took the receiver down from its hook.

The caller sounded far away, with an extraordinary voice. Off-key. Or off-pitch. Not like any voice I'd heard in years . . . I couldn't think what it reminded me of.

"Hello? Hello?" It sounded tight, as if under strain. "Mister Mac?"

"He isn't in now. Please call back later in the day."

"No, now, very important. Tell him it is Lew. You understand? It is Lew who calls. A most important matter."

I said I would, and he hung up. Still trying to ferret out the oddness of that voice, or rather, what made it sound odd, I turned around without looking and knocked over the chair behind me. As I set it in place against the table I noticed a white tag sewed to the underside of the chair cushion: "VALENCIA STREET LEASING."

Either Valencia Street Leasing sold furniture as well or most of this house and the furniture that had not been here originally was a stage set, created by that prominent member of the Giralda Acting Troupe, Mr. Howard MacPherson. I looked around for a telephone directory and found the large catalog-sized book under the south window. I searched along the endless line of Valencia Street merchants and found what I was seeking. A little shakily, not from fear but from awe of this unaccustomed black monster into which I spoke, I gave the company's number. The operator got it for me rapidly and I was talking to a man employed at Valencia Street Leasing.

"Yes, ma'am, we have a record of Mr. Howard MacPherson's transactions. Quite recently. Last week, matter of fact . . . Otto, get me the sales record on a Mr. Howard MacPherson." It was as I expected. "The furniture you refer to was leased for a month. That is our minimum period. I'm afraid we couldn't give it to him for less. It is all insured, of course, but we do hope no damage has occurred. Some of the pieces are hard come by since the war."

So Howard expected my affairs would be wound up in less than a month. "I understand," I said. "Only I haven't received the bill yet, nor paid the deposit. I wanted to be sure we have the furniture for the time we need it."

"But Mrs. MacPherson, the charges were made to and paid by Mr. Lawrence Brubick of Cafferetto and Brubick. According to our records, the check is made out on the account in trust for your daughter, Miss Merideth Hyde."

I thanked him and set the receiver back. Whatever was going on, I seemed destined to pay for it by one means or another. A visit to Brubick was clearly indicated.

I heard the hall door swing open and Eve Carpe came hurrying in. "Was that the telephone? I had the water running. I thought I heard—"

"They hung up when I answered. A wrong number, I suppose."

One of her wet hands reached for the support of the china closet beside her. She had turned quite pale.

Apparently the mysterious caller for my stepfather was of more than passing importance to her as well?

NINE

I MIGHT HAVE KNOWN I wouldn't be able to leave the house without objections. My mother came out of her room in answer to Eve's call.

"Oh, Merideth, you aren't going out so soon, surely! You should be getting your rest, not wandering all over the neighborhood, wearing yourself out."

Eve offered "Perhaps I could go with you, Miss Hyde." She caught my glance and went on innocently, "Then you'd at least have someone to talk to."

"Yes, that's true," Polly put in, "you don't know the district, you might get lost."

I laughed at that, and giving Polly a quick hug, I went out of the house and down the endless flight of front steps. Those steps were more than I had bargained for and by the time I reached the sidewalk my knees felt a bit weak. I stood there taking long breaths of fresh air, heard the door open at the top of the stairs and started off briskly before they could make any new objections.

In spite of the problems surrounding me I felt increasingly better as I walked down toward the streetcar line on Mission

Street. The vacant lots of the Hyde Place ground were dotted with buttercups. I had been so accustomed to the blooming of seasonal flowers in Nevada, and especially the display of wild blooms over the desert floor on only one day a year, that I found these plain little buttercups exquisite. I picked one, intending eventually to press it in a book, but right now I stuck it into the buttonhole of my coat. It became my reassurance, a cheerful sign that everything would be all right. Several children, digging big holes in the dirt and mud at the northwest corner of Grandpa Hyde's block, looked up curiously, watching my antics with the buttercup, then giggled and resumed building a fort with the mud.

I certainly needed some outside assurance. When I left Nevada, Polly Hyde was mostly just a name and a small memory, half bright, half painful. Today she was a very real person, apparently mired in what seemed a terrible marriage and an unsavory attempt to get hold of at least a part of Grandpa Hyde's property. It wasn't that I resented mother's having a share of it, or, indeed, most of the money from the sale. I had never expected to get anything like the amount of money Miss Falassi had quoted—so I wouldn't miss it, but I was *not* willing for people like Howard MacPherson to intimidate her—or do worse to me—in order to get their hands on my property. For her to be intimidated was not like Polly Hyde, a woman of starch whatever her once bad habits. Her husband had turned her into an apparently quite submissive person.

I took the first car that rattled by, went downtown and walked over to the Monarch Building, struck by how the city had totally changed from the way I remembered it before the fire. It was necessary to look hard down every side street before I saw even one horse-drawn wagon. And there were, of course, many buildings higher than ten stories. I shuddered to think of those giants under the onslaught of another earthquake.

People were so well dressed, too. All the ladies in their hats and gloves and neat suits that had feminine gewgaws to relieve the general businesslike look. Even in my new clothes I felt like a country mouse. I should have worn a hat. Was my dress right?

The color was good, and I loved my romantic new pumps and my coat.

Another man was on duty at the elevator. Not nearly so obliging as Calvin. He looked old and bored and merely nodded when I asked for the fifth floor. Things on that floor were much livelier by daylight. I could hear an occasional voice behind the doors that had looked so mysterious the last time I passed them. Lights were on, even in daylight, glinting through the glass in the doors.

I walked in on Miss Falassi, who was at the telephone.

"I'd love to. Fortunately, I just happen to be free for lunch. I go at twelve. Wonderful!"

When she saw me she was still exuberant over her telephone call and seemed delighted to see me. She got up, walked around her desk and pumped my hand vigorously. "And what brings you down to this dreary old office? I know! You mustn't be shy. You are here to ask about an allowance. Just until things are settled. And you're surely entitled to something. That's just what Mr. Brubick said when Mr. Cafferetto—but that is neither here nor there. I'll tell Mr. Brubick you are here. I'm sure he can squeeze out a few minutes for his favorite client."

She raised her hand to rap on the inner door but I said sharply, "Mr. Cafferetto didn't want you to pay me any money?"

She looked uncomfortable. "I'll let Mr. Brubick explain. It's just that Mr. Cafferetto is very old-fashioned. He knows that according to law your mother should be handling your affairs until you are twenty-one. However, there is also your grandfather's express wish that Polly Hyde not be made your guardian in the event of your father's death."

"He never liked my mother," I said, and added, "I am not going to let the MacPhersons handle my estate. I don't care what your lawyers say."

"Quite so, that is the assumption. Your dear father made it quite clear to Mr. Brubick long ago that we should handle your affairs in the event of his death. And now, any day, the matter of that little document will be completed, and you will be wealthy. Until now we have allowed Mr. MacPherson to handle things for you, but we do initial every expenditure. By next week we will have the full list of those expenditures itemized for your perusal."

I had not come here today to get money, even my own, but on the other hand I wasn't going to let Howard MacPherson play the role of protective father with me. I said nothing more and waited while Miss Falassi went into her employer's office and closed the door.

She came fluttering out almost at once, waving her arms. "Go in, Miss Hyde. He can see you right away." Before she had finished, the lawyer was in the doorway behind her, adjusting his pince-nez and smiling his prim smile. He extended his hand, and took mine.

"Close the door, Miss Falassi."

We sat down facing each other on a stiff, uncomfortable leather settee and he said in what he doubtless fancied was an avuncular tone, "Our Miss Falassi tells me you need a bit of spending money."

He proved to be quite perceptive behind his pince-nez as he amended, "It's not only money you came to see me about?"

"If I do ask for any money, it will be as a loan against the money from my property when it is sold. I might need about twenty dollars to get back to Reno and then to Virginia City. And while I am at it, I understand I owe your company the amount it cost for the time I was in the hospital."

The glasses fell through his fingers and he fumbled for them. "My dear Merideth—if I may call you that—all of this is purely inconsequential. Once the property comes into your hands . . . and that should be shortly, shortly . . . there can be no question of repayment. It will be automatic."

I looked about the room. Its severe elegance didn't much interest me, but the door between his office and that of his partner was ajar, which made me nervous. I wondered if Mr. Cafferetto, who didn't like me anyway, was listening in that office.

I lowered my voice. "Could you please tell me what you know about Mr. MacPherson? I understand he and my mother came to see you in answer to a column by that Passerby person."

He nodded. "I assure you, it was all quite proper. I recognized her at once, the near-image of the charming little Polly Hyde I last saw in 1905 before she left your father. Why, I saw that girl perform at the Poodle—" He cleared his throat. "Must have been nineteen years ago, before you were born, and yet she hasn't really changed a whit. Same delightful—"

"But she has changed."

He was startled.

"I don't mean that I mistrust Polly. It's the people around her. . . . I don't mean to be difficult, but what proofs of her identity did they offer?"

To my surprise, Mr. Brubick wasn't annoyed by my question. He got up and brought me a file folder from the center drawer of his desk. It had been handy to his reach, and I wondered if it was handy because he was waiting for my question. I decided I was becoming impossibly suspicious.

He read off a list from the top page of the file. Beneath that page I could see grandfather's will written in his beautiful, flowing script, the kind he must have used when signing his name to a dance program, or a lady's fan at the Tivoli Opera. Although I had never known grandfather, the sight of that writing moved me and I looked away, toward Mr. Cafferetto's partially open door.

"Ah, now we have it. All very well documented. A wedding ring belonging to one Polly Hyde. So tightly squeezed into your mother's flesh that it wouldn't come off. It would have had to be cut off. A plain gold band with a—"

"Tiny wreath engraved on it?"

"Precisely." He considered the document again. "An ivory fan. Every stick had the name of a song performed by Polly Hyde."

I nodded.

"And a dress . . . Now, here, I must allow myself to be the greater judge than you. They brought a dress that I distinctly remember. It wouldn't fit Mrs. MacPherson now, of couse, but it was the gown she wore when I once took her and Mr. Hyde to the Lakeside Country Club for dinner. Exquisite creation. Near falling apart now, but unquestionably the same gown. Black and white, gauzy material with a kind of bustle, and taffeta underskirt. And Mrs. MacPherson also had a sewing basket with a pin cushion—you recall that pin cushion, my dear?"

"She hated it," I said, remembering the pin cushion very well, because whenever she had to get out the darning things to mend one of my stockings or my father's shirts, she always cussed and complained. "Was the pin cushion red felt, with the insides spilling out? The insides were an odd color."

"Green stuffing. Yes. Now, we come to memories. I can tell you, Merideth, we put your mother through quite a course. She didn't always remember, but when she went home and thought it out—and neither Frank nor I had given her a single clue—she usually remembered. Even the details of our dinner that night at the club—the chandeliers, she particularly mentioned, described their special luster." He looked at me for a minute before closing the file, then said gently, "Are you satisfied, my dear?"

"Yes, I didn't *really* doubt it, except—"

"Yes, except we must have it all out. All the doubts and fears looked at and gotten out of the way. I do understand."

"Well, it just seemed to me that if she went away because she drank too much and father had complained once too often, then she wouldn't look the way she does today. Older, yes, but I couldn't see any signs of dissipation."

"Nor could I, Merideth. Frank pointed that out, too. But I believe we may safely conclude that once she realized what she had deserted—and I make no excuses for your mother in those days—she stopped drinking and became a most respectable lady—which you must admit, she is today."

I looked up at him. "And what about Howard MacPherson? Was he in the YMCA? And was he hurt overseas in a bombardment at St. Mihiel or something like that?"

We were both startled when Frank Cafferetto came into the room, his portly stomach preceding him by several inches.

"Miss Hyde, you are no fool. I think I may pride myself on having checked into the man's antecedents at once, although strictly speaking, he is not involved here except as the person who handles your mother's affairs. Incidentally, she seems to revere him. She looks to him for every opinion."

"He is what he claims to be?"

"As nearly as we can judge, yes. He was overseas. He did act in a capacity to aid our soldiers and was wounded. I can also say that he has been fairly well known from time to time as an ctor. He played the Alcazar here some years ago, and is at present playing the lead in some mystery or other at the Giralda Theatre. It was through his theatrical connections, I believe, that he was able to refurnish your house in order to make you feel you had a home to return to, after your hospital stay. It also was intended to refresh your memory so that we may have your deposition witnessed. You conclusively prove your identity and we issue a directive to the effect that your identity is unquestioned and, well, there you are—the well-to-do Miss Merideth Hyde. I may say the notion of taking you to your former home after your release from the hospital was an ingenious one. Mr. MacPherson tells me that you have related innumerable incidents which establish the relationship between yourself and your dear mother."

The purpose of which, I felt certain, was to validate her and thereby his position, as much as mine—two birds, as it were. . . . It was indeed ingenious of Howard—more so than Mr. Brubick could or, apparently, would suspect. I thought again of that dream which I now believed to be a genuine conversation overheard. Howard had talked about making things seem natural. He was doing that, all right. And what would happen the day I received my estate? Afterward? I thought of Polly's uneasy attempt at a warning. If they got their hands on that money through Cafferetto and Brubick, what then? But could they get the money without my consent? Surely not! Unless I was not around to withhold it, and my next of kin, my mother, and her husband *were* around to claim . . .

I had to find someone I could trust, someone who at least believed in the possibility of my suspicions. The only prospect I felt I knew in San Francisco was Dr. Demos.

I gave the two lawyers my sweetest smile and said, "I'm afraid Mr. MacPherson may have exaggerated just a bit. You know, I can't seem to place all those things they tried to remind me of. Sometimes it's as if they're talking about a different girl. . . ."

Cafferetto and Brubick exchanged glances, Brubick looking pained and taking off his glasses to rub the indentations on either side of his thin nose. Mr. Cafferetto, however, studied me intently. I wondered if he suspected me.

Mr. Brubick coughed, got up and put the Hyde file into his desk. "Well, perhaps we are being precipitate. We shall see."

"Yes," Mr. Cafferetto agreed in his harsh voice, "we certainly will not rush into anything." He didn't like it, though, not at all. His office stood to lose a considerable sum if I turned out to be some nobody who only pretended to be Merideth Hyde. I now felt I had tried their patience long enough and got up to go.

Miss Falassi watched me, her head almost revolving as I passed her. She had just powdered her nose with a puff from her boxy vanity case and waved the puff at me as I passed. I remembered her appointment and said, "Have a good lunch." She beamed. I envied her that excited glow.

Out in the hall I wondered what I could do to avoid returning to Hyde Place after I had accomplished the one errand I had planned for this afternoon. I had forgotten dozens of things I meant to ask the lawyers. For instance, was it their idea to buy me all these clothes? Miss Falassi had suggested them, but if the property sale didn't go through, or my inheritance failed to come to me, would I be in debt for those large bills too? One more debt against a possible fortune which even before possession made me prey to all kinds of most unpleasant—and dangerous?— ambitions.

I heard men's voices coming out of the elevator around the corner. I hesitated, feeling out of place as usual in this building full of businessmen, but there was no place to get out of sight and then I almost ran into the two men when we met just as they rounded the corner of the hall.

The man I saw first was Howard MacPherson, still carrying my blue-covered lease papers. He was with Neil Burnham, the columnist, both men laughing at an exchange of remarks.

So much for Neil Burnham's supposed well-intended warning to me! After a brief, surprised frown upon seeing me and a slowing of his pace, it was almost as if he failed to recognize me.

TEN

My STEPFATHER, ON THE CONTRARY, appeared so delighted to see me that one never would have suspected we had said goodbye to each other with utmost indifference only an hour or so before. He clasped my fingers so vigorously I winced.

"You've been talking with your father's lawyers. Good for you. And I'll wager you've told them all the details you recalled after spending only one night in your old homestead. I said right along you were a bright girl . . . By the way, you haven't met our old friend, the Passerby, have you?"

"Once," I said. "In my back-yard. I believe you might say the Passerby was trespassing."

Howard laughed at my small irony. Actually, I had told him the truth because I assumed Eve Carpe would have done so. Neil Burnham and I approached the introduction as if we had never exchanged more than the most casual remarks, and I didn't know whether this was deliberate on his part or whether he had genuinely forgotten his curious warning to me. As I looked at him coolly, I confess I found it difficult to dislike him as much as I should have in these circumstances, yet I also felt a man of his assets could be especially dangerous if he were teamed up with the likes of Howard MacPherson.

My stepfather reminded me, with the subtlety of an elephant, "You owe it to friend Burnham here that your mother and I heard about your search for her."

"Thank you," I said to Mr. Burnham, hoping the words sounded as toneless as I intended.

The exasperating man seemed to read into my lack of interest a clear enthusiasm. His green eyes flashed and his smile was far too engaging to be sincere. Hadn't I read the cynicism in that clever face the first time I saw him on the streetcar?

"My dear Miss Hyde, I really don't deserve all this, not just for a few words strung together to make a column. A string of clichés, as I'm sure you will be the first to agree."

"Yes, indeed," I obliged him pleasantly, and walked away as they stood there. Having turned the corner, I slowed my rapid pace and made my steps as silent as possible in order to hear the dialogue that followed. I couldn't make it out, though. They must have lowered their voices or stopped talking entirely. I wondered what secrets these two men had. Or if it was my imagination, after all . . . ?

I rang for the elevator and was just stepping into it when a man's hand reached over my head from behind to keep one of the doors from closing. It was Neil Burnham again, favoring me with his patented vaguely surprised, lifted eyebrow, as if I were the last person he expected to see.

"What *do* you want?"

"Just to go down. This car is going down?" he asked the operator. The man nodded and continued his staring into space.

There appeared to be no answer to Mr. Burnham's juvenile humor so I tried to ignore him, but he was the kind of man women were automatically aware of. I hadn't forgotten all the absurd flutterings of the girls in the hospital ward and of Miss Falassi herself. On the ground floor I started to hurry past him but the buttercup fell out of my coat buttonhole and he picked it up.

"Yours, I believe, ma'am?"

"I never saw it before," I said, and went on, hoping I appeared more sophisticated than I felt. I was both flattered and uncertain when he came along after me, uncertain because I believed him to be untrustworthy and probably a party to Howard Mac-Pherson's plans for my inheritance. Clearly, he was immune to a snub. Worst of all, he diverted me when I knew I should remain suspicious of everyone connected with my stepfather.

He caught up with me on the sidewalk. "You haven't thanked me yet." And though he must have known perfectly well he was talking in riddles to me, he added in the same manner, "You don't like it. That's the trouble . . . you just don't like it."

What an actor! I felt that the wrong person was in the Giralda Melodrama Stock Company.

"Thank you for what? I don't like what?"

He took a folded newspaper out of his overcoat pocket and handed it to me. Prominently displayed was a black-and-white sketch of a vaguely rendered building. It did look, however, as though it might be the back of the house at 379 Hyde Place. A girl was looking out one of the windows of my back bedroom. A girl with long, rather tangled hair and plaintive eyes. Not someone you would expect to find in a sketch under a headline: "BEAUTY DREAMING."

I tried to clear my throat without his noticing. I said, "It's quite a good picture of Miss Carpe, but the hair is too long. Miss Carpe is very modern, you know. She has bobbed hair."

He sounded impatient. "I know very well what Eve Carpe looks like. Don't you know your own likeness when you see it? God knows, I did it over enough."

There was no article underneath the picture, just a few paragraphs captioned "Passerby on the Go." I couldn't hide my interest any longer. "How did you do it? I mean—when? I was only at the window a few minutes."

"Good memory. I added a few details to the sketch after our rendezvous in your delightful back garden."

"Don't be sarcastic. It's nothing but a mud slough. Anyway, thank you. May I keep this?"

He waved it aside. "Let's go. If we wait any longer, all the lunch places will be full and I hate to eat standing up."

"Lunch!" I considered the newspaper. Luckily I had an excuse to give in. "I suppose I do owe you something for this."

"Quite true. The paper, by the way, cost me a nickel. Bought it myself. Come on. You're headed in the wrong direction." He took my arm and we started along Market Street.

"Where are we going?" I asked, and quickly knew as we turned the next corner and walked into the Palace Hotel, that symbol of majestic elegance.

The lobby appeared to be full of homecoming soldiers still in their khaki, still with their legs bound up in the khaki strips they called puttees.

"One last fling for them in the City before it's home to Salinas and Fresno and Petaluma," Neil Burnham commented.

I said suddenly, "Was he really a hero at St. Mihiel?"

"Who?" But I thought it a little suspicious he understood almost at once. "Mac? Yes, or at any rate he was there. An accidental hero, I imagine. I don't know. I was home long before that, but the police say the record is clear." So he had checked with the police.

He took me through the long, crowded lobby to the elegant restaurant. We sat at a table where people could look at us and some did. They recognized the Passerby as soon as we were shown to the table with its stemmed glasses on a cloth with damask threads. I ran my fingers over the cloth, noticed him watching my hand. It was odd to see him look away, as if he were ashamed I had caught him at it. I needed to remember that watching was his profession, after all. Watching and then telling the world about it in ridiculous Laura Jean Libbey terms. Still, he was being kind and friendly and at least for this luncheon I would try to forget my suspicions that he was up to something with Howard MacPherson.

The out-size menu was in English, but there was such an assortment that I finally dismissed it with a defeated wave. "You order. I usually eat at counters."

I readied myself for one of his flippant remarks, but he only said, "Good, we'll see if I can guess what you like."

Two women in gorgeous hats were sitting at the next table and obviously whispering about him, putting up their menus to cover their mouths, glancing at him and then away. He caught them at it and gave them one of those mannered smiles I had disliked that first evening on the streetcar. Then he resumed ordering lunch for us and paid them no more attention. I couldn't help feeling flattered when he concerned himself with whether I liked seafood or the elaborate soups, while the women did everything they could to attract his attention and got nowhere. The only thing we disagreed on was dessert. I wanted some and he didn't.

When we had worked our way to the dessert, he said, "I suppose, as Mac says, you've cleared your inheritance with Cafferetto and Company."

"No. Isn't it too bad?" I had surprised him and I liked that. I went on eating my lusciously rich lemon-cream pie until I decided he had stared long enough. "I'm afraid I seem to have forgotten several things they thought I ought to know."

"What are you up to?"

"Up to? My mind just goes a bit fuzzy sometimes. It may not recover until I am old enough to handle my property without relatives hanging about with their advice."

"Merideth Hyde, look at me."

I did.

"What game are you playing? Mac says you remember every detail."

I finished eating my pie quickly, and between bites reminded him, "You told me to take care. It apparently frightened everything right out of my head."

He stared at me and then began to laugh, which was embarrassing because the few people who hadn't seen us before certainly noticed our table now. I said, "Don't you have to go back to work?"

He admitted it. "I can't keep writing about imaginary golden-haired little orphans forever."

As we left the magic precincts of the Palace, he said casually, "You must be lonely in town. What do you do with your evenings?"

I was proud to tell him with his own degree of casualness,

"I am very busy. Tomorrow night, for instance, I am dining with Dr. Demos' family, on the Heights."

He turned up the collar of his elegant, slightly shabby tweed overcoat, frowning into the windy blue sky. "That should be exciting."

"Why are you being sarcastic?"

"Me? Why should I be sarcastic?" Then he added after a few seconds, "I must admit I'd like an interview with the Demos pair. Quite remarkable. Why don't you interview them for me?"

"I'd love to. He's a wonderful man. He saved my life, I really believe it. And I'll be happy to interview him for you."

"I'm not talking about our noble surgeon. I am talking about his parents. Much more interesting."

"We have different opinions on that."

"Just don't make any engagements for later in the week." He started away breezily without even saying goodbye, but then, I hadn't thanked him either. I did now. "Thank you. I really did love my lunch."

"Nothing at all. And now I have to do it all over again."

"What?"

"I've a luncheon date with Miss Falassi."

"Good heavens!" So he was her date! "Aren't you rather late?"

"Less than an hour. Business interview detained me, of course. Where are you off to now? Can you get home?"

I had a very special errand but I didn't think it wise to tell him about it for fear he would relay it to his good friend Howard MacPherson.

"I am going window-shopping."

"See you soon, dreaming beauty."

In a private glow I walked to the nearest corner, where a policeman stood directing people across the enormous width of Market Street. Many people paid no attention to him and ploughed right across in the middle of the street, remarkably adroit at missing automobiles and the streetcars that rumbled by on all four tracks. Still, I didn't feel up to all that leaping, running and scooping my posterior in to keep from being hit by a car rattling by in the opposite direction. I crossed in a reasonably ladylike fashion and walked north toward the California Street cable car.

The street was terribly busy. I felt closed in by the large buildings representing enormous fortunes in this Wall Street of the West, a district which seemed unfriendly because it was totally alien to my past life. I walked several blocks without seeing anything that looked familiar, and was beginning to wonder if that whole evening trip to Chinatown had been a fantasy of my illness when I reached the cable-car line. That suddenly looked familiar. I jumped on the little car just as it was about to pull across Montgomery Street, and rode up through Chinatown. It looked a good deal less glamorous by daylight. The cable car was crowded, as always, but I found nothing in the least sinister about my fellow passengers.

The young Chinese looked exactly like the stockbrokers from Montgomery Street, but the older Orientals, male and female, wore trousers and padded blouses, and had the unnerving ability to look directly at one without appearing to see anything at all. I still imagined that they were staring at my defenseless back and I could almost feel between my stiffened shoulder blades the ax of the Tong hatchetman.

I watched for Dupont Street, the main Chinatown thoroughfare, which crossed the cable-car line. Then I belatedly remembered that it was now an extension of Grant Avenue. Once past Grant, I recognized the little Chinese grocery store and hopped off. Nothing in that damp, evil-smelling alley had changed except that the running rat had been metamorphosed into a cat only slightly larger and just as wet. Fortunately, the cat appeared well fed. I had second thoughts before starting up those stairs, but when I heard a woman's voice singing off-key in the landlady's apartment I got up my courage and climbed up.

A tousled, red-haired woman shuffled to the door in a flowered wrapper. She yawned, and asked, "Looking for a room? We're full up right now." She looked me over. A little of the friendliness I had seen that first night began to seep through. "Come around next week, I'm expecting two vacancies Saturday. A sailor first floor back, and a real nice sunny room on the top floor.

Rented by an old Tong Boo-How-Doy, but he's getting married to a little China girl from Weaverville so—" She got a better look at me. "Don't I know you from somewhere?"

"I was here about two weeks ago. I rented a back room for three days but I got sick."

She pulled the door open. "Lordy! You're the . . . Hyde girl. Come in, come in."

"I'll only keep you a minute. I just wanted to ask if you remember anything about that night."

She was already pulling me inside the double-room apartment I had seen once before. "If I put my mind to it, I can probably remember. How about a little glass of red wine? Homemade by some friends of mine out in the Excelsior. Better drink it now, hon. Along comes this summer and there'll be no more wine—not legal, anyway."

I refused, saying I had just eaten, but told her to please have one herself. She did so, pouring a water glass full and enjoying every long swallow as I looked about, trying to figure out what really had happened the night I was taken to the hospital.

"I came here with an older lady that night, didn't I, Mrs.—"

"Ybarra, Angel Ybarra. Yes, there was a woman with you. Wow!" She rolled her eyes elaborately.

This was how I had expected my mother to look—hard-drinking and a bit blowsy, but still pretty, still the attractive and pert Polly Hyde she had been when I was a child.

"I did see her," Angel Ybarra said, "but she didn't stay around long. Not after you came down sick."

We were getting to the crux of things. "Who phoned for the ambulance that night?"

"She did, I guess." She waved her glass. "Said she had no money and tried to get it from me to pay for a taxicab. As it happened, I wasn't so flush that night. Between rents, you know. Anyway, I guess the woman got an ambulance instead of the taxi. She also lifted a bottle of my best whiskey that I was saving for the dry times ahead, and away she went. Guess she found the money she was looking for same way she found my hooch. I heard all the commotion when they came for you and helped them get you off to the hospital. The woman was drunk as a lord by that time. If I'd known about the whiskey being gone I'd have understood how she got drunk. Anyway, she went off and I watched them take you away and then, later, I read about you in the Passerby's column. I was glad to hear you came through. Wasn't much I could do, though. You were real sick that night. Right out of your mind."

"You don't know any more about the woman? Did she show any sign that she knew me as more than a casual acquaintance?"

Mrs. Ybarra laughed. "Not the way she was putting it down! She'd already been pulling at my whiskey bottle when I saw her staggering off down Dupont Street . . . Grant Avenue, I mean to say. No, ma'am, far as I could make out, the only thing she was interested in was the booze."

I got up, thanking her again, and gave her two dollars for the missing whiskey. I left the house with her good wishes trailing behind me. It seemed evident that my strange first night in San Francisco had led me up a blind alley in more ways than one, along with the unpredictable woman whom I had thought of, almost without realizing it, as Polly Hyde number one. There was, I'd have to accept, only one Polly Hyde, and that was the woman unfortunately married to Howard MacPherson.

I walked the long way down Grant Avenue to Market Street, not feeling satisfied, even though now I could be certain about Polly MacPherson being Polly Hyde. I kept thinking how that disheveled woman had only taken a few dollars from me but not the rest of my money. If she had been a complete reprobate, a hopeless drunk, wouldn't she have taken all my money? I finally dropped my defense of her and decided she was probably curled up somewhere around a bottle at this very minute. Sentiment was fine, but I was letting it get out of hand. . . .

On Market Street I faced a minor crisis. I could take one of the municipal streetcars and if it didn't go out past Geneva Avenue, I could transfer. On the other hand, the first car approaching from the Ferry Building was on the inner track. A crowd had lined up along the narrow strip of pavement between outer and inner tracks, and I could overcome at least one of my fears by getting on that car.

I crossed to the center of the street beside two women loaded with packages from the Emporium and Hales department stores. I found myself hoping we could all get on before the first municipal car arrived on the track behind us. A crowd had already begun to gather for that car. I felt like a race-track bettor urging on my horse . . . please get here first, inner-track car. . . . Obligingly, it arrived. Less obliging, it stopped yards ahead of me. I found myself caught up in the rush for the entrance door, pushing and being pushed. I was wedged in front of a fat woman loaded down with paper bags and just behind a little man with a protruding stomach, which he was using as a battering ram.

I heard the roar, the rattle and crunch of the municipal car coming up on the outer track and gritted my teeth, swearing to myself I wouldn't look around, would ignore the monster roaring toward my back. I began to feel shaky. A step, a single long step backward and—

Had I wished it upon myself? Screaming, "Who pushed me?" the fat woman with packages suddenly hurtled into me. I grabbed at empty air, conscious of space and the whirling sky. I was pushed backward . . . back and back . . .

My shoe heel skidded on the track behind me. The rail trembled with the weight of the oncoming car.

ELEVEN

I WAS TOPPLING back onto the outer track when the little man with the stomach grabbed my arm, nearly pulling it out of the socket.

I recovered my equilibrium, clutching frantically at the little man's lapels, while the municipal car clanged in a fury.

The little man grinned. "Easy, lady. You nearly got your head cracked like an eggshell."

I mumbled my thanks, but he could only guess what I was saying as passengers and packages poured up the steps into our streetcar. The seats were all taken, and the fat lady lumbered in to stand beside me.

She puffed breathlessly as she apologized. "Really, I don't know what this world is coming to! Before the war this rude behavior would never have been allowed."

"Did you see who pushed you?" I asked.

She shifted her packages. "Must have been a child. Anyway, a small person. Nobody else behind me."

Just for a moment or two as she was speaking I had wondered, looked out the window. . . . She was right. At least from the tracks to the curb no one as big as Howard MacPherson was visible among the crowd. Perhaps someone smaller . . . ?

But even assuming my suspicions were not overheated, there would be no reason for anyone to try to murder me—not yet . . . the property wasn't mine yet, so my death wouldn't profit anyone . . . unless by Grandpa's will my next of kin, mother, or the lawyers would be in line. Even so, it was such a clumsy, uncertain attempt . . . if it *was* an attempt, which seemed unlikely. Clumsy, or shrewdly contrived so that the identity of the assailant was easily and quickly hidden in a crowd. . . . Whatever, no denying it was a near thing.

Still shaken and with my shoulder aching badly, I was half inclined to pack up and go home to Nevada. However, by the time we reached Valencia Street and I had recovered my senses, I decided I was indeed being melodramatic and that in any case I didn't want to leave my mother only a few days after I had found her again. The years of separation had been too long. I decided again to make plans for instant departure but to hold everything in abeyance, and above all to be watchful but not excessive in my suspicions.

The first thing I did when I reached home, if a houseful of strangers could be called home, was to pull out father's carpetbag and check its contents. I put in the attractive pair of kid pumps my "family" had bought for me with an advance on Grandpa Hyde's inheritance, and the most practical of the lovely dresses in my closet. I had brought underwear, stockings, night things and other clothing with me. And because it brightened my day, I also stuck in the newspaper that had my picture sketched by the Passerby.

When I had set my carpetbag back in the darkest corner of the closet, I felt much more secure. Now, if only I could be sure Polly would be safe if I left her. Impossible, as I kept thinking of her husband and those pale eyes of his, the way he smiled while his eyes went right on clicking away money like the counters on a Chinese abacus.

A Chinese abacus . . . I had seen many of them in the mining camps, operated by Chinese who were in business there, but now I suddenly remembered a time when I was a child and father and mother and I went to Chinatown for a dinner given by the members of father's singing group and I recalled how most of the men I saw there wore the oiled queues. They seemed far more attractive to me than the whites in father's group, who had ugly handlebar mustaches and striped suits.

I closed the closet door. What *was* this obsession of mine with Chinatown? I had seen how little that first night meant. Something a great deal more important had happened to me today after I left Chinatown. I had almost lost my life.

Polly knocked on my door. "Are you all right, dear? Howard suggested we have a little music before dinner." She gave a small embarrassed laugh. "He thought I might sing a few of my old numbers. Probably I'm all out of voice, but Howard is always so sweet about complimenting me."

I felt the pity she stirred in me nowadays. Heaven knows she never did before! She had been direct and devious and charming all at the same time. Life must certainly have tamed her, along with breaking her of her drinking habit. I opened the door and put my arm around her, drawing her into the room.

"I'd love to hear you sing, but in a minute. I'm surprised Howard is home. Won't he be needed for rehearsal?"

"But dear, he rehearsed all afternoon after he left the lawyers' office."

"And Eve Carpe?"

She puzzled over this. "I couldn't say because I was out for an hour or so. I walked up to the old dairy on the hill at the end of the street."

"Then she was here alone." And Eve was not a very big girl.

"Really, Merideth, I don't understand you. Of course she wasn't alone. Mrs. Halston, the cleaning woman, was with her until about fifteen minutes before you arrived."

So the fat lady had probably been right . . . the pushing and shoving was doubtless a routine thing and my near-accident was simply part of it.

"I'm sorry," I said. "I do want to hear you. Let's go."

Polly and I went into the front room together in considerably restored spirits. Even my stepfather looked tolerable to me, smiling and enthusiastic, applauding Polly as she went to stand by the piano, where he was to accompany her. I sat down on the sofa in the front alcove and soon had my feet curled up under me, reliving moments from my earliest years. Except, of course, for the obvious differences between father and Howard Mac-Pherson.

It had been a long time since I'd heard Polly sing. I had never heard her sing professionally, but it seemed to me that she was a better singer now than before. A better singer, but perhaps lacking a little of her old zest and sparkle. I could understand that, though. After all, she hadn't appeared before the public in years.

She began with a rousing "Hello, My Baby," went into "Love Me and the World Is Mine" and brought up in a finale of "Grizzly Bear," all to a lively accompaniment by Howard. During this pleasant hour Eve Carpe stood in the doorway arch, listening with an attention that surprised me. I had no idea she would be so respectful to Polly. Eve joined in during an interval of applause. She really appeared to care that Polly's little recital was a triumph, as it certainly was, with me.

When Polly had sung an encore, this time nearly moving us to tears with a war medley including "Keep the Home Fires Burning" and "There's a Long, Long Trail," Howard gave the piano one last banging chord and swung around to face me.

"Pretty good for a girl who hasn't appeared in public since before the war, wouldn't you say?"

"Wonderful," I said, and was immediately surpassed by Eve Carpe's, "It was wonderful indeed, Mrs. MacPherson, especially the old pieces. They made me think back to when I was a little girl . . . when I was a little girl," she repeated softly.

A silence followed, just long enough for me to become aware of the big case clock in the hall ticking away. As before, they were waiting for me. They all looked at me, even Polly. I smiled dreamily.

"You're right. It does take you back. I can still hear Father singing those very words from the illustrated slides in the Goldfield Casino."

Howard started to say something but Polly frowned at him and he subsided. They were, of course, expecting to hear me reminisce about Polly and our past together, not about my father. Howard fiddled with the piano keys as Polly said, "Don't you remember hearing me sing those songs while you were cuddled up on the sofa? Sometimes you hummed along with us."

I was furious that they had once more tried to use what appeared to be an unselfish moment of pleasure for their own purposes. I looked at Polly, all perplexed innocence. "Really? That long ago? But I thought 'Home Fires Burning' was a war piece from England. And 'Long, Long Trail'—does that actually go back to my childhood?"

For the first time I saw a show of the old Polly Hyde temper. *"I did not mean the war songs.* I meant—" She seemed to think better of this mood and smiled with an effort. "Howard, it's getting on and tonight is your dress rehearsal. Don't forget."

Howard got up and bounded for their bedroom, calling as he went, "Damn, you're right. We were having so much fun I nearly forgot *The Pine Box* opening Friday night. Merideth, you want to be sure and see it. It's a mystery. Plenty of secret passages, that sort of thing. You'll like it. Polly will take you."

I wondered what he would say if I told him I'd feel much more comfortable going to a theater matinée alone than entering this very house.

I called after him, "Thanks. I'd love to see your show," and felt like adding, "especially on a proper stage instead of in my home." He waved and vanished into the bedroom.

After that Polly and I attempted small talk about her husband's return to the theater and what it meant to him. All evening, whenever I tried to discuss Polly's future, I ran up against the imposing barrier of Howard MacPherson. I tried to get around it, even venturing to ask if she and her husband were ever apart, or ever had quarrels, difficulties.

This produced not only surprise, as if we had never had our discussion a few hours earlier in the attic, but also an almost too firm denial. She rushed to say it was impossible and I mustn't even think that they would ever be separated. It wasn't until I went to bed, early as before, that I glanced at the telephone in the dining room and remembered the phone call, the anxious voice asking for "Mac." I had lied about it once when Eve Carpe came in too late to get the call, and I felt no particular guilt in keeping it secret. No one had called since, so Howard's caller must have been less desperate than he sounded. It was curious, though, and I wondered if I might not know a great deal more about Howard MacPherson if I understood what that call was all about—and who had made it.

I awoke several times and on each occasion worried about dinner the next evening with Dr. Demos at his home. He hadn't told me the hour we would meet, or where, but he was a gentleman and I knew he would come for me at 379 Hyde Place. What should I wear? I wanted to look my very best for the father and mother of Anthony Demos. It wasn't bad enough that they were the parents of this fine man, but, according to Neil Burnham, Mr. and Mrs. Demos were even more famous than their son.

Thursday morning I went through all the new clothes in my closet and couldn't make up my mind what would please the young doctor and not antagonize his parents. I had just begun getting dresses out and putting them back when I heard the big touring car leave the basement-garage. Howard MacPherson, off to rehearsal, no doubt. He did not slam the basement doors, which meant one of us would eventually have to close them.

About half an hour later I heard a series of muffled crashes somewhere inside the house. There seemed to be a few seconds' pause before the last crash. I went out into the hall. The kitchen was empty. Polly had rushed back from the front room.

"What was that? Merideth! Are you all right? Oh, God, I thought—"

"Never mind me. I'm fine. You know what that sounded like, don't you?"

She shook her head. "Somebody falling. Maybe down the front steps. Oh, Mery, I hope not! Things have been going well with us and now this!"

"You know perfectly well that noise didn't come from outside."

I opened the door onto the staircase that ran from the basement to the attic. Polly pushed in behind me. I heard her quick gasp. There was no one on the attic half of the stairs, but beneath us, halfway down the stairs to the basement, Eve Carpe was getting painfully to her feet. She was disheveled and wincing as she climbed back up toward us.

"Eve!" Polly was trying to see around me. "Whatever happened?"

The breathy voice reached us with mingled anger and fear. I understood the anger, but the fear was so real it was nearly contagious. "I fell down the damned stairs . . . caught my heel and just tumbled down." She was coming rapidly up the stairs and ignored the hand I extended until she reached the dining room. I helped her to her room while mother went to look for salve to rub on what she predicted would be some nasty black-and-blue marks.

When Eve finished doctoring her bruised hip and the ankle she had twisted, she waved us away with the fretfulness of anyone who suffers such an accident, but as I left the room and looked back at her in the doorway I realized that in her manner was more than mere bad temper. Apparently something had badly frightened her—surely something more than the fall.

I went into the kitchen and finished the dishes. Afterward, I began to clean and polish the stove. It was a new gas range and very impressive to me. I had been working a little while when the telephone rang and as I reached the kitchen door I discovered Eve Carpe at the telephone. I hadn't heard the door of her bedroom open or her footsteps on the squeaky boards of the hall. She motioned to me and I came running. It had to be Dr. Demos, and it was. As I listened to him I saw that the door to the basement stairs was standing open. I thought I had kicked it shut when I helped Eve to her room, but since she couldn't possibly have been foolish enough to go back down those stairs with her bandaged ankle and bad hip, I decided I must have failed to close it properly. I could think of no other explanation.

Dr. Demos, perfect gentleman, was apologizing for not having told me what time he would drive by to pick me up, and told me that a last-minute hospital meeting had come up which would delay him until seven, which in turn would upset his mother because it was cook's day off and she had everything planned for six-thirty. Not too promising a beginning, I thought.

It was always bad luck to start out with a man's mother upset.

"Is everything all right, Merideth?"

"Fine," I assured him hastily. "Seven o'clock. I'll be ready."

"Good. By the way, my parents don't always, well, understand my friends. Different generations, you see."

Obviously his parents were formidable, in spite of all Neil Burnham could say. In fact, I almost wished Neil was going along with me to get his interview. I could always exchange insults with him if things got difficult with Dr. Demos and his parents.

"I'll do my best not to be too modern," I assured him.

He told me I needn't worry, that "as a matter of fact, if I may so, it's one of the most endearing things about you, Merideth, that you aren't modern."

With this crushing compliment he said good-by and left me feeling even less sure of myself than before. Eve Carpe had stayed to hear my half of the conversation. Now she pulled the door to the basement steps open wide, remarking, "This time I'll get those damned garage doors closed or else."

"I'll do it," I said. "You rest your ankle." I'd almost reached the door before she stopped me forcibly, a strong girl for her size.

"It's my job. Let me get to it." She was so emphatic, and appeared so upset—frightened—that I shrugged and left it to her. Her fall had obviously affected her nerves, but if it was that important to her to tramp up and down to close doors after Howard and his splendid car I certainly would not interfere. I went back to finish my work in the kitchen only to have Polly come fussing in to say the regular woman would be here tomorrow and I mustn't deprive her of her work. "She has eight mouths to feed."

I agreed that I wouldn't dream of taking the food out of eight mouths, but the truth was my coming date that night worried me so much I wanted to keep busy in the meantime to divert myself. I finally asked Polly what she thought I should wear for the occasion and she responded with far more interest than I would have expected, although her own nervousness "because I want you to be at your very best, dear," seemed excessive or my own lack of confidence about the exciting was contagious.

I noticed that her fingers were shaking just a bit as we studied the green-barred muslin dress. She talked rapidly, almost rattling. "Gentlemen with old backgrounds like the Demos family still prefer modesty in a young lady," she told me, and added as I started to object, "in spite of the war. Now, your lovely arms can be seen through the sleeves and with the high neck your bosom will be intriguingly suggested, because the material is rather thin. Isn't that sly? Very effective, I promise you."

I hugged her and she reddened with pleasure. "Don't forget, I was young once."

"Indeed you were. And the belle of San Francisco, too."

"Oh, that! No, I meant . . . off the stage. What a pretty skirt! The new length, you notice. It shows so much of your limbs. Silk stockings! Thank heaven you have silk stockings!"

Though I was grateful for her comments, she worried me with all her fluttering and her inability to settle down and rest. "Please, mother, you musn't worry so much about it. It's only a visit, not an engagement. A member of the Demos family isn't going to get himself engaged to me."

"And why not? There's no one prettier in Frisco."

"Frisco" . . . That was strange . . . outsiders' talk . . . she'd been away so long she nearly sounded like one of them.

"There is Eve, for one," I reminded her, but she only smiled at this. I wondered what, if anything, she suspected about her husband's relations with Eve. They once had been friends. . . . I thought of my dream of Howard's conversation with some unknown that I was now certain was no dream. Howard MacPherson was staging a charade of affection for me to get control of my property. Polly had to know about her husband's hopes and, although perhaps manipulated, was going along with him, if reluctantly. And yet I felt she cared about me. Since we left the hospital, she had repeatedly shown she was concerned about my well-being. I laid the barred muslin dress across my bed and got out my new pumps. I still hadn't figured out how to tell her that there might not be an inheritance, not for some time. I could tell her I was taking her uneasy advice of yesterday morning, not to rush my remembrance of the old days—a warning I had come to believe was a sincere if momentary impulse, forgotten or at least regretted shortly after.

Much too soon the cool, crisp afternoon gave way to evening and Polly set strict instructions to the rest of the household not to enter the bathroom for half an hour while I scrubbed away in the bathtub, which was a delicious change for me from my more customary galvanized tin tub.

When I finished dressing, with the skilled help of Eve Carpe who did my hair, it was close to seven o'clock. I think my mother was more excited than I was. Howard, who had come home for an early dinner, was in an uncharacteristic anxious mood. It seemed to me that he had taken on some of Eve Carpe's upset after her fall, although she herself was much calmer now, as if her problems were solved by Howard's arrival.

Polly whispered to me, "Rehearsal went badly. That's always a good sign, actually, but I can't make him believe it. I've never seen him so worried, though. It's ridiculous because he's really a very good actor and the women, especially at matinées, just love him."

I understood his stage fright, something Father had told me affected everyone, no matter what his experience, but Howard's interest in getting me out of the house and successfully off on my date seemed rather out of the ordinary. I decided it must be that he hoped I might marry into the wealthy Demos family and shower some of their Comstock Gold on him and his wife.

Shortly after seven a modest black Ford drove up in front of the house and Dr. Demos stepped out, looking even taller and stronger than I'd remembered. Howard was still home, though Polly kept reminding him he was expected at the theater before seven-thirty to fill in for a lead in the current play who had come down with the flu.

Standing in the hall and peeking through the glass in the door, Howard nudged me. "Don't let him climb all those stairs. Go out and say hello. Let him know you're glad to see him."

I was fully as nervous as he was but I muttered, "I never saw anybody so anxious to get rid of me."

He laughed, and opened the door practically in Anthony

Demos' face. To my ears he sounded much too effusive as he greeted the doctor. I was so uncomfortable I wanted to crawl under the doormat, but the doctor seemed to find nothing embarrassing in it as he shook hands with my stepfather and Polly and gave me a posy of spring flowers.

"Well, now," Howard cut in, "we don't want to keep you two so run along and have a fine time."

I was grateful Dr. Demos' eyebrow didn't go up as Neil's would have done, or that he didn't make some pointed comment about Howard's odd behavior. On the other hand, when I had kissed Polly and gone down the long stairs with Tony Demos, he didn't understand me at all when I remarked, "He certainly seemed anxious to get me off his hands."

"I'm sure it's because he wants you to be happy tonight." He smiled. "And I do, too. You look enchanting, Merideth."

I was terribly pleased at the compliment but at the same time aware that talking all evening to Tony Demos without ever saying what I really thought was going to be a strain. I was not, as he was, naturally given to seeing the best in human beings . . . especially not under my present circumstances.

As we drove away I felt my fingers getting colder, my mouth dry. We were about to meet those awesome parents of his, with whom it would be even harder to be myself. At least that uneasy anticipation helped divert me from the peculiar happenings and atmosphere at 379 Hyde Place.

TWELVE

We drove out toward the beach just as the city shifted into a darkness now emblazoned with gleaming white lights. Even on the great highway bordered by the beach on one side and rolling sand dunes on the other, I could look back and see the white glow of the city against an unusually clear night sky. It was cold out at the beach, but a pleasurable, exciting cold, if only I could have been myself.

"There are the Heights, straight ahead," Tony said, and I saw how the highway swung to the northwest and started climbing to avoid the huge, rocky prominence ahead of us. Those rocky, jutting heights were covered with trees, dark evergreens, eucalyptus and cypress, the other giant growth unidentifiable to me, forming a barrier around the forbidding fortress that was the Demos house.

"Sorry the Cliff House is still closed," Tony said as I kept staring at the Heights ahead and wondering if I had done absolutely everything to look my best, "but the Baths are open, on the left of the highway just above Seal Rocks. If you've never been in them, you'll be amazed. Healthiest place in the world, fresh- and salt-water pools. Father and others worked hard to build these up—monuments to the last century. For what they are I don't think you can find better."

"I understand. My mother was born in Virginia City, and her father was a miner on the Comstock. He actually was there, I'm told, the day they struck pay dirt with the Con-Virginia. I'd love to have been there."

He laughed, but apparently not with any intention of making fun of me. We began to climb around the great cliff, the glass roofs of the bathhouse on the left, and on the right, high above our highway, the Heights themselves. He put one hand on mine briefly. "Excited? You'll like my parents. They really are wonderful people."

"That's what Neil Burnham said. He wants to interview them."

Tony frowned. "I met the fellow once at the hospital. He came to bother you, remember? Not a pleasant type. Sarcastic." He glanced at me. "I hope you won't mind. I've no right whatever to give you orders but I wish you wouldn't see him again. I think he's a cynical fellow who mostly makes fun of life. Convenient for him, but life is not a fun house or an amusement park. It is a pretty serious business."

I sank lower in my seat and hoped he would not persist in talking this way. Still, he was attractive—especially his eyes, almost enough to forgive him his rather dreary view of life.

"I spent a lot of my childhood there." He pointed to the Baths perched on the last spit of land and descending the rocks to the tidal foam below.

I sat up straight. I felt the most peculiar sensation, as if I had lived this moment before. I didn't want to look at that side of the road, or anywhere near the great glass-topped building. I could hear them in my imagination now—echoes and weird sounds, the hollow atmosphere and the smell of the old wooden benches and the chemical quality of the water.

"I don't like indoor swimming," I said a little shakily, and kept looking up around the cliff toward the dark, tree-shadowed Heights.

He was surprised and I think a little hurt. "You've been to the Demos Baths, and you don't like them?"

"I don't remember ever having been there. All my life I've

felt this dread of enclosed places like it, but nobody, including me, remembers a good reason for it. Father said it was some fear I was born with. I don't like to talk about it."

I couldn't blame him for pressing. "But you can swim?"

"Yes. Something must have happened . . . or I saw something happen . . . before I was old enough to remember. I'm not sure . . ."

He nodded and kept silent, and then he was swinging the car around a curve and onto the grounds of Demos Heights. "Here we are, Merideth. And I warn you, if I don't persuade you to try the Baths one of my parents will. They believe the Demos Baths are a kind of wonderful cure-all. They don't take 'no' easily."

I forced myself to smile, but my heart was distinctly not in it as I now felt once again an old and familiar fear of those precise rectangular indoor pools as we came in sight of the glass domes of the Demos Baths. And yet I couldn't remember having been to the Baths before. I would have to ask Polly . . .

Meanwhile, we drove up to the three-story building, stone façade over wood at the rear, framed entirely by elaborate Corinthian pillars. A tall man with white hair and an imperious face stood between the pillars under the porch lights as we stopped. Tony got out, came around and helped me down. I looked up at the chill eyes of the tall man who received us and began to offer my hand when Tony said cheerfully, "Good evening, Gibbons. You can tell mother I've made it home only an hour late, and with Miss Hyde."

While I was digesting the welcome fact that this awe-inspiring individual was the butler, a stocky dark man came hurrying out behind Gibbons. This had to be the doctor's father, although I was surprised when Tony embraced him as though they had been separated weeks instead of hours.

"Father! How is Mama? Losing her temper over the meat sauce, if I know her. Merideth, this is my father, who built those Baths you are so afraid of."

Mr. Demos appeared shy, something I hadn't expected, but it made things much easier for me. I took the large fleshy hand he extended, found it warm and firm but not, thank goodness, overpowering. He also retained some hint of an accent, which I liked.

"It is good to meet Tony's friends. Such a popular boy he is! The best doctor in San Francisco, I always say."

"Oh, yes, indeed!" I hastened to add. "The very best. He saved my life, and many others, too."

Tony drove off into the heavy-scented eucalyptus grove to park his car and left Mr. Demos and me alone to appraise each other.

"You do not look so dangerous," he said finally. "Always he brings home these fine ladies, so elegant one feels like the poor fisherman one started out to be."

"I am one of your poor fishermen," I told him. "As you can see, I am not one of his fine ladies."

Which seemed to please him as he led me into the house. It was odd to walk into an expensive house and find no old-fashioned vestibule, no entrance hall, just a huge staircase of dark, highly glossed wood and two wide halls flanking it. Gloomy, unlighted paintings in heavy frames kept the halls from looking bare but I thought it a shame they seemed ill cared for. I had a feeling someone had collected them mostly because it was the thing to do.

An elderly housekeeper stood on the staircase, not appearing at all like the French maids I had seen in the movies. She accepted my coat in fingers whose contempt for the coat's material and cut I could read by the way they pinched the collar as she went abruptly upstairs with it.

I took a deep breath and went with Mr. Demos through the doorway into a heavy, dark dining room set with a delightfully informal red tablecloth and crimson wine glasses. The silverware was thick and expensive looking. It had been given a lot of wear. I got the feeling that these people did not buy light temporary things. Probably Mrs. Demos, at least, did not like light, frivolous people either. I straightened up and was careful to look serious as Mr. Demos brought me through a small hall-pantry into a kitchen where marvelous odors filled the air. It was a huge, old-fashioned kitchen, the kind I had seen in many Nevada ranch houses, utilitarian, light and roomy.

119

A slightly plump dark woman of middle height was bending over the oven.

"Burned!" she announced as she covered her hands with old flour sacks and yanked a pan out of the oven maw of a big black stove.

"Teresa, the young lady is here. You will frighten her with all this violence," Mr. Demos said.

"Frighten, indeed," said Mrs. Demos, dropping a bread pan into the sink. "If she is frightened that easily, she's no business in my house." She swung around to face us. I could tell that she must have been pretty as a girl, and in a mature way she was downright beautiful now.

"Excuse my hands," she told me straight out. "If it isn't flour, it's the meat sauce. . . . So you are this dreaming beauty the Passerby keeps writing about."

I started a denial but she waved it aside. "Wouldn't miss him for the world. My son despises the fellow, but if I don't get his column every day I am not fit to live with. Now, tell me, Miss Hyde, is it true that your stepfather is actually Howard MacPherson?"

This was even more astonishing than the fact that she liked Neil Burnham's column. "Yes, ma'am. Do you know him?"

"Only from my box at the Alcazar. I loved him in those plays he did before the war. Such a handsome rogue as he was! I haven't seen him for ages. Nicholas, will you please leave us? We have all sorts of confidences to exchange."

I hadn't the least idea what confidences she and I were to exchange, but I thought I might learn to know her better if I didn't have to worry about pleasing her and her husband at the same time.

Mr. Demos stroked his mustache and backed out. "I think—yes, I hear Tony. I will leave you women to your proper work."

"Bah," his wife said, obviously not meaning it. She sighed over the bread but when I went to examine the disaster, I suggested that half a loaf could be saved.

"It is disgusting. The bottom, ruined,"

"But the top is all right. You could use it for bread pudding. And this half is good clear through."

She looked at me briefly, nodded and cut off the better half of the loaf. "You are not one of Tony's heiress friends. I can see that."

I laughed. "I was reared in every petered-out mining camp in Nevada. If I am an heiress, ma'am, it will sit very uneasily on me."

"I guessed that." She was lifting kettles, emptying pots and pans while I tried, mostly with little success, to assist her. It was an odd dinner for a Greek family—spaghetti, meatballs, sauce, artichokes . . .

I stared at the spaghetti. "Excuse me, but is this a Greek dish?"

She gave me a big smile, revealing white, healthy teeth. "Of course not. I assumed, since you are from the mining country, that you like Italian food. My husband is Greek. I am Italian."

It was true. The Italians I grew up with came west in the tracks of the Union Pacific and remained to build up on solid foundations. I told her my mother was born in Virginia City, and before I knew it we were exchanging reminiscences about the Comstock. It seemed that Mr. Demos, a San Francisco fisherman, had heard about the gold strike on Sun Mountain in Nevada and rushed to get his pick and shovel, as well as a bride, Teresa Salvini, whose father was mayor of the city. The rest, as she said, was history.

We were just beginning to get along famously when we were startled by a raucous honking sound that cut through the great dark eucalyptus grove and put Mrs. Demos in a sudden bad temper. She swore in Italian.

"*That* will be Gerda Edwards. Her father gives a great deal to Tony's work on the charity wards. Beautiful creature, and knows it."

I felt like a pricked balloon. Everything had been going so well and now my rival had appeared to overshadow me.

Mrs. Demos whispered, "Have you ever seen that movie woman—Theda Bara?" I nodded, staring at her. She went on, "This one reminds me of her. Absurd creature! I call her 'the vampire' behind her back. But Tony is such a stickler for good manners!" She sighed and winked. "I am a great trial to my very proper son."

I found myself laughing. I felt I already knew her well, and I had to remind myself that I scarcely knew her after all, that she was an ex-mayor's daughter and one of the richest women in San Francisco, and yet in spite of all that I felt more at home with her than with my own mother, Polly Hyde.

Mrs. Demos took me in and introduced me to Miss Gerda Edwards, who was everything promised: beautiful, raven-haired, with sloe eyes and the complexion of one who had not recently been out of her shroud after sunrise. She broke this spell of fascination when she opened her mouth.

Languid and not interested enough to shake my offered hand, she murmured, "Miss Hyde, of course. Neil has been running one of those boring series of his, you poor thing. I do wish you could stop him. I know you must find it as tedious as—my dear Mrs. Demos, hard-working as ever, I see."

"Gerda," Tony interrupted, "you know perfectly well that Burnham fellow makes up all that trash he writes."

I was interested in their relationship and perhaps even more in her relationship to Neil Burnham. I thought it very unfair of her to be involved with both men. She and Tony seemed to know each other awfully well, I thought, and noted her fingers dug in around his wrist.

She addressed me again. "Well, surely you can do something. . . . Can't you refuse to see him? As long as you pose for his sketches and—"

I reversed my own previous stand on Neil Burnham's column. "Really, Miss Edwards? I wonder what I should do. It's awfully hard to refuse to pose when he persists in drawing a sketch purely from memory."

Mrs. Demos pinched my arm, a gesture I rightly interpreted as approval. Tony started to dismiss the matter of Neil Burnham's work by explaining that Gerda Edwards worked on the same newspaper as Neil and couldn't avoid him.

"It's for fun that I work there," Miss Edwards explained as she looked me up and down and clearly found me wanting. "When I went to work at the paper Neil did several sketches of me, against my wishes, of course. I had no idea. Such a tiresome man!"

"Too tiresome to keep us away from the dinner table," Tony said. I wondered if Gerda Edwards was the cause of the dislike between Tony and Neil Burnham.

I found myself wondering what Neil thought of his vampire colleague. The relationship between Tony and Miss Edwards seemed so close I was surprised that I had been inveigled over to the Heights, since Tony must see that my presence displeased Herself. On the other hand, and from the sound of Mrs. Demos' complaint, Gerda Edwards was here on her own hook.

"You will be staying to dinner, won't you?" Mr. Demos asked, adding a trifle anxiously, "It was very kind of you to bring your good father's agreement out here tonight. It will just save the new wing."

Mrs. Demos added, "Very kind, my dear. And clear out here to the Heights . . . at this hour."

I felt perfectly at home with Mr. and Mrs. Demos. Strangely enough, I was still struggling to say something that would interest Tony. I could sit by the hour studying his handsome face, his splendid physique, but studying him did me no good. It only made me feel inferior, so I spent dinner talking with Teresa Demos and answering her enthusiastic questions, while Gerda talked to Tony in a low voice. He didn't say much, but he seemed content. He looked over at me once in a while and smiled, then returned his attention to Gerda. She really was beautiful; I envied her that.

Toward the end of the evening Mrs. Demos' questions began to bother me. They seemed to return incessantly to my stepfather. Tony finally protested as we sat in the big living room drinking some strange, green Greek concoction in tiny glasses.

"Mama, give Merideth a chance to know Mr. MacPherson. She only met him a few days ago. He's a great deal more respectable than that newspaper fellow who seems to take delight in hanging about Merideth all the time."

"Gerda's friend?" asked his mother with a slight emphasis. "The Passerby has tried to interview us, you know, Merideth, but I don't want clever young men seeing through me. However, we were talking about Merideth's stepfather. My child, you must have gained some knowledge of his voice offstage, and those little mannerisms he uses. How does he behave to you? Nicholas"—she turned to her husband—"you may as well know I do envy Merideth, living in the same house with Howard MacPherson."

Gerda Edwards smiled, then dabbed at her full lips with her napkin.

Tony was half angry, half amused. "Mama, in front of Merideth? She may take you seriously." He was much more upset than his father, who smiled fondly but showed no signs of jealousy. As for me, I wondered how I could get over to her some inkling of what I really felt about Howard. I had known people with dispositions like Teresa Demos'. When they were shown an opposite fact, their volatile natures switched them right over to the other side. And as long as I felt so diffident with Tony, I wouldn't bring him my suspicions. I knew I could talk to his mother, though.

When we were setting our small cordial glasses back on the tray, Tony said, "You will have to do what you can to conquer Merideth's prejudice, mama. She has taken a dislike to bath-houses."

Gerda appeared shocked. "My dear, how odd. I adore the Baths, wouldn't miss my Sunday dip for worlds, would I, Tony?"

Mrs. Demos was inclined to agree with Gerda. "We must prove how wrong you are, what pleasure—"

"No!"

Everyone looked at me. Red-faced, I apologized. "I beg your pardon, I just meant that I never go into those . . . buildings."

"It is a pity," Mr. Demos said in his gentle way. "The Baths are open Thursday nights and you might see it without the weekend crowds."

I hated myself for this cowardice but I couldn't help admitting, "I would rather see it when it is crowded. . . ." As this surprised them, too, I tried to change the subject. "It must be getting late, I think I had better be going. I've had such a nice time, I can't tell you how I appreciate it."

"Hilda is probably in bed reading *Science and Health with Key to the Scriptures*," Mrs. Demos said, and got to her feet. "I'll get your coat, Merideth. Come along and we can have a little chat." She lowered her voice but everyone in the room heard her. "About your fascinating stepfather."

I noted that Miss Edwards made no move to depart.

As Mrs. Demos and I went up those splendid stairs together, I ventured onto the dangerous subject I suspected would startle her.

"Do you believe it would be possible for Howard MacPherson to do anything, well, underhanded?"

Not for the first time that night she astonished me. "Easily. I'll never forget him as the handsome villain in *The Wooden Kimono*. And if you could have seen him seducing the girl in *Sign of the Cross* at the Alcazar . . ." She glanced at me. "Don't tell me he has tried to seduce you!"

"Just the contrary. I'm rather sure he dislikes me, but apparently is doing everything he can to see that I get my grandpa's property as soon as possible."

"Very proper."

We were on an upper floor now. It was lined with life-sized copies of ancient statues which I privately thought were a bit overpowering even for this high-ceilinged and spacious hall. Besides, they all appeared to be staring at me with their empty eyesockets.

"You don't understand, Mrs. Demos. When I get my inheritance, I have a feeling he may do something drastic to get his hands on it—my mother, *his* wife, would be next in line for it. . . . I do have lawyers but Howard seems to have them under his thumb. . . ." I waited for her shock, surprise, even indignation, but she appeared thoughtful as she opened the door into a beautifully furnished bedroom that had the spotless look of a guest room, or spare room, as I would have called it. The furniture was all heavy, mahogany and inlaid. I was impressed but not comfortable.

Mrs. Demos got my coat from a closet and put it on me, turning up the collar around my neck. "You will find it cold if you return by the beach and the Great Highway."

Looking into her warm eyes I said anxiously, "I hope I didn't offend or upset you by what I said about my stepfather."

She made me more apprehensive than ever when she patted

my shoulder in a kind of unthinking gesture of agreement.

"No, not at all. One really never knows . . . he's been off the stage for some time—the war, of course—and there weren't many jobs. He had the scars of that wound. In any case, I *would* like to meet him." She smiled at me. "Just say I'm a fan."

I remembered something I'd both dreaded and anticipated. "We're all going to see his opening tomorrow night—*The Pine Box* at the Giralda Theatre."

"Good. I'll see that Nicholas and I have a box, and you must introduce us. I'll soon have his true number!"

I had to be satisfied with that. At least, I had an ally. We went down the stairs together, and I saw Tony waiting at the bottom, talking to Gerda. It seemed to be a casual conversation between long-time friends. I again found myself wondering about her relationship to her fellow reporter, Neil Burnham. Was that as casual?

Mr. and Mrs. Demos came outside to watch us drive off, while Gerda Edwards stood to one side, elegant in her swath of velvet wrap, which she had thrown around her shoulders. As we chugged past the porch, Mrs. Demos called to us, "You must come during the day and I'll give you a tour of the grove and the gardens. Enchanting. And you'll love the statues." I doubted that, but was pleased with the invitation. I started to remind her about Friday night but was especially grateful when she did so before I could. "Don't forget tomorrow night. Look for us, we'll meet at the theater."

As we drove out of those gloomy, dark grounds which rather inappropriately sheltered a happy pair like Mr. and Mrs. Demos, Tony said, "You were lovely, Merideth. I want to thank you. Few of my friends find it easy to cope with my mother, but you hit it off at once."

"She's one of the nicest people I've ever met. I can be at my best with someone like her. In fact," I rattled on, unthinking, "since I've come to the city I can only be completely myself with her and—" I didn't dare name Neil Burnham, knowing Tony's feelings about the columnist.

He looked over at me and smiled. "And?"

It occurred to me that Tony thought I was referring to him. I owed him the polite lie. "And you."

"Thank you, which brings me to something else. Do you trust me?"

My open mouth and my stare must have answered him, but I said almost indignantly, "Of course I do."

"Good. As your doctor, I do know what is best for you. Agreed?"

Bewildered, I nodded.

It was then he stopped the car, right in front of the lighted entrance of the Demos baths. I drew back. I even caught myself holding tight to the car seat with both hands. It was not his insistence when he opened the door on my side but shame at my own cowardice that forced me to let go of the seat and get out of the car.

"We're not going swimming at this hour!"

"Certainly not. But when you fear something, you must face up to it. We'll just go in and look around inside. Maybe walk around, that's all. I promise you."

There was nothing for it but to give in. I felt stiff as a poker and very cold, but I took hold of his hand and, once inside the doors, we started down the wide stairs together. Oddly enough, he bought tickets, explaining, "It's father's enterprise and I am, after all, only a visitor."

It was all very honorable and just like him, but all the honor in the world didn't help me when he persisted in thinking my fear could be conquered by a quick plunge.

I was immediately aware of the bathhouse atmosphere—the enormous hollow interior where distant playful screams and the splash of water by friendly combatants reverberated from every point in this private world. The smell of chemicals, of salt and of wood that was weathered by wind and spray reminded me forcibly of my terror; yet I had never before in my life walked down these stairs of my own volition, nor those of the many balconies hanging from the walls of the great bathhouse.

I said slowly, more to myself than to Tony, *"I have never*

walked into this place in my life. Never!" Then why this chest-tightening fear? I felt stifled. Breathing grew more difficult.

"You see? There is nothing to be afraid of."

I couldn't find an answer he would understand. We were now at the cold railing, sticky with salt. Tony was pointing out that we had passed a side chamber with a model display of one of the coastal missions. I scarcely heard him. There were a number of other visitors around us, and I was looking far down into the largest pool, where a lone swimmer was making a race toward our end. A huge diving platform cast a shadow over a patch of the green water. With mingled fascination and horror, I stared at that platform, which opened off one of the hanging balconies. I could explain neither reaction. I could swear I had never climbed such a place in my life.

"Too bad mother didn't come with us," Tony remarked suddenly.

I started to agree but realized he was not making a social observation. I followed his glance and saw a big man standing half-way up the wooden stairs on the north tier. There was nobody else in that tier at the moment and I could not possibly mistake Howard MacPherson. He was not looking in our direction, and so I doubted he saw us. Clearly, though, he was looking for something . . . someone.

"He must have just gotten here," I said. "He had a role in the play tonight. I wonder why he's here."

Tony shrugged. "To relieve tension, perhaps. We have many performers who come here. He doesn't see us. Too many people around here." He started to wave to my stepfather, but I stopped him.

"Please don't. Let's go."

"No, Merideth. You mustn't run away from a challenge."

I seemed to have forgotten his iron determination. Or was it stubbornness? In the hospital when I couldn't seem to find strength during my recuperation, Dr. Demos had persisted, kindly but unshakably.

In this great, hollow bell-jar of a building I felt his strong will and, though resenting it, obeyed because I couldn't bear that he should think of me as a hopeless weakling.

"What do you want me to do?"

"You said you were afraid of indoor tanks and pools. All you have to do is walk down beside the tanks and over to that tier, to your stepfather. While you are doing that, you will find that tanks are quite harmless."

I looked at him, wondering if my suspicions had finally included this good man who had only recently saved my life. I think, but I am not sure, I was about to agree to his order when the woman behind the ticket window called down to him.

"Doctor Tony, could you come here a minute?"

Annoyed, Tony looked up the stairs, then patted my hand. "I'll be right back. *You* start walking."

I watched him go up the stairs as I made a few tentative steps along the railing. He glanced back, waved me on. I squared my shoulders and started. I was aware, even though I did not look down, that the waters were rippling in the lights and shadows, with endless little troughs, in one of which I had almost died once, long ago. When? Must have been when I was a baby. I remembered the horror of my world dropping out beneath me, of falling . . . falling, then swallowing bitter chemical-tasting water, strangling on it. I remembered piercing noises, echoed cries of fun and laughter, shrieks of other swimmers that hit at me from every wall, terrifying me even more. I remembered my chest and my throat feeling they would burst. . . .

But nothing before or after.

Having descended another tier farther along, I looked up and back to where Tony stood by the ticketseller's window. I hoped I would see him coming after me, but he was tossing a half-dollar, then testing it with his teeth—I guessed he'd been called because the four-bit piece might be counterfeit, a common-enough occurrence in a city where almost all the money was in gold or silver. No help from him.

I was beside the low rail now, the nearest tank so close there were signs hanging from it which prohibited diving from this level. I did not look at the water but up where we had seen my stepfather. Others were moving along that tier and onto the next, but he was gone. He hadn't had time to leave. He must be close by. There were so many potted palms, the fronds gently weaving and swaying as if to the music that started up from somewhere. He might have been behind any of them. Little decorative pagodas about the size of a grown man were on higher elevations. Howard could be anywhere. Had he seen me?

I planted my foot firmly on a north flight of steps and started up. I saw a door in the distant north wall standing ajar, revealing the night sky and heard a distant roaring splash from the high surf which must be very far below. On the door were the painted words "KEEP THIS DOOR CLOSED." It appeared to open onto the ocean and Seal Rocks. Had Howard for some reason disappeared into the cold night? Maybe he didn't want to be seen by *us*.

It seemed to me from the view I had that the Pacific Ocean was far less menacing than the great hollow interior of this glass house. I moved up to that level and stepped carefully over to look out. The ocean wind almost swept me off my feet, but not before I saw the huge spray from the rocks below and the tidal pools in levels on the way down. I started to move backward to avoid the spray.

Something sharp stabbed between my shoulderblades. I swung around. The instrument had been Howard's forefinger. He loomed over me, smiling. I tried not to let him see he had startled me or that with the slightest additional effort he could have sent me hurtling to the bottom of that series of tidal pools to the rocks below.

"Don't creep up on me like that. I don't like it."

He was all apologies.

I wanted to keep him on the defense. "What are you doing here at this hour?"

He waved a big, thick hand. "I died in the second act. A gruesome business. Shall I describe it?"

"Don't trouble."

"But the truth is, I have been bothered by something Polly said. Thought I'd investigate. Something about your being afraid of the Demos Baths. But nobody here seems to have any record of an accident you might have had as a youngster. Of course, most of the employees have only been here the last five to ten years. What with the war and all, there has been a considerable turnover."

"Doesn't Polly remember?"

He recovered rapidly. "She says not. Might have been some second or two when you went under and then revived—so short a time it has slipped her memory. She only knows you are afraid of the tanks."

I didn't believe it had happened that way. Whatever happened to me had seared itself upon my consciousness even if I couldn't remember the circumstances. And after I was able to walk, Polly and I never came here. It was before that. It must have been.

"Let me show you that marvelous view of the Pacific down below," Howard said. "Your doctor friend will find us eventually."

"No, I've seen enough. Besides, he'll be here any minute."

I felt I was being maneuvered closer into the open doorway, in spite of dragging my feet. Still, I didn't want to call out, or make a scene.

"There's a good view of the Seal Rocks beyond the breakers," he said. His grin looked frightening, especially in this darkened corner cut off from the rest of the Baths. I jerked away from his hold.

"I told you—no!"

"My dear Merideth, you act as if I were going to—" He appeared shocked, hurt, the full arsenal of his tricks. "What could happen to you here in full view of the entire bathhouse?" Ignoring that for a minute or two we had been unseen by anyone, he went about his playacting, or what I thought was very like playacting. "Ah, Dr. Demos, I certainly am glad to see you."

I moved slowly. The doctor's tall figure was coming toward us. He looked a trifle surprised.

"Mery has been telling me how she has some fear of indoor tanks. Now, Mery, you walked clear over here and none of those pools did you any harm, did they?"

I wouldn't even answer that.

He went past Howard, closed and locked the door in the corner. "This goes down to the tidal pools. There's quite a drop.

Strange, the workmen are usually more careful. It isn't supposed to be left open." Then he shook hands with Howard, assuring him, "I'll have her home safe, don't you worry. We are leaving immediately."

"Sorry," Howard called after me. "I wouldn't have frightened you for the world."

I felt it wouldn't do to let him know how deeply I did suspect him, so I looked back, waved and said I knew but really was tired and would see him at home.

I may have been wrong but I thought he looked relieved. On the way out Tony asked me what had been going on.

"Howard wanted to show me the view from the utility door."

"He means well, I suppose," Dr. Demos decided with no help from me. Then he added something that chilled me with its implications in the event I had difficulty in the future. "I've noticed, Merideth, ever since your illness, you are very nervous. It is natural. But really, you can cure it only by at least allowing those who love you to take care of you. Your mother loves you very much, and your stepfather was in the hospital repeatedly to ask about you. He often sat for hours, hoping that you might be well enough to meet him."

"I can imagine."

He looked at me sternly, like an old-fashioned flogging schoolmaster.

"Merideth, girls your age often imagine for one reason or another that the world is their enemy, that they're in great danger. It's romantic and it's natural, but you must learn to rely upon those of us who are older and know a little more about human nature. Your stepfather, for instance, was overseas, and did a fine job. He seems a good man who cares for you and it's rather painful to see you showing so little respect for him."

"What would you have said if I had fallen down into one of your wonderful old tidal pools tonight?"

"That would be highly unlikely. You might as well say I could throw you off these stairs. You could, after all, meet with an accident in any one of a million ways. We all could. This would not mean that those who love you were trying to harm you, which I suppose is in your thoughts. You even have my mother wondering. Mother, by the way, has the most over-active imagination in the world. So please don't get her started."

As we went back up past the cashier's window we met several latecomers rushing down the stairs. Among those entering, casually buffeted by others in a greater hurry, was Neil Burnham. He was looking off toward the tier where we had left Howard and didn't see us. He certainly wasn't in a hurry, but he was keeping close to the other wall, as though he didn't particularly care to be seen. My heart almost stopped beating. I guessed he was on his way to meet my stepfather, and I felt sick all over at the implications of that.

THIRTEEN

I RUINED the otherwise pleasant drive home by constantly relapsing into silence as I tried to explain to myself Neil Burnham's late arrival at the Demos Baths. There were a hundred—well, a dozen—reasons why he might be going to the Baths just before closing time. A story, perhaps. Even a late swim. He tended to do things on the spur of the moment. Half an hour before, I had been ready to suspect even Anthony Demos of ulterior motives. Maybe he was right. I was becoming too imaginative.

"You see? It wasn't so dangerous, was it?" Tony asked as we cut away from the beach and turned inland.

Caught in the middle of my complicated thoughts about the actions of Neil and Howard at the Baths, I said, "I won't know that until I know why they are meeting there."

An unexpected jerking of the car made me realize I had said something that startled him. "Who was meeting where?"

"Nothing. I was thinking about something else." Which was obvious, but I didn't want to go into what that something else was.

We drove in silence through the deserted streets until we

reached the Hyde Place neighborhood. This silence was apparently Tony's usual nature, and it suited me very well at the moment because I had much to figure out and wasn't very far along with it. There didn't seem any logical reason why my stepfather should frighten me—or worse—tonight because I hadn't yet received my property . . . unless my mother and thereby Howard would be next in line should anything happen to me at any time . . . ? More likely, I felt, it might have been to produce in others the belief that I was subject to wild and unfounded suspicions, or that I was prone to accidents. Then, if anything did happen to me, people could reasonably say, "She was so terribly nervous, she probably brought it on herself." Or was this even more preposterous than my usual suspicions?

"This is getting to be a very nice district," Tony said suddenly. "Your inheritance should be worth a considerable sum. Aren't you anxious to get it?"

"No. On the contrary. I am scared to death to get it."

It was something impossible to explain to a man like Tony who obviously couldn't bring himself to believe the rest of the world was somewhat less well-intentioned than he was. Suddenly I felt quite a bit older than Tony Demos.

He laughed at my fear. "Don't be frightened of money. Be frightened of what you may do with it. But you will find a use for it. Money is very important. Don't forget that it can often buy health and even make life more bearable. I have seen too much poverty to believe it sanctifies a life."

All true, but he didn't know what I feared once I received my property and sold it, or conceivably even before the property could be sold. There was Howard's angry insistence the night he thought I was asleep: "Quick and natural?" Natural what? My demise? Really, I thought . . . I am getting impossibly melodramatic, as bad as Howard's melodramas at the Giralda Theatre. Did I believe that? I wish I could . . .

Having reached the foot of Hyde Place, we crossed Pompeii Street, which was the northern boundary of Grandpa's Hyde Place block. Pompeii Street was split in two by a little park running down the center, with beds of seasonal flowers surmounted by a pergola made of Greek-style pillars. The early spring flowers were in the process of being replaced by summer roses and had been dug up and set aside in low crates. The entire ten or twelve feet of ground was turned over. Some children had already started to put up a fort here at one end of the little traffic island, as in the corner lot of the Hyde Place block across the street.

"I used to play there, too," I remarked, thinking how odd it was that in those days the pergola and its surroundings had seemed gigantic, like an all-concealing forest.

Tony let the motor die in order to escort me to my door, where he took my hand and thanked me for a perfect evening, cutting off my own gushing thanks. He said warmly, "It may have been a rough business, your catching the flu, but it was certainly a lucky day for me."

"A good omen," I said. "I noticed that nobody at the Baths tonight was wearing a flu mask."

"We must do this again soon. Good night, Merideth, and thank you once more. . . . Do you think your mother will object if I kiss you good night?"

How like him to ask me! And worse, to ask if my mother would object! What had Polly Hyde to say about my kissing someone? I doubted Neil Burnham would ever ask. He would take. But then, Anthony Demos was much more of a gentleman in his behavior; whereas Neil, who looked like the typical gentleman about town, gave me the feeling at times that his slim, unathletic look concealed a piratical soul. All the same a question about a kiss was embarrassing. I smiled and shook my head. Tony correctly took this for an assent and kissed me softly, and warmly, on the lips. It was a protective kiss, I thought, as was the arm he slipped around my waist. I almost wished I hadn't returned his kiss with such enthusiasm. By comparison, it made me seem forward.

"Promise me you won't imagine any more wickedness tonight."

"I promise," I lied. He hugged me, then went down the stairs. The last I saw of him he was cranking up his car to start for home.

The door opened behind me, and Polly stood there waiting, for which I was grateful. It made me feel less isolated. She kissed me on the forehead, hoped I had enjoyed myself and asked if I would like some hot chocolate.

I laughed, a bit shortly. I didn't feel very humorous, haunted by what I was still convinced had been a prearranged meeting between Howard MacPherson and the man with whom I had hoped to discuss my fears, the man who had even gone to the trouble of warning me once. It didn't make sense.

I said abruptly, "Where is Howard?"

"But dear, where would he be? You heard him say he is replacing one of the leading men in the last performance of the show tonight."

"Is it a long role?"

She was getting more agitated as we walked through the house to my back bedroom.

"I—I couldn't say. Why?"

"Because he wasn't at the theater tonight."

Eve Carpe's voice came to us from the darkness of her room. The door was open and I thought of it as a cavern filled by the unknown. "I understand the part calls for him to be killed off at the end of the second act, Miss Merideth. At least that's what I think he said. . . . Where did you see him?"

If so, it probably made his story true—at least about the part in tonight's show. "I ran into him when I was out with Tony," I said. "How are your aches and pains?"

"Aches and pains?" A tiny pause. "Fine. Much better. Thank you for asking."

Say what she would, she had apparently forgotten all about that presumably bad fall down the stairs. If she hadn't hurt herself, why did she pretend otherwise? I went on to my room and managed to convince Polly that I didn't need her to talk me to sleep, as she showed every sign of doing.

I went to bed at once, with Polly hanging on my every word as if it were engraved. When she insisted on tucking me in "as she had when I was a child," I reminded her with some amusement that she had seldom fussed over me when I was young.

Her fingers dropped my blanket as if it were woven of fire and she stepped back from the bed apologetically.

"I'm sorry. It seemed so—well, natural."

I took her hand. "It was lovely of you all the same. . . . Polly, your hands are nice as ever." I remembered the Christmas candle accident years ago and turned her hand over. On the under side of her arm, below the elbow, was a tiny burn scar, my mother's scar, triangular in shape, almost as vivid as if the whole business had happened yesterday. I caressed the scar with one finger and she smiled.

"Does it ever hurt?" I asked.

"Certainly not, my dear. Not for years and years." She waited for me to say more about it but I must have shocked her when I asked, "Do you think you could come to visit me in Nevada? Just you?"

"I might," she said vaguely. "Some time when things are . . . running smoothly here."

"No. I mean right away. If I just picked up and left at once. This week."

That seemed to upset her. "I couldn't, not possibly. Aren't you happy here? We've done everything we could to make you feel at home. And we're finally getting close now to—"

"To what?"

"To each other, of course."

"Polly, what do you remember about a bathhouse? Demos Baths, for instance?"

My change of subject startled her. "I don't remember. It's just that you made a remark—I forget when—and I wondered . . ."

"You must have taken me there when I was very little. Could I have fallen in? It's very odd, because I remember you said the other day that you didn't swim."

She clasped my hand so hard I winced and she let go, still looking frightened. "I don't swim. I—I hate it. It terrifies me. I've never liked it. Not in rivers or indoor tanks or anywhere. It's just something I've always felt. Even crossing the bay on a ferryboat is an effort."

A little light illuminated this murky business. I now thought I might have the explanation for my own fear.

"I may have inherited that fear of yours. I don't know exactly how things like that work, but it could be true."

"I'm *sure* that's the answer, Mery. Now, I'll let you get some sleep."

"All this talk about water and fear reminds me—I had a close call downtown yesterday."

"Close?" She paled and I touched her hand, which was restlessly tracing an imaginary circle on the counterpane.

"But I'm here, so don't look so scared. I just mean that I am grown up now and I should make a will of my own. Accidents can happen, you know."

Apparently this was not the first she had heard of a will. "You needn't worry about that. Mr. Brubick has one drawn up, a mere form, ready for your signature as soon as you come into the property. He thinks it is a—what did he call it?—a wise precaution. Of course, you alone must decide on leaving your property. It will be yours exclusively."

"Dear Mr. Brubick . . . he thinks of everything."

"Yes, doesn't he?" she agreed, apparently missing the irony. "He drew up a will for me and I've already signed mine. I felt very important, I can tell you. I'm leaving all my worldly possessions to you, dear."

"*Me*? Why not to your husband?"

Polly had certainly grown more naïve in her middle years. "But Mery, it was Howard's own idea that I leave it to you. He says he can take care of himself. There are always acting parts, he says."

"What a remarkable man! I had no idea he was so unselfish."

She seemed to take my remark at face value.

We both heard the front door open and the low hum of voices. I wanted to say "speak of the devil," but did not. Polly kissed me and was leaving when I asked abruptly, "Why did you warn me the other morning in the attic?"

She laughed. "I was awfully silly, wasn't I? I suppose I was worried about you remembering the past too completely—you know, remembering about how I *used* to be. . . . I was afraid it would come between us. But that was wrong, and I'm relieved Good night now, dear."

139

The minute she had closed the door, I got out of bed and opened it a crack. Eve Carpe had taken Howard's coat. Howard yawned and said to Polly, "Did she get in yet?"

"A little while ago. She is in bed now."

"What mood? Do you think she discussed anything with them?"

"Oh, no, dear. She was in a fine mood. Tired, but very good to me."

"I see. Well, I've taken the first step for tomorrow. We've got to move things along. . . . God, what a day! I'm off to bed. Good night, all."

I accepted this as good advice, and went back to bed myself. If ever I had any doubts about him, they were dispelled that night. Until I could convince mother to leave him, I wasn't about to oblige him so that he could "move things along." I assumed he meant to see that I received my property, then made a will that would leave it to him (after all, he'd so graciously made me his beneficiary, as Polly dutifully reported, no doubt just the way she'd been told to do). Or make Polly my beneficiary . . . either way, he'd be in a commanding position. Or, worse, if I remained too difficult, move more directly to dispose of me and hope Polly, his wife, would inherit in any case . . . ? It was a difficult game I'd decided to play out. Also—again I feared I was not being too dramatic—perhaps a dangerous one. . . .

Wait until tomorrow, Howard MacPherson, I promised him silently . . . "You may be an actor, but you've never seen such a performance as I'm going to put on tomorrow. I hope."

Tucking myself in with this comforting thought, I eventually went to sleep and in the morning was pleased to find that my determination to outwit Howard MacPherson still held. I only hoped Neil Burnham wouldn't bring himself into whatever was going to occur today. The two of them would be too much.

I didn't know what Howard had in mind that should be done on this of all days, when tonight he was opening in a new play and one would think he had enough to be concerned about. But he was up fairly early, with a great deal of energy, nervous or otherwise, and announced that Eve Carpe and Polly were to see that the house looked its best because we were having guests.

I knew I was expected to ask questions and express some sort of excitement but I couldn't bring myself to it. However, I joined in the cleaning and dusting with pleasure. It was something to do, and shortly after I heard Polly and Howard discussing Mr. Cafferetto, so I had a fair idea that our visitors would be here to put me, in a sense, on the witness stand, reciting old memories. I hadn't decided what to tell them, but I meant to give my stepfather a surprise.

A rough-faced, hard-voiced woman whom Howard addressed as Mrs. Halston arrived shortly afterward and was introduced as the cleaning woman. I didn't understand her gutteral accent —I assumed she was German—but in view of the recent hostilities, Howard introduced her merely as a refugee from the terrors in that part of the world. She must be the woman with eight mouths to feed.

I was dusting the front room, reliving my childhood connected with each item of furniture, when Howard came in to ask me, "What kind of phonograph did you have when you were a child? Remember when you used to tuck yourself up on that sofa, or one just like it?"

I knew what he was getting at and just nodded and shrugged. I was growing more anxious by the minute to find out what the visitors would ask me, and how I could put them off, but I didn't want my stepfather to guess how concerned I was.

"Good girl," he congratulated me and actually chucked me under the chin. I found it startling that his touch brought on a feeling of such revulsion. Neil Burnham's similar action—but there was no point in remembering the columnist or I would start wondering all over again what he and Howard had talked about at the Demos Baths.

While Eve Carpe worked outside, clipping what she called the Cecil Bruener roses that grew up the side of the house, the rest of us worked at making the old house sparkle. Mrs. Halston, muttering to herself, was busy with the carpet sweeper when I went to find a broom. There was none in the kitchen closet and then I recalled that father had kept such things in the basement in the old days. Maybe the people who followed us into this house had left theirs in the basement also. I went down the stairs behind the dining room, careful not to catch my heel as Eve Carpe had said she'd done the day before.

The basement itself almost sparkled, it was so clean. Although it had begun to rain, a spring drizzle actually, there was still plenty of light through the glass in the garage doors and the windows at the back. The day we arrived there had been a reasonable clutter around the foot of the stairs; now not a single item was out of place. Probably, I thought, Howard was so crazy about the car he had bought—or leased?—with a loan against my anticipated inheritance that he polished everything in sight along with his car.

I found the smell of gasoline very strong. Curiously enough, the smell was even stronger away from the big car. Yes, I thought, someone certainly is a fussy cleaner to use gasoline for cleaning the basement. Unless gas had leaked over to the door of the enclosed stairs and it had been mopped up.

I went over to the corner where we had kept the broom when I was a child. No broom, but a dustpan had been dropped here. Particles of glass stuck to the pan. Most of it had been pulverized, but what remained appeared thin and of light weight. I dumped the particles into an ashcan by the back door and found a broom lying nearby.

By the time I returned to the activity upstairs, Eve Carpe was at the front door looking down the street. She ducked inside and said, "Those 'Nosy Parkers' across the street! Every time we so much as sneeze in this house, they have to spy on us. The damned children are filthy, too. Mud all over. Mac—Mr. MacPherson should keep them out of our lots and send them home."

In the hall Howard was saying something to her about her language. I managed to pick up . . . "control yourself, damn it" . . . which I thought was almost funny, except that their apparent intimacy was disturbing and even a bit threatening. I was baffled by my mother's apparent total lack of interest. She was even closer to them—she'd been busy dusting the victrola, which stood near the archway opening into the dining room and the hall. Polly also hummed off-key, very low. All the same, she was not deaf. Why then did she display no jealousy or even interest in the two?

Shortly afterward Howard shooed us all into our bedrooms to get ready for our company. Being by nature contrary, I washed up but came back in the same dress I'd worn to dust and sweep. I caught his frown, and said in my sweetest fashion, "You do want me to be *myself*, don't you?"

He managed to contain his anger and agree that this was exactly what he wanted, but it amused me to see how his natural temper struggled with what he knew to be the careful attitude he must take with me. When Mr. Cafferetto's chauffeured Pierce Arrow drove up the street, I saw the heads of the children living across the way turn from their game of jacks that they were playing on the steps. I had no doubt their mother would shortly hear the whole story if she wasn't, even now, watching through a window somewhere. I waved to the three children; the girl waved back, apparently less shy than her brothers.

Eve went to open the door for the two lawyers and the ever-obliging Miss Falassi, who was armed with a thick notebook and a box containing ink, an assortment of pens and an indelible pencil. All very legal, very official, this visit.

Howard was right behind Eve, greeting the men in his expansive, theatrical way. After Eve had taken their hats and coats and the subject of the unusual showers so late in the season had been covered, everyone adjourned to the front room. Even Eve Carpe found a straight chair and sat down in the archway to listen. I took my seat in the window alcove but was careful not to curl my feet up under me. That would be one of the habits to connect me with the child Merideth—and my purpose just now was to put off being legally identified until I had persuaded mother to leave Howard . . . at least for a long enough period to separate him from the mother of the so-called heiress. Once we were in Nevada I felt that we would not be threatened by his plans.

Meanwhile, with a splendid professional air, Miss Falassi spread her materials out on the writing desk while Howard pulled an armchair over for her. She uncorked the ink bottle, tested the pen point and dipped the pen into the bottle.

"Now!" she said triumphantly.

Mr. Brubick cleared his throat. "You are Merideth Hyde, correct?"

"Yes, sir."

"Can you tell us what your earliest memories are?"

My earliest memories were actually concerned with a Christmas tree in this alcove and the little white fence around it. I mentioned, however, the sunlight shining through these west windows. Miss Falassi wrote busily.

Mr. Cafferetto said in his hoarse voice, "Anyone might say that. It's of no consequence."

They proceeded. What did I find missing in this room? Mr. Brubick asked this, looking in the direction of the sofa behind me. I suddenly remembered a green-satin sofa pillow with the words "Midwinter Fair—1894" embroidered across its face in pink floss. Its bright, glossy surface had especially fascinated me.

Instead, and keeping this memory for when I would want to use it, I looked up smartly and said inanely, "An old phonograph with a horn?" The two lawyers exchanged glances and nods, so I added, "Isn't that what you reminded me about this morning, Howard?"

I had to give him credit for recovering quickly enough to say, "No, it wasn't quite that way, Mery. It was *you* who told *me* about the old phonograph."

The lawyers, of course, did not believe him. They put their heads together, looked over a list of subjects Miss Falassi had drawn up. Then Mr. Cafferetto asked me what I remembered about my mother's departure.

"She walked out," I said, "and left a note for father. He kept looking for her, and I think sometime in April of that year—1906—he thought he might have located her at the Thalia on the Barbary Coast. He took a room for the two of us in a little hotel on Sutter Street for a couple of nights. I was asleep there when the quake struck that morning. Father had been out all night going from place to place on Pacific Street. She wasn't at the Thalia."

"And your father came home and rescued you," Miss Falassi put in.

"No. I was thrown out of bed by the quake. I scrambled up and when the shaking stopped for a minute I ran downstairs to the street in my nightgown. Some neighbors took me to Union Square. That's where father came looking for me," All very detailed, and yet impossible to verify, now that father was dead. I *could* have been making it up.

Polly cut in, "What a dreadful thing I did . . . my poor baby . . . I can never repay—"

Her husband interrupted, full of impatience, "That has *nothing* to do with the matter at hand. Go on with your questions, gentlemen."

The questions that followed were generalized and I did not hesitate to answer them since I might have learned the answers from some other source. Then Mr. Brubick asked me what I had remembered about my last birthday spent in this house. "Anything in particular about your gifts?"

He was talking, I knew, about the big stuffed woolly dog he'd brought me. The stuffed dog had been as tall as I was. No one present knew about it, including Polly, who had already left us by the time my birthday came around in January.

"I remember dolls, paper dolls," I said finally, as if remembering with great difficulty. "And the candles on the cake."

Mr. Brubick was crushed. "Nothing more? A special present?"

Poor man, he hadn't the faintest idea why I was behaving like this.

"It's all rather vague. I think I remember more when I was back home. I mean home in Nevada. . . ."

Polly came to her feet anxiously. "We're pressing her too hard, confusing her."

"Keep quiet!"

Everybody looked at Howard, who recovered quickly and apologized to Polly. I was thoroughly disgusted with Mrs. Demos' matinée idol, and only wished she could see him now. The lawyers and Miss Falassi were embarrassed and chose to disregard his bad manners. I found myself in difficulty again with their questions. Not, of course, that I didn't know the answers, but rather that it was hard not to answer correctly.

By the time I had exhausted their questions, I was exhausted as well, and the double-thinking grew more difficult. I had become accustomed to Mr. Brubick's easy, hesitant manner when Mr. Cafferetto attacked suddenly and, to me, unexpectedly.

"Do you not remember the gown your mother wore at the Valley Country Club the night you three were Lawrence Brubick's guests?"

That was easy. I could pretend Polly coached my memory. "Yes. It was a—what was it, mother? A jet-beaded skirt with a blouse . . . or did they call them corsages in those days? . . . made of green georgette. You mentioned the material. And a gorgeous plumed black, jet-beaded hat. We've discussed that outfit often lately, haven't we, mother?"

I wanted to watch Mr. Cafferetto, but I was too busy congratulating myself on outwitting Howard, who stared at Polly as did Miss Falassi and Mr. Brubick.

Mr. Cafferetto finally said, "No, no, that was the gown she wore to the Olympic Club when you were dressed in that white silk affair."

"Ridiculous," I said. "Polly wasn't at the Olympic Club. Nobody went but Father and me. And I didn't wear white silk. It was pink organdy, which wasn't my color. And I looked awful."

Mr. Cafferetto shook his head. "I cannot believe that. I had the description from someone who saw you there that night."

"Well, he must have been blind! Polly wasn't there. And I wore . . . pink." Too late, I knew I had been trapped.

"Just so, in every detail," Mr. Cafferetto agreed. He adjusted his ponderous weight and stood up. "Did you record that, Miss Falassi? Very well. I am now quite satisfied that the Hyde Place property belongs to you."

I got up too. "No, wait . . . how do you know it's true about the Olympic Club?"

He announced, "I was the person who saw you at the Olympic Club that night, you and your father only. And you were in pink, just as you say."

I caught just a glimpse of Howard staring at me. He knew perfectly well what I had been trying to do. It was as if he were making me a promise of trouble for having put him through some most uncomfortable moments. I was so angry with myself that I did not go to the door with the lawyers. Everyone shook hands with me, including Howard, who then saw the lawyers out.

I hardly waited for them to get into Mr. Cafferetto's Pierce Arrow before I grabbed my coat from the hall-rack and went out to walk off my anger and panic. I would have to make plans, and quickly. Polly's talk of wills suggested one way. Surely he couldn't actually get at my property without my death or the lawyers' consent. And my death wouldn't serve him unless Polly inherited. If I wrote no will until I had decided what to do about her, what would happen?

Polly was still congratulating me, and Howard was looking at me with marked distaste when I went down the steps in the drizzling rain and started walking, and thinking. When Mr. Cafferetto declared me to be the real Merideth Hyde, the property was all but mine. And that meant things would quickly come to a crisis. Damn the property!

I debated going home to Nevada, even if I couldn't persuade Polly, but I would never be sure that Howard's treatment of her would not extend to other cruelties beyond his indifference and bad temper. There was also the very nice Dr. Tony Demos. And there was the doubtless untrustworthy but most exciting Neil Burnham. A few more days in San Francisco, just a few more days . . .

A voice called to me and I glanced around, surprised. It was a very young voice, and when I looked over at the vacant lot where the mud fort was sagging with dampness, I saw the three children who lived across the street. Bundled in yellow raincoats too big for them, the three were trying to repair their fort. It was the girl who had called me. I crossed the lot, trying to avoid mud puddles. While the girl watched my approach, one of her brothers picked a beaten-down buttercup and handed it up to me, stretching mightily for the purpose. The knees of his stockings were crusted with mud. I only hoped that before she spanked him his mother would take note of those enchanting green eyes that looked up at me with an innocence and devilry that reminded me of someone.

As I thanked him and took the flower, his older sister announced, "We saw your friends with the Pierce Arrow. That was a Pierce Arrow, wasn't it?" I said it was. She nodded and said, almost sing-song, "We know something you don't know . . ."

"I'm sure you do," I agreed pleasantly, though I wasn't thinking as much about what she'd said as I was about the changes in the neighborhood since I was a child and had built mud castles on this vacant ground.

"Did you ever see a real live Chinaman?"

"Chinese," I corrected her automatically.

"Uh-huh. A Chinaman. He went right by here."

It was unusual, at that. "You saw a Chinese in this district?"

The other boy spoke up, seeing that I did not look dangerous. "He was looking for Hyde Place. We told him."

"Hyde Place? What on earth—what would he want at our house?"

The girl said, "That's silly. He was looking for the street. Not your house. Chinamen are very mysterious. See? He's coming back down Pompeii Street."

I looked around and saw a good-looking, well-dressed young man walking along the street toward us, the children's mysterious "Chinaman." It might be unusual to see him out here in the suburbs of the city, but it was certainly his right.

The boy who had given me the little sodden buttercup said, "We made this fort. We started one over in the . . . the . . ."

"Pergola," the girl said, indicating the narrow dug-up patch under the Greek columns that divided Pompeii Street. "But they are putting in new flowers when the ground isn't so soppy. The trouble with this ground is that water keeps running into the holes when we dig them."

I looked skyward. "It may be soppy for some time." I thanked the boy for the buttercup and he explained his gift with, "You picked one the other day, I saw you."

I started on, intending to circle this block of the Hyde property. Behind me I heard the girl speak again and I stopped, thinking for a minute that she had called to me.

" 'Lo, did you find your cook?"

A male voice corrected her quietly. "I do not know that he is a cook. I believe he must have come to this district for some purpose, which may be employment. I want to see him. That is all."

"Does he have a pigtail?"

I wished I had not heard all this and started on my way again. I needn't have been concerned. The young man said, "No, not a pigtail. But he is my father. Well, thank you."

His footsteps came toward me. I was more than a little curious but carefully kept my eyes on a distant point of the Hyde block. He passed me and eventually got into a Ford parked on Geneva Avenue and drove away.

While my own problems had nothing to do with the good-looking young Chinese, this business was intriguing. It kept my mind off more serious matters for the rest of my walk. When the old problems returned, I soon forgot about the young Chinese and his search. His problem was none of my business, after all. Or so I thought.

FOURTEEN

SOMEWHAT TO MY SURPRISE, the opening of Howard's new play was taken very seriously by the family. Polly told me it would mean, as she had predicted, evening clothes, which was a bother in the rain that continued to fall during the late afternoon and evening.

"We'll go out to supper afterward," Polly told me with pride. "And maybe, if we are up late enough, we can read the morning reviews in the *Chronicle* and the *Examiner*."

"Will the evening papers be represented at the theater?"

She said they would, and I wondered who was coming from Neil Burnham's paper. Since the Demos family would be represented and very possibly Neil might be there, I was delighted by Polly's announcement that we should choose our best low-necked gowns with trains or demi-trains, as had become popular since the end of the war.

My most daring gown was a flame-colored peau de soie with low décolletage, no sleeves and a tight belt of the same material compressed to look like a sash and display a narrow waist. I had a small waist but certainly hadn't the bosom for a gown cut any lower than the flame-colored silk. Luckily, the square neckline suited me—my neck would have looked very bare otherwise—and the flame color did something for my hair and eyes, in addition to making me feel considerably more cheerful than I had been lately.

It was not surprising that Eve Carpe, who was not going and had probably picked out these very clothes for me, found herself with a headache and could not help me do up my hair. I did it myself as simply as possible in a loose club on the nape of my neck, going on the theory that if you hadn't a talent for the job, the simpler the better. Polly gave me a small hair ornament in the shape of butterfly wings, which I set into the hair over my forehead. I pulled tendrils out around my face so I wouldn't be thought too severe and plain and used some of Polly's rouge on my lips and cheeks. I also traced my eyebrows and lashes ever so faintly with an indelible pencil and was fairly pleased at the results. Even Elsie Ferguson in the movies couldn't look much more sophisticated than I did—well, at least considering the material I had to work with.

When Howard got us all in tow, Polly and I followed him down the inside stairs to his car in the basement-garage. We exchanged satisfied smiles that must have appeared rather smug. I remarked on how clean the basement was and Eve, who came down complaining of her head, reminded us, "That's because I was cleaning it all day yesterday." Polly looked perplexed, as if it would never occur to her to clean the basement, as indeed, it probably wouldn't.

It was still raining at dusk. When we drove out and down the street, Eve grumpily closing the doors behind us, I saw the three children across the street returning from their fortification at the end of the long block.

"I feel sorry for them," I said. "They wanted to build a fort in the pergola on Pompeii Street, but now the city will soon have flowers growing there."

I hadn't supposed this idle gossip about neighborhood children and a mud pile would interest Howard, but he remarked unexpectedly, "They were chased off the pergola ground. They aren't supposed to be on the Hyde property either. That's private ground. Better tell them, next time you see them."

"They aren't doing any harm. Builders will do a lot worse." I added, "Maybe I won't sell my property, after all."

I could well imagine the state Howard was in, considering the enormous expenses he had already run up against the expectation of profit from the Hyde Place sale. I wanted to smile but did not.

When we'd arrived at the little baroque theater on Geary Street, it was Polly who first aroused a buzz of attention, especially from the women in the lobby. She looked her very best in green and black with a fantastic little jet-beaded black silk turban that fitted over one hazel eye.

Shortly after we arrived, the door opened and we were ushered in to our seats, third row center of the orchestra. I was feeling so vain in my flame silk and velvet evening wrap that I wished we could have arrived late, at least later than the Demos family, so that they might see Polly and me at our best. As it was, we were within ten minutes of curtain time when there was a slight commotion in the aisle as a newcomer arrived. I looked around and saw Neil Burnham walking down the aisle, looking as if his black-and-white dinner clothes had been moulded on his body. I suspected that he was fully aware of the interest he aroused, but he behaved exactly as he had at our previous meetings, amused and sardonic, with a faintly aloof quality. At sight of him I found myself hoping against hope that his friendship with Howard MacPherson was dictated by the desire for a good story, or some other equally innocent reason.

He was looking directly down into my eyes and I could not help myself. I had been so surrounded by suspicion, accidents and depression lately that I found his sudden smile irrresistible. I thawed in spite of my reservations about him. He reached the fourth row and was ushered to the aisle seat behind me. I had turned to face the stage again but was intensely aware of him. A minute later there was a little metallic "click" behind me, followed by a tug at the hair gathered on my neck.

I turned. "What on earth—"

His face was close by. "Have one?" He had put a coin in the metal box on the back of my seat and taken out a little package of chocolate peppermints that he held out to me. Hypnotized by that persistent gaze of his, I found myself eating the wafer, and with my mouth full unable to say a word while he exchanged pleasantries with Polly. Wisely, she had refused the candy.

He broke off to ask, "Do you feel you are being observed?" He made an upward motion over his left shoulder. For a second or two I pretended to ignore him. Then, as Polly looked up, I did the same and saw the Demos family in the front box on the left of the theater. Others in the orchestra section were also looking at them—Mrs. Demos and Tony and another woman being the most visible. Mr. Demos already seemed settled and half asleep in the background.

Between Mrs. Demos and Tony was my recent acquaintance, Miss Gerda Edwards. The black-haired young woman with sloe eyes was heavily made up. Her evening gown was a beaded black crepe and she carried a black feather fan that Mrs. Demos obviously took exception to. Every time its gentle waving feathers reached her she put her finger under her nose as if to prevent a sneeze.

"Heavens," Polly said, "who is *that*?"

Neil grinned. "I believe you know Gerda Edwards, San Francisco's answer to Theda Bara. She will be writing the review of this play."

He probably hoped I would think she was Tony's special property, and I did wonder.

Teresa Demos, with her small, mother-of-pearl opera glasses, was studying the audience. She stopped suddenly, remained focused on us and as I smiled a bit hesitantly she waved at me with a ripple of her fingers. "Merideth! I promised to drag them here."

Everyone heard her, but I didn't mind that. I felt a sense of at least borrowed importance. She said something to Dr. Tony but he had already seen us. I think he would have smiled, but Neil Burnham looked at him that minute. Neil's head was very close to mine, which may have been why Tony looked off in another direction. Mrs. Demos, in quite another mood, struck her son's hand with her glasses and Tony was forced to give me a belated smile, as though he had not seen me until that moment. Mrs. Demos said something to her husband, who gave a start, roused himself, and moved forward between his wife's shoulder and the bare one of Miss Gerda Edwards. He nodded to me in his genial fashion, and at that minute the asbestos curtain went up onstage. He settled back, a bit flurried, but Mrs. Demos leaned onto the padded rail and called to me: "After the second act."

The velvet curtain was already on its way up now and there was a chorus of "shushing." I crunched down in my seat, but Mrs. Demos looked around at her critics with interest and animation, waving to various acquaintances, not the least bit crushed. I thought she would have made a perfect mother for Neil Burnham. He would have reacted in the same way. Tony, on the other hand, said something apparently severe to her over Miss Edwards' elaborately feathered head, which bent toward his behind a fan. I wondered how well acquainted Tony really was with this beauteous vampire. I made a bet he didn't ask *her* before he kissed her good night. Or were they even more intimately involved?

I decided to pay more attention to Howard's play, and reluctantly shifted my attention from the interesting tableau in the Demos box to the stage. The curtain had risen on the traditional murder-mystery setting, a rich man's library. Like all rich men in melodramas who make the mistake of being caught in their libraries, the rich man in question ventured too near the stacks about ten minutes into the play. A pair of translucent hands, thanks to the blue lighting, reached out of the stacks, closed around his throat—and our mystery was launched. Niece arrived in Scene Two for the reading of the will, and along with assorted suspects Howard MacPherson now strolled into the scene. His fakery and larger-than-life gestures were well suited to the stage, and he wasn't bad at all as a romantic suspect.

I liked the play. It was full of spooky thrills and the acting was good, especially Howard's. I was a little puzzled by Polly, however. I had expected her to be conspicuously proud, even possessive, about his performance, but she settled back after a few minutes and even closed her eyes occasionally.

The second act was exciting enough to hold my attention, but I began to get anxious about the between-acts meeting with the Demos family and its devastating friend. Meanwhile, the stage rocked with melodrama. In the midst of a thunder and lightning storm (much rattling of tin behind the scenes) another heir was pushed off a balcony, and the noise of this assault covered the villain immediately afterward in a concealing raincoat and sou'wester hat as he pretended to take a tumble himself.

How all this would turn out I couldn't really care—Did my hair look all right? Was my dress wrinkled? I devoutly hoped I wouldn't step on the fish-tail train of my dress.

By the end of the second act I was once again interested in the plot, which found Howard trapped in a sou'wester and raincoat, though he was obviously not the fiend who had tucked his victims into The Long Box. The stage lights dimmed to eerie green this time as the curtain descended. Like most of the audience I was left shuddering pleasurably, when Neil Burnham tapped me on one of my unaccustomed bare shoulders.

"Time to face the lions."

How he knew I was nervous about the meeting I couldn't imagine, but for some reason his breezy reference to it made the moment easier for me. I got up, asked Polly to come with us, but she refused, smiling.

"You young people run along." She swung around. "I know I can count on you to look after my girl, Mr. Burnham."

"You may be sure of that," he told her. Mother had been gracious and friendly to him and so I was surprised at the decisiveness in his voice as he answered her. It also lacked that easy lightness I'd noted in most of his conversation. Was he possibly revealing that sincerity I had only guessed at once or twice before? I was delighted as he led me out into the aisle, where he got a good look at me from head to toe. His·eyes seemed to widen as he said, "Good God!"

I was, to put it mildly, pleased at his reaction. Walking up the aisle on his arm, I was aware of the intense interest of those around us and caught scrambled remarks about who the Passerby's girl was.

"They're jealous of me," I told Neil.

He was nodding casually to right and left, but said to me out of the corner of his mouth, "They are jealous, but not of you."

I was so pleased my fingers curled up over the flawless sleeve of his coat. He glanced down, then looked at me, at my eyes and, more slowly, seemed to see my mouth. I felt the pulse in my throat beat and wondered if my feelings about him were that transparent. During the endless time we strolled through the ornate little lobby and up the staircase I forced myself to remember the other women who had found Neil Burnham fascinating, and all to no purpose. Still, it was not difficult to find excuses for his so often being found in my stepfather's company. Since he had once warned me, he might be staying about with Howard in order to find out what Howard was up to. On the other hand, Neil's so-called warning to me might refer to something quite light and innocuous.

"Be careful of San Francisco, Merideth" . . . or "be careful of your virtue, Merideth" (mocking) . . . or even "be careful of *me* . . ." That last was probably good advice. Thinking about it, I displayed for him my biggest, brightest smile just as we saw Tony Demos coming toward us. I took Tony's hand and really startled Neil when I let Tony kiss me on the cheek.

"Mother is asking for you," he said. "You look lovely . . . Evening, Burnham." With distinctly less enthusiasm. "Coming?"

Neil said, "By all means. Wouldn't miss it for worlds." It apparently took a great deal more than an exchange of kisses between Tony and me to put Neil Burnham out of countenance. He followed us right into the back of the box where Mr. Demos had gotten up and was motioning me to take his chair behind his wife.

I was anxious to see the relationship between Neil and Gerda Edwards, but when I did it gave me no pleasure—apparently they were thick as thieves. Neil became the casual charmer and Miss Edwards began a great flutter over something he said to her, rapping his knuckles with her fan and behaving exactly like a soubrette in a French farce. It was disgusting.

I could hardly concentrate on what Teresa Demos and Tony were talking about. I was shaken out of my preoccupation when I heard Mrs. Demos ask me suddenly, "You can make it, can't you? That boy of mine particularly says he wants you along."

What on earth was she talking about?

"You are very kind. When—what— time—?" In fact, what *day* was this invitation?

"Immediately after the show. A midnight supper. Naturally we want your mother and father along too." They glanced over at Neil, and with rather pained reluctance Tony introduced the columnist to his mother.

"I know this young man quite well from his writing," Mrs. Demos said as they shook hands. "I wouldn't miss his column for anything."

"If only you meant that and would give me an interview," Neil said, pursuing his opportunity, but Teresa Demos shook her head.

"You aren't going to make a golden-haired little orphan out of me the way you did our friend here."

He laughed and gave me a quick, rather puzzled look, but I made it my business to have my full and undivided attention upon Mr. Demos. Poor man, having just concealed a yawn, he was complaining that he wished plays would start earlier and end quicker.

No one invited Neil Burnham to the midnight supper, although, without him, there would be an uneven number—I was certain either Gerda Edwards or I would be without a partner. However, it was no concern of mine. A midnight supper sounded gay and festive, and I did want to wear my flame-silk gown as long as possible. Heaven knows there were few enough occasions when one could really dress up and be glamorous. Unless one were Gerda Edwards, of course. A little heavy-handed, I thought, but she certainly was beautiful. I couldn't deny that, although indeed I tried.

Teresa Demos nudged me. "You're going to introduce your stepfather to us, aren't you? I've promised myself to play Sherlock Holmes. I'll smoke out that rascal. If, of course, Mr. MacPherson is all you say."

"Mother," Tony Demos said in a low harsh voice I'd never heard him use. And then he added something in Italian—a warning? I hoped so because for all Neil's joking with Miss Edwards, his attention had been caught by Teresa Demos' uncautious remark. He was no longer smiling. In fact, he seemed quite grim.

FIFTEEN

MRS. DEMOS REMINDED me that Polly and Howard and I were to join them immediately after the last curtain. "Tell that fine villain of a stepfather that we'll only wait for him to remove his makeup and then we're off."

As Neil and I left the box he said to me, "I did my best to hint but no invitations to romantic midnight suppers were forthcoming."

"What a pity! Now you and Miss Edwards will have to save your business for working hours," I said, and instantly regretted my show of pique.

He assured me "that would ruin everything. I don't especially like things made easy for me. No sport in that."

I didn't trust myself to respond. The curtain was already up and our passage down the darkened aisle was watched by many a frowning face. We sneaked into our seats in time to disturb the onstage villain, who peered fearsomely out at us through the murky green glow.

In spite of Teresa Demos' betrayal of our suspicions to Neil, whom I still had to consider a possible accomplice of my step-father, I was having a marvelous time. I only wished he had been included in the invitation for midnight supper, but I supposed Tony's dislike of him was behind it.

The thriller onstage reached its peak, and the villain was unmasked. After an embrace with the heroine in which Howard aroused appropriate sighs from females in the audience, the curtain came down.

Polly went backstage to see Howard. Neil Burnham was looking for the glove I had lost, and I used this as an excuse to remain behind. By the time Polly was out of sight, Neil had found my glove. Several people had stepped on the elbow-length white kid, which he held up a bit ruefully.

"Never mind," I said. "I'm not elegant enough to eat with my gloves on anyway."

"Pity I couldn't persuade them they are going to be short a male at their precious supper."

We looked at each other at the same time. He cupped his hands around the back of my head, drew my face to his as Teresa Demos' full voice called down the aisle.

"Oh, there you are, Merideth. Where are we to meet the MacPhersons?"

Flushed, flustered and distinctly disappointed, I broke away from Neil, who calmly placed my wrap around my shoulders and escorted me up the aisle to the Demos family. I had only one satisfaction. Neil, who never let anything fluster him, showed a higher color than usual. I hoped he'd been as frustrated as I was.

Mrs. Demos was her usual lively self but I saw her pinch Tony's hand and Tony's scowl softened a trifle. I thought she liked me, but I suspected I was being used by her to divert her son from the vampire. In any case, there was nothing to do but to let Neil say good night to us all, lingering too shortly over my hand, and then I watched him stride through the lobby into the rainy night.

Polly and Howard arrived, with Howard being trailed by two middle-aged women and a male photographer. After I'd introduced him around he gave Mrs. Demos news I secretly welcomed.

"I'm afraid I must refuse your good invitation. As you can

see, the press is at my heels for an interview. Silly business, but part of the game."

I think Teresa Demos was genuinely disappointed but she rose to the occasion by saying she understood perfectly. "I only hope this will not prevent your stepdaughter from accompanying us. Or . . . your charming wife."

This was obviously an added thought about Polly Hyde, but Howard seemed to jump at it. "Nothing could be better. Polly is always bored by this sort of thing, interviews, the lot."

"I'll get them home," Tony volunteered. "Please don't let that bother you."

So Howard and his entourage retreated to a nearby saloon for the interview while the rest of us were driven by the Demos chauffeur through the misty night toward what had been the Barbary Coast before the fire. What remained of the old Coast was reached by Columbus Avenue, which cut through the modern Italian district below Telegraph Hill and ran on to old factories, ultimately ending near the Sausalito ferries crossing the Golden Gate.

I had never, to my knowledge, seen the Barbary Coast and was disappointed when Polly began to point out old dance halls, saloons and assorted dives which had been rebuilt as replicas of the prefire buildings. She and Mrs. Demos argued in a friendly way about the location of the originals. Everything looked dark, and there was a dead appearance to the district. Even the street lamps were sparse and far between.

I wondered if this was the area Polly had run to when she deserted father and me. She did not seem to be drawn to it now, as she and Mrs. Demos continued their rather loud discussion while Mr. Demos quietly announced, "Ah, we are here."

Tony had said absolutely nothing to either Gerda Edwards or me during the trip but he was more than usually attentive in helping her out of the car, and the lavish way she responded made me also wonder whether her real interest was Tony or Neil Burnham. Probably she wanted both. I knew the feeling myself.

The restaurant we had come to, one of the very few lighted at all, was small on the outside, obscure, dimly illuminated and hardly imposing. Its name was spelled out on a small replica of a roulette wheel: "MONTE."

We approached by a long outside passage at the side of the building. The passage was covered over by a tin roof that in turn was disguised by vines. I heard raindrops intermittently on the tin and was fascinated by the sensation of being in some exotic, tropical place, far from the Monte Carlo suggested by the name, but to me in this misty, foggy night the air was truly romantic.

Tony put his arm around my waist. "My parents love this place for its Old World feeling. Sometimes their sentiment runs away with them."

"There's a terrible draft here, Tony," Gerda reminded him, and caught between our opposing views of the night, Tony apologized to her and stepped back, as though to shield her. As Mr. and Mrs. Demos were being greeted by a stout little man who proved to be both owner and headwaiter, I came up beside mother, who was shivering. It seemed a refreshing, brisk night to me in spite of the darkness that enclosed the little tin and ivy arbor through which we had reached the Monte's entrance.

When I asked if she were too chilly, Polly shook her head. "It's everything. This neighborhood. The darkness. Shadows . . . anything could be out there."

I teased her, "You can't have darkness and shadows too. One or the other. Anyway, we won't let them hurt you . . . whatever is out there." The area beyond the ivy-covered trellis looked completely deserted, just the side of a vacant building and no lights whatever. I abandoned my light mood as her fingers gripped mine and she whispered, "I would never do that again, Mery."

"Do what?"

"Never leave you for—this awful place."

I squeezed her fingers affectionately. "You're married and some-day I'll be married. We must leave each other sometime." This was certainly not the right minute, but I had to take every opportunity. "Polly, *are* you happily married? If you're not, we can go—"

"No! Oh, God, no!"

I was shaken by this sudden outburst, as by their looks were Tony and Gerda.

"No, you aren't happy with him? Or no, something else?"

She looked about, as if to compose herself, then: "I'm sorry. I just don't know what came over me. It's just—I don't know." But she added quickly, "Of course I'm happily married! He's been so good to me—I think Mrs. Demos is motioning for us to come on."

It was all very unsettling, but we went on to meet the proprietor, Mr. Monte, and to be ushered into a dark, warm, well-filled room that looked enormous considering its unprepossessing exterior.

I felt Tony's touch on my shoulder to guide me to my chair at a large table near a postage-stamp dance floor, where he seated me between Polly and himself, with Gerda on his other side, Mr. Demos beyond, and then Teresa Demos.

I shouldn't have been surprised at the way Polly and Teresa Demos got along. Almost drowning out the music of a Victrola for the dancing, Mrs. Demos talked incessantly about the San Francisco of the war years, but when she wanted to bring the conversation back to the days before the fire, my mother said very little. She was in her depressed mood again . . . thinking of the lost time just before and after the fire, no doubt.

We all let the delightful if overpowering Teresa order dinner for us. The restaurant's cuisine was Italian and Greek but the vote at our table was for the Midnight Speciality of the House— an omelet with fresh oysters, mushrooms and other ingredients of interesting color and size, exotic but hardly guaranteed to settle the stomach at that hour. With it we had a red wine that everyone pronounced the best ever. I didn't know. The wines I was used to in the mining towns were harsh and strong and I had been taught to drink them watered.

Gerda said, "Prohibition will destroy all this. No more good wines to give that certain something to a meal."

"Prohibition won't stop mama," Tony remarked, raising his glass to her.

Mrs. Demos grinned mischievously. "Certainly not. I have already made a deal with a family out in the Excelsior district.

Just everyone's making deals with them out there. They've promised to sell me the premier vintage each year. Fermented in their very own cellar."

Polly drank very little. When I urged her to finish her glass, she shook her head.

"I don't like it," and as I looked at her, she repeated, her lips scarcely moving, ". . . not anymore."

I touched her hand, resting on the table, and she smiled faintly. To change the subject I asked Tony *what* we were eating.

"Hangtown Fry, Monte's version." He waved his fork threateningly. "And I don't want you spreading the word that Dr. Demos prescribes Hangtown Fry for all his patients at midnight."

"A little Ouzo. That is best of all," Mr. Demos put in, and I noticed for the first time that a small, extra glass filled with what looked like a potent dark liquor had been set beside his plate. He downed the contents with gusto. "Ouzo! All around!" he told Monte, with an expansive gesture that was uncharacteristic.

I, for one, would have been quite happy without the Greek drink, which seemed too thick to be a wine and was too strong for me at any hour. We had not finished dinner before Mr. Demos was on his feet claiming he would sweep Gerda through the fashionable tango. We all applauded as they went onto the floor, where he demonstrated his version with the skilled assistance of talented Gerda. Tony took my hand and led me onto the floor under the faint crimson lights.

"Don't be afraid, Merideth. Just follow me."

I was happy that I had learned to tango two years ago in college, but I let him think he had taught me with a few quick directions. It was pleasant dancing, moving seductively with him. Pleasant and comfortable. He was not a bad dancer, though I felt he regarded it as a therapeutic exercise, not romantic by-play. He was so businesslike about the dance that it shook me a little when we came together in the pattern of the movements and he said, "I never liked this dancing business before; it's you who make the difference, Mery. *You.*"

But I didn't want to be serious with him tonight, so I laughed and pretended to read in his voice the lightness, the flirtation a girl might expected in such a dance. "Thank you indeed, sir, you are too—" I started to say and saw his face darken. I knew I was on the wrong tack and quickly got out, "I'm glad, Tony. You have been kinder to me than anybody since—"

"Since?"

"My father and I were very close. I beg your pardon, I don't mean to imply that you are like my father, Tony."

"No, please, I don't mind at all. I know you loved your father. And you need a man of substance in your life, someone who understands you and you can be safe with." We swung away from each other in the dance and when we were together again, he said, "Mery, my mother is very taken with you. I guess you noticed."

"And I with her. She is a wonderful lady."

The dance ended, and barely in time. He was dear and protective, but I wondered if that was enough for a whole lifetime. Obviously a woman could do worse. Far worse.

Someone changed the Victrola record and we sat down to finish dinner. I had enjoyed the dance and the opportunity it gave me to be in Tony's arms. I also had some troubling thoughts to sort out about the man who, in my view, had saved my life.

We made our way through the rest of our dinner carefully concealing yawns, and when we left the restaurant sometime after one in the morning we were all glad enough to be going home. None of our party seemed too intent upon making a night of it out at a beach resort where Mr. Demos, still full of the Old Nick, wanted to show the rest of the world how to tango.

Gerda suggested that Polly and I be driven home first. She didn't mind waiting, she said, taking Tony's hand. "It will give me a lovely ride in the cool night air, and with such good company."

I wasn't in any condition to argue the matter. My stomach already hurt from this midnight assault on it.

There were no lingering good-night kisses on our high front porch that evening. Gerda and Tony's parents were watching as Tony got out and escorted Polly and me to the door. On our way up the stairs, I saw the front curtains abruptly close and assumed that either Eve Carpe or Howard was watching for our arrival. Mrs. Demos had held my hand briefly as I left the car, and I was pleased when she said, "We must see you again soon, Merideth. Remember."

I had promised, but by this time my stomach ached so much that I was anxious only to get to bed. I didn't even look back as we reached the top of the stairs.

The door was opened by an unseen hand and Polly ducked in. I could well imagine Eve buzzing to ask her how Howard's play had gone over—not one of us had thought to check the morning papers for reviews.

Meanwhile, Tony kissed me his friendly kiss and asked how I had liked the night life.

"Gives me a stomach ache," I confessed unromantically.

He became the doctor on the instant. "Maybe you are a bit young for wine. I'm not sure this prohibition law might not turn out to be a good thing, after all. It will certainly save a lot of livers that were headed for cirrhosis."

I managed to smile. "On this romantic thought I'm afraid we must part company. For tonight, anyway."

"Take a packet of those powders I gave you if you feel a head-ache coming on," he told me.

I went inside, saw that Polly and Howard were talking in low tones in the front room. He had a morning newspaper spread out in front of him. He raised his head as I was tiptoeing across the dining room to the swinging door of the hall.

"Have a good time?"

"Fine. Ate too much. Your show was great."

He grinned. "*Examiner* says so too: 'Howard MacPherson has never been better. He returns in his most invigorating and at-tractive role since he played Marcus Superbus in *Sign of the Cross* before the war. He is the most'—"

"Excuse me"—I was being rude to him as usual, but, feeling the worst of my stomach ache I went on to my room, hearing behind me Howard's "What the devil . . . ? What ails her?"

I didn't know whether it was the wine I had drunk or the con-glomeration of food, but I didn't want Howard to know about it if I could help it. By the time I got to my room and lay down,

I felt much better, but I did have some belated thoughts: Why had I eaten that awful stuff at this hour?

Polly must have come into the room before I realized her presence. "Darling! Are you sick?"

"I'm all right now. It was mixing drinks and eating that stuff."

"I'll get you something. Dr. Demos left us several things when we took you home from the hospital."

"No, really. I'm fine."

But she rushed away, and I heard voices, including Howard's resonant tones. . . . "It's all in the bathroom . . . powders, pills, the rest of it. Never mind . . . I'll fix it for her."

I sat up, hearing Howard's voice repeating, "I'll fix it for her. . . ."

By the time Polly came in with the glass and held it out to me saying "Drink it down," I decided I didn't need it.

"What is it? It's all cloudy."

"Howard put the powders into water. You're supposed to drink it down. It will settle your stomach."

I looked up. He was standing in the doorway staring at me.

I told Polly, "I'll drink it. You run along and I'll drink it and go to bed. Good night, mother."

Polly kissed me good night, put the glass in my hand and left the room. I waited until I was certain they'd gone to their own room, then got up, still in my beautiful flame-colored silk dress which I'd been so proud of and which was now wrinkled and wrapped around my body, making it almost impossible for me to move.

I put my finger into the glass, tasted the contents. There was a vile, bitter taste. But wouldn't medicine taste bitter? As I recalled, the powders in the hospital were equally revolting. At any rate I wasn't going to drink anything furnished by Howard MacPherson. Until I could get the contents of this glass to Tony, I made up my mind to preserve it with great care. Surely Tony could tell by some means or other if it contained any poison.

I unwound myself from the silk dress, kicked the train out of the way and crossed the room. I carefully set the glass down in the back of the closet, undressed and went to bed. To what dreams, I wondered.

SIXTEEN

THE RECENT DRIZZLE and showers had let up and the blue sky was swept clear next morning, but its brightness didn't communicate itself to my companions at 379 Hyde Place. I came out of my room to find all three of them in low spirits. Whether my appearance brought on their low spirits, I couldn't say. But after staring at me with his mouth open and remarking that he hadn't expected me to be so bright and cheerful after coming home sick, Howard complained that he was feeling none too good himself. It seemed he had gotten a review in the *Chronicle* which referred to his "mature years and noticeable weight . . . hardly the answer to a maiden's dream." Well, I could have told them that. They read the whole thing again during breakfast, first Howard, and then Polly, like an echo.

Howard wadded up the paper, threw it on the floor only to have it picked up by Eve, whose pretty face showed no emotion at all. She had set down our plates of bacon and eggs and now started out with the crumpled paper.

As if she had said something, Howard called at her, "No maiden's dream . . . it says 'no—' "

She said coolly over her shoulder, "Mr. MacPherson, you knew you couldn't go on playing Prince Charming forever. All your eggs in one basket, remember?" and she went out through the swinging door. Howard looked after her, laughed shortly.

"All in one basket. Eve's right, eh, Polly?"

I wondered what that was all about and waited for her usual sycophantic agreement, but she said nothing, just stirred the egg around on the plate, then said abruptly, "Mery, I'm glad to see you got over your sick stomach."

"That stuff young Dr. Demos gave us did the trick," Howard said. "I'll bet on aspirin every time, providing the patient took her medicine."

Did he suspect I hadn't taken all of the drink? Did he also know something about it that—had I indeed taken it all—would have kept me from showing up so well- recovered this morning?

Polly spoke up quickly. "I read the other day they're starting to put crosses on the aspirin tablets they sell. You know, the name of the brand and all."

"Were they aspirin tablets you dissolved in my glass of water? They do seem to have done the trick, though I didn't drink so much of it . . . too nasty tasting . . ."

"It must have been those mushrooms that made you sick. You can get awfully sick on bad mushrooms," Polly said.

"I wonder if anyone else came down sick. I'll have to find out from Mrs. Demos. Somebody should tell that Monte fellow," I answered.

"Just getting ready for Prohibition," Howard said, reaching for the enamel coffee pot. "All these saloons are charging all and more than the traffic will bear. They know they'll all be closing down by July."

I looked across the table at him. "Then you think it was the restaurant that made me sick."

"What else?"

"I thought it might be the flu coming back." I could be just as disingenuous as he. "Well, I think I'll get some air after breakfast. I'll feel better out in that sunshine. Isn't it lovely?"

For some reason the sunny weather depressed him as much as the bad review of his performace.

"I don't know, Mery. With all the new building going on out

here there are a lot of drifters about—regular South-of-Marketers. Eve or your mother will keep you company if you want to get out."

Since by now I was nearly convinced he had tried to give me some kind of drug or unpleasant substance the previous night I didn't think it especially clever to annoy him if I didn't really have to, so I shrugged and sulkily agreed. The most important thing was to get my evidence (of the "medicine") to Tony Demos. Did mother know what she'd given me last night? Was she aware that it may not have been aspirin but something more deadly in that glass? Howard had acted either very surprised or very worried this morning. Was it my quick recovery? Or something else? Something I hadn't even guessed?

I honestly prayed that Polly didn't know about any attempt to drug me . . . please let her be innocent . . . please . . .

And all the time she sat there looking worried about Howard's mood and saying now with near-pitiful eagerness, "That's true, I'll go with you, Merideth. Just tell me where and when you want to walk."

I said, "Thanks, Polly. You're being your old sweet self."

She appeared startled, perhaps not understanding what in particular I found that was like her old sweet self. At her best she had been salty in my childhood.

I got up from the table and went to help Eve with the dishes. Whatever put my mother under her husband's control, they couldn't forever keep me away from the telephone, and all I needed was Tony's proof that the glass Howard prepared for me last night was poisoned with something or other, possibly not fatal. Why he should poison me with anything at all if it wasn't to be fatal puzzled me, but I didn't put any connivance beyond him.

By mid-morning, however, I was pretty nervous. Howard did not leave the house and Eve Carpe busied herself polishing furniture in the dining room. I decided aloud that I would go up to the attic and see if I could find some of my childhood toys. I waited until we heard a newsboy come up the street yelling "EXTRA!" about the capture of a murderer in San Jose. Howard went out and bought a paper, turning instantly to the second section for the interview he had given after the show last night. I could almost feel sorry for him, he was so anxious. Almost. While he read I took a clean preserve jar from the kitchen, washed it again to be sure, poured in the contents of the glass I'd hidden the night before, then sealed it with the complicated jar top.

I got my coin purse and, with the jar hidden in my jacket, went to the inside stairs. Under Eve's casual eye I started up toward the attic. The moment the stair door closed I switched directions and hurried down to the basement. I went to the big garage doors and opened one, startling myself more than Neil Burnham, who apparently had heard the door being opened and preferred entering the house by the inside basement stairs rather than the long front steps.

His smile as always made it difficult for me to suspect him of anything worse than viewing mankind with a general, amused kind of scorn. He appeared to think I needed some sort of manual assistance as he found me bolting out, and caught me by both forearms, almost shaking the preserve jar out of my pocket.

"Oh, Neil, I am glad to see you," I told him breathlessly.

He chose, not unreasonably, to take this as a personal endorsement. "That's the kind of greeting for a sunny day. And were you about to deliver that depressing jar of soup to me as a token of your affection?"

Though he refused to recognize my attempts to wriggle out of his hold, I could not let him remain under this illusion about my cooking. "I ought to let you drink this stuff . . . which I suspect is poisoned."

"Wonderful! Curare, of course."

"I've no idea. I do know I want Dr. Demos to have it. To find out what—"

"To analyze it."

"That too."

His smile did not vanish, but it stiffened a little. "What makes you think it— Well, Mac, old man! Thought you'd like to see the write-up hot from the dangerous Gerda's pen."

One of his hands had dropped from my arm but the other

firmly prevented my nervous start from being noticed by my stepfather, who must have seen us from the front doorway of the house. I told myself that this effort and the sudden change in his voice to light cordiality counted for something. If he were genuinely Howard's friend, he wouldn't likely go to these efforts to conceal my own emotions from the man. Would he? Unless he were clever . . .

He went further, whispered to me, "Patience," and went on up the stairs to Howard, who'd started down holding his hand out.

"What does she say? Is it good? You know, Burnham, it's just possible that little show could make it to Broadway. With the right backing, money, supporting cast. . . . Where is it, what page?"

His hand shook as he tore at the pink pages of the afternoon paper. While he read Neil called down to me, "Where are you off to? Need an escort by any chance?"

"Just going out."

Howard, still absorbed in his paper, was finally stirred to suggest, "Why don't you run along with Mery? She wants to go for a walk."

"Since you insist." Neil looked over the banister at me again. "Ready?" He came on down to join me while, with some difficulty, I tried to hide my pleasure.

When we were beyond my stepfather's hearing, I asked Neil if we were on our way to meet Tony Demos at the hospital.

"I'll get it to the noble Tony myself. Don't worry. Though to be frank, I don't think you will send old Mac to San Quentin with this unappetizing looking soup."

"Maybe *you* don't want your friend to go to San Quentin. By the way, where is your car?"

"Don't be childish. Now we are going to inspect the rest of the acreage of the celebrated heiress, Merideth Hyde. Next, I never drive, so we are going by taxi if we can get one on Mission Street. It's not precisely known for its available taxis."

I looked at him and asked flatly, "Why?"

"Why look at your acreage? Or why no taxis on Mission?"

I did want to know why he didn't drive. From what I'd seen

since my arrival in town, almost every man in San Francisco had a car and used it. But he seemed intent on making jokes so I kept my conversation in the neighborhood he'd chosen. "Why go to all this trouble for Heiress Hyde when there are Crockers or Sutros, or Athertons or heaven knows what real heiresses in California?"

He helped me off the curb. "They are so much harder to approach. Also not so pretty."

I ended by laughing and gave up my inquisition.

"Was my stepfather's notice in that paper actually a good one?"

"To quote Gentle Gerda: 'A splendid relic of the great prewar matinée idols. Gives a fine performance worthy of any man his age.' "

I groaned. "It will be a gloomy house tonight."

"Don't worry. He has a matinée today. All those little old ladies sighing as one will make things right for him." He was still smiling when he asked me abruptly, "What legal arrangements have you made in case of your death?"

That shook me. "I haven't. I'm not going to until I make up my mind. Why? What do *you* know? Did Howard tell you something? Do you believe he gave me some kind of poison last night?"

"What excuse did he have to give the medicine—or poison, if it was—to you?"

I explained about the food at Monte's, which puzzled him.

"I've never known Monte to serve bad food. And certainly he knows a toadstool when he sees one. I rather doubt the mushrooms could have been bad, but I'll check on some folks who ate there last night."

He had been looking for a taxicab and as predicted found none. He did signal a private car about to turn onto Pompeii Street, and I got my first ride in a jitney. When we had settled ourselves in the back seat he remarked, as if there had been no interruption, "He is not a complete fool, you know."

"Who?"

"My old friend honest Mac."

"How old a friend is he?"

"At least three weeks. Since, in fact, he brought his shy bride to Brubick's office to make their claim on you. My informant there—"

"Miss Falassi."

"—my amiable informant told me about them and I smelled a story."

"Then you aren't really old friends?"

"I am always an old friend of any man who puts in a claim for a hundred thousand dollars."

I had given up telling him he was impossible. I merely crowded over to make room for another rider who had signaled from a corner two blocks west of the Hyde Place house.

I never ceased to be surprised at the changes I saw in this district, which had been so heavily built up since my childhood, and so I wasn't awed as I might have been when we got out of the car on the edge of a beautiful meadow dotted with wild-flowers and bordered on the south by a series of hills still with their primitive wild loveliness.

"Behold! The rest of your inheritance. What are you going to do with it?"

Even I could see what this area would mean to developers. Street after street had been cut through from Hyde Place onward to the very edge of this meadow and hillside. Row upon row of houses. Those nearest my meadow were spacious and beautiful— some of rich stone and spreading out over several lots, most of them wooden but of generous size.

Still, I liked my meadow as it was, full of grass and buttercups and acacia trees. And my hillside, which had the look of high-nap lavender velvet, covered as it was with tall flowering lupine.

"I love wildflowers," I said, which wasn't quite the remark he must have expected.

He thrust the preserve jar down into my jacket pocket as he said lightly, "I haven't forgotten the buttercup you dropped. Matter of fact, I still have it somewhere." He neatly turned me around to face him. "We have some unfinished business." And he kissed me.

Because I was surprised, I was caught breathless, but during those next seconds it hardly mattered as I was drawn to that sensuous mouth which had troubled me from our first meeting. I was, though, properly dizzy when he let me go and had to clutch at his coat lapels until I got my breath. Not precisely the most romantic finale.

He watched me. "I spent most of the night planning that."

"You might have warned me. I almost strangled." All the same, I was highly pleased to see that he was a trifle out of breath himself.

"An army doesn't warn the citadel before a surprise attack."

"And how many citadels have you taken?"

"Countless." He reached into my jacket pocket and took out the preserve jar. Even the brief touch of his hand in my pocket excited me, but I managed to look around casually at the beautiful grassy meadow. There were some, I knew, would have encouraged him to continue where he'd left off in the confines of that meadow.

"Come along," he said, "before this stuff blows up in our faces."

I caught sight of the preserve jar and wrinkled my nose in distaste. He had put a singularly unromantic end to what, for me, had been a delightful encounter. All the same I had the notion as we walked back along the curving street that he too was very disturbed by our encounter, that it had meant nearly as much to him as it had to me. Or was that only wishful thinking on my part? It was hard to tell about Neil Burnham, but his silence was uncharacteristic.

We had walked several blocks occupied by heaven knows what thoughts with nothing said between us, though I sensed him glancing at me several times. I hoped this was a favorable sign. We presently heard an auto horn honking, and I recognized Howard's touring car headed out of Hyde Place into the wide double lanes of Pompeii Street. I wanted to avoid him, but Neil looked around.

Howard called, "I'm off to the matinée. Going downtown, Burnham?"

Remembering the preserve jar Neil had palmed and which now was only partially covered by his coat sleeve, I was terrified

174

that my stepfather would see it and guess its contents. To make matters worse, Neil asked me, "Can you get home alone?"

"Certainly." I clipped off the word with as much indifference as I could manage. Only the street with its pergola in the center separated me from the foot of the Hyde Place block.

He stopped long enough to brush my fingers with his, giving them a quick, gentle pressure which, I assumed, was meant to reassure me. Then he got into the car and they drove off, with Howard adding insult to injury by waving at me. So the man I was infatuated with had driven off with the man I was convinced was my enemy.

I should have known I could never really count on Neil Burnham. I wondered how many other women had discovered the same thing, but this was not the way I had expected love to come —a painful, gnawing, aching desire to see and touch a special man. Love should have been the pleasant warmth I felt in Dr. Tony Demos' presence. Nothing fiery or hurtful there.

I started across Pompeii Street. I was so busy trying to convince myself of the difference between real love and a painful physical infatuation that I paid no attention when the neighborhood children called out "Hello" from within the white-pillared pergola. They had to call me twice before I looked over and saw them.

"Hello," I said. "What are you up to?"

What they were up to was mischief, I suspected. The turf under the many low crates of bedded flowers had begun to dry out in the bright, wind-swept sunlight, and the girl was digging up individual pansies and violets from one crate with a toy trowel. Her usually silent brothers took each flower as it was dug up and planted it in the turned earth after shoving the crates along.

"The flowers were all wilting," the girl informed me with considerable justice. "The city just left them all to die. By Monday they'd be dead if it wasn't for us."

"You are absolutely right. May I help?"

The boy with the green eyes raised his head and smiled shyly, but as he didn't seem to be the foreman of the crew, I looked to his sister for my permission. She said, "Sure," and I began to shift the first empty crate out of the way. When I moved the crates holding the bedded plants I uncovered a considerable portion of ground beneath that was still churned up and wet from the recent rains.

My friend, the green-eyed boy, helped me shift other crates out of the way so we could clear the ground to plant the bright-faced pansies in rows which, our foreman specified, "must be neat. That's not a very straight row, Binky."

"I have to go around a dumb old sack," the older boy explained, and stuck his toy trowel hard into the earth.

His sister stopped all operations to watch him. "It's a rock, you Silly-Binky."

"It is not. Think you're smart!" Binky stuck his tongue out as he pulled up a gunnysack with a flower nursery name stamped on the end. "The rest won't come up."

I pulled the corner of the gunnysack with him. It resisted and began to split between our hands. Binky looked upset and tugged so hard I suggested hurriedly, "It must have rotted away during the rainy spell. We can plant the flowers around it as you have done."

"No! Right here!" and he went on tugging, having already torn the sack in two places. I could see that regardless of age he would be the stubborn kind of male who never gave up. His sister and his green-eyed brother must have shared my feeling because we all joined in the efforts and gradually dislodged about a foot more of the sack. In lifting up that end of the sack we'd turned over considerable ground.

The sack was not empty.

Binky's eyes widened. "It's treasure. Buried treasure! Like pirates."

His sister scoffed, "You are dumb! Why would pirates bury anything this far from the Ferry Building? It's—" she felt of the sack, her voice trailing off—"I thought it was a cabbage, maybe, but it's . . . long."

I reached between her and Binky. I needed little more than the merest touch to guess what they had uncovered. I felt stiff and thought for a minute I wasn't going to be able to move.

I finally managed to say calmly, "Do you or your brother know where the nearest telephone is?"

The girl looked at me. She had paled so that the freckles stood out on her small pug nose. She understood. "I'll go. You take care of the boys. You want me to call the police, don't you?"

Binky yelled, "I saw it first. I get first dibs on the treasure."

I looked over their heads at the girl. "Tell them to come to the pergola on Pompeii Street, honey. Tell them a lady named Merideth Hyde told you to call."

She nodded wisely. "Shall I tell them what we think it is?"

Before I could answer, she was off and running across the street to the big Tudor-trimmed house on the far corner. I felt over the gunnysack again. Oddly enough, the boys did not scramble to investigate what was wrapped inside the sack. They squatted there in the dirt, staring at me. I wondered if they finally knew that between us was a human body in the water-soaked gunnysack.

SEVENTEEN

THE YOUNG GIRL, whose name proved to be Violet Deutsch, was just as calm, efficient and admirable as I'd expected her to be and in no time our quiet district was pierced by sirens and swarming with police. As for Violet, who was about nine, she assured her young brothers that someone had been buried in the pergola because he had asked to be buried among the flowers. They took this as reasonable, although Binky pointed out, as a mounted policeman rode up and down clearing away curious bystanders, "Even if the person wanted to be buried here, it wasn't right because the city owned it." Forever precocious.

"Very true," I said, and watched as another mounted policeman said he would escort the boys home while a plainclothesman questioned Violet and me. Her little brothers almost burst with excitement and immediately began to argue over which of them would grab the pummel of the saddle and ride home with the policeman. With the judgment of Solomon, the mounted policeman agreed they should take turns, and off they went up the block with a clatter of hooves.

While we explained to the plainclothesman how we had happened to find the gunnysack, other police slit the sack carefully and looked at the contents. I was very relieved that we were not allowed to see those contents but to my amazement one of the police muttered, "An Oriental. And pretty old, too. Look at that wispy beard, Gino. Couldn't have been in here very long, I'd say. What the hell was he doing out here in this neck of the woods?"

I was still explaining to Lieutenant Jacopo, our questioner, about seeing the crate-beds of flowers ready for transplanting a day or two ago and Violet was interjecting corrective points when the girl suddenly said, "That's it! We saw a young Chinaman come by yesterday, looking for another Chinaman."

I agreed. "That is true. I saw the man myself. He had been walking all over this district looking for his father, he said."

"Hold it, Gino," one of the police ordered as he pulled out of the sack what appeared to be a small club covered with mud. The police seemed especially disturbed by the sight of it.

"That'll do the trick," one of them muttered.

We all stared at it. Violet gasped. Lieutenant Jacopo swore lightly under his breath. I asked, "What is it? Why is everybody so excited over a club?" Not because they had discovered it was murder, surely! That had been obvious from the first.

"This, Miss Hyde, is no ordinary club," the lieutenant informed me. "Get a little of that mud off the blade, Tim, but be careful you don't remove the blood." As Lt. Jacopo had stated, the weapon was no club but an ax with a small head.

"A tong hatchet!" Violet said, her eyes like saucers as, I'm sure, mine were. But young Violet was enjoying this. I wasn't.

"I've read about them things. They killed people all the time, daddy says."

"Well," one of the policemen said, "Looks like the young Chinese boy you girls saw was actually a *Boo-How-Doy*."

At my blank expression the lieutenant explained, "The Hatchet Man for one of the Six Companies—the Tongs. They're like a lodge, Miss, only more so. Most of the *Boo-How-Doys* have had to take up better paying jobs these days, but this was one busy boy."

"I know what Tongs are," I announced a trifle heatedly. And I couldn't believe that the well-dressed, respectable young man we had seen was a Hatchet Man.

"This means trouble, all right," the two policemen agreed. Lieutenant Jacopo sighed. "Why a Tong War now? We haven't had a real one since the fire. Hard to believe, but it looks that way. This is the first ax. We'll have to have a thorough description of that fellow you saw, Miss."

Violet cut in. "I saw him plainer. Plain as I see you. So did my brothers."

Lieutenant Jacopo looked at me, his eyebrows arched as if he doubted the girl's assertion, but I agreed with it, explaining that they saw the young man going and coming and that he had spoken with them both times.

"I didn't talk to him at all, though I heard him exchange a few words with the children. He obviously hadn't found his father when he passed by me and he got into his car down on Geneva Avenue and drove away."

"What kind of car?" the lieutenant asked. "And which direction?"

"Downtown, I suppose. A Ford."

One of the policemen took notes on practically everything I said, which I found unnerving. . . . A tall young man? Well, how tall was he? I did the best I could, adding, "If he had just killed somebody, why would he have lingered around this district asking questions, calling attention to himself?"

"There's something in what she says, Tim. Now, Miss—"

"Violet Thelma Deutsch, 380 Hyde Place. I saw him real good." And she raced on, mentioning details so fast the note-taking policeman had to say "Whoa!" several times. She knew almost the exact number of eyelets on the shoes of the young Chinese. Every detail was filled in and, as nearly as I could remember, it was accurate. Her memory of their dialogue was livened considerably, however. She was a born successor to the popular mystery writer Mary Roberts Rinehart.

"He was real sinister. He had slanty eyes and they looked daggers at me, and his voice was deep and mean."

Lieutenant Jacopo glanced at me and I shook my head. He smiled but asked her to go on. She did. At length. Presently, one of the police interrupted after studying the unfortunate victim in the gunnysack.

"Little girl, all this happened yesterday? What time?"

Violet looked at me. I thought it was late in the morning. I remembered it was right after the lawyers had left my house that I had gone out walking and the children had told me about the Chinese man. I told him so.

The policeman said, "Then, lieutenant, I doubt he's your Hatchet Man. This body's surely been dead longer than twenty-four hours. I'll bank on it."

Shortly afterward Violet and I were dismissed upon our promise to report to Lt. Jacopo anything we recalled later and to be available for identification. As the two of us walked up Hyde Place Violet looked at me knowingly.

"They'll call us when they capture the fiend."

"The fiend?"

"The Chinaman who pretended to be so nice to us. He's the fiend, all right. And then, when we point him out, his Tong will get after us and we'll have to get out of the country. I'll ask them to send me to the Anti-podees. That's way down under the equator."

I thought this sounded like a pretty grim future but it was clear that Violet Thelma adored it. When we separated at her house and I went across the street to mine I noted her two young brothers peering out the big bay windows, and behind them the shadowy forms of several grown-ups. I imagined Violet's joy when her family bombarded her with questions about the beginnings of a new Tong War.

The front door was locked when I came home, and I had to ring to get in. If I had been in a bad mood before, I was more so now. First, I had apparently let myself begin to fall in love with an unreliable charmer whose every deprecating remark about himself was probably true. Then I had become involved in the murder of a poor old man. (I refused to believe that good-looking young Chinese had killed his own father, but no matter how little the crime may have involved me, I was haunted by the awful end of the old man. Did Tong Wars really extend to quiet suburbs like this?)

"You look awfully pale, Miss Mery," Eve said as she looked up and down the street before closing the door. "How's the stomach feeling?"

"Fine. Where is my mother?"

"Out." Apparently Eve Carpe was feeling just as sullen as I was. I must have given away my surprise and suspicion at her manner because she stared at me, cleared her throat and added in her usual syrup-sweet voice, "I mean—out looking for you, Miss. You being so late, and all. Did something happen? We saw you walk off with that reporter. We knew he didn't drive, and we couldn't figure where you could walk all this while."

I ignored that and proceeded to wash up for lunch. I left the bathroom door open and saw her go to the front room and try to see down to the corner of Pompeii Street, where there must still have been quite a commotion. She was very efficient, however, and had everything on the dining-room table by the time I came out. After my suspicions about the medicine last night, I did not want to take a chance, and invited Eve to share my lunch. The surprising thing to me was her lack of surprise. She brought in dishes and silverware, sat down opposite me and calmly began to eat. I think she was also wondering why I didn't tell her about all the police on Pompeii Street.

I said suddenly, "What do you know about the Passerby?"

I had thrown her into confusion. She was expecting talk about the police out there in the street. She glanced toward the front windows, then answered me vaguely.

"Very little. Mr. MacPherson knew him in France, I believe."

. . . Three weeks ago, Neil had told me. . . . He met Howard three weeks ago. . . .

"Why doesn't Mr. Burnham drive?"

I had the feeling she was pleased at my questions, but couldn't imagine why.

"Because of the war," she said. "He was covering the early Hun advance in Belgium for his paper and some others. As I understand it, he was driving three other correspondents. It was around Louvain. The Huns blew up a cathedral and Burnham's car. Everybody in the car was killed except Burnham. He recovered. He's never driven since."

I was constantly being torn two ways about Neil Burnham. He had lied about his acquaintance with Howard, which should have convinced me I couldn't trust him. But then there was the Louvain bombing, and my heart turned over at the idea of his suffering.

Eve's curiosity about the body in the pergola was satisfied when Polly Hyde came hustling in to report a garbled version of the affair. As for me, while the afternoon crept on, I waited for the phone to ring and to receive word on the contents of that preserve jar Neil had taken away with him to be analyzed.

The call came just as I was about to give up. Eve came to tell me I was wanted on the telephone. I rushed into the dining room. Polly stood in the archway to the front room, stiff, tense. A look at her suggested she expected trouble from my caller—and that she knew something about the subject of the call. That was what worried me.

The man calling was not Tony Demos but Neil. I was both delighted to hear his voice and worried by the beginning of another concern.

"Hello," he said. "Is it you, darling?"

Darling. The word might be as commonplace as "hello" to Neil Burnham, but all the same his use of it excited me.

"Neil! Did you find out about it from—" I remembered my audience—"Did he tell you?"

"I found out. It seems you were being fed a dose of aspirin crushed to powder and dissolved in water."

I almost dropped the receiver. I had been so very sure! Even Howard's manner had been obvious, pointing to something wrong about that glass of "powders."

"I don't believe it, don't joke. Is that what he said? You know who."

There was a brief silence on the line.

"Neil! Are you there?"

183

"Yes. Mery, I wish you would trust me, just once. Believe in me and do as I say." He sounded different—serious and even unsure of himself. I could hardly believe it was Neil.

"I don't understand. What should I do?"

"Are they listening?"

"Naturally. As always."

"Don't mention this poison business to anyone. Not yet. Will you promise me?"

Don't mention it because it might make difficulties for Howard MacPherson? His friend. The man he had known since the early days of the war . . . the man he'd told me he'd known for only three weeks.

"Yes, but I want to discuss it with— Maybe he made a mistake. They can make mistakes about things like this . . ."

Neil almost cut into my question. He was upset. "No! Above all, not Demos. Don't you realize he already thinks you are imagining things? This would only confirm his belief about you. The fragile child, the helpless girl. Is that what you want?"

I almost hung up on him. Something I had never thought I would be capable of doing. "So you didn't take it to him! Neil, you knew how much I wanted him to check on it."

This time there was no mistaking his anger. "Mery, I'm doing my damndest to save your property and maybe your life. Now, will you please have a little faith in me and do as I ask you?"

"If you meant what you say, you would have taken that to my friend the way I asked you. But to try and tell me that he would gossip about me, say I imagined—"

How quiet the room was around me. With the two women standing there motionless, hardly breathing, I still felt them intensely, surely listening to every nuance. I thought of my mother, apparently so under the spell of her second husband that she would allow him to attempt fraud and theft, maybe murder, against her daughter. At least I wouldn't be *that* weakened by an infatuation. I had nearly let myself come under Neil Burnham's spell, that famous power Miss Falassi and even the women in the hospital had bragged about. Nearly. But not quite.

"Mery! Are you there? Do you understand what I am saying?"

"I understand perfectly."

"Will you do as I ask . . . keep this quiet? Don't say anything to anyone until we have proof we can use. I'm working on that now. Promise me you won't say anything to anyone else."

"Except you."

"Be sure and get any developments to me at once. Find an excuse to leave the house and make a telephone call to me no matter what happens. Have you a pencil?"

"I don't know. Why?" I felt around, found a stub of a flat pencil, the kind contractors use. I tore off the corner of a page from the telephone book and wrote down the two numbers he gave me.

"Now, darling, promise me you will call one of those numbers at the slightest suspicion. Someone will deliver the message. They can reach me at any time."

I heard that voice saying "darling, promise me," and it cut me to believe I couldn't really trust either the voice or the words.

"But no one else?"

"No one, and that specifically includes Polly."

"And Tony?"

He sighed. He was holding onto his temper. "Especially Tony. He's too clinical, sees everything clinically."

I said nothing, which he took for assent. As I was hanging up he said, "I'll see you tonight. And don't worry. Incidentally—"

"Well?"

"I do love you, you know."

"Thank you so much," I said, and hung up.

I wanted to cry so badly my throat hurt, but there were those two staring at me, waiting for me to tell them something—some lie—about my phone call. All I did say was, "Mother, how would you like to go to a show with me tonight?"

Polly relaxed perceptibly. "You want to see Howard's play again?"

I picked up Howard's discarded *Chronicle,* which was already turned to the theater page. "No, mother, I had a movie in mind. Something with—with Jack Barrymore. 'Scheming young lawyer conspires to win girl in *Here Comes the Bride.*'"

Anything to be out of the house if Neil Burnham did come to

185

see me. I was still afraid of his influence if he tried to reason with me. After all, I was Polly Hyde's daughter, and look what happened to Polly.

Howard returned to Hyde Place after his matinée feeling delighted with the world. His popularity with matinée-goers seemed to be as great as ever. Over a quick dinner he chided me with something of his stagey matinée aura still around him.

"You know, Polly, you missed an amusing little scene last night in the Demos box. It seems Teresa Demos had some notion that I was the villain in the play."

Polly looked at him, completely at sea. "But that's silly. She knew quite well you were the hero, the star of the play."

"That's not what she said, I'm afraid. She must have gotten a twisted report from someone . . . I wonder who?" He was being coy as an elephant. "Because she said she was going to—how did she put it?—'smoke out that rascal,' if he was all that his stepdaughter said he was—in short, a villain. She meant me, of course. My dear Mery, where did you get the idea I played the villain in *The Pine Box?*"

I said blandly, "I must have heard it somewhere." But this was one more nail for the coffin of my trust in Neil Burnham. Howard did not know the Demos family. But he had driven downtown with Neil Burnham just before his matinée, and Neil had heard Teresa Demos make that remark about the villainous stepfather.

EIGHTEEN

❧

I HATED THE MOVIE. I didn't really see it so I shouldn't make such flat judgments, but I kept picturing events that must have been going on at Hyde Place that evening. Only Eve would be home. Neil would arrive. Would he be very disappointed because I wasn't there? I did him the justice of thinking he might be a little sorry to miss me, but on the other hand I didn't have a doubt in the world that if he spent much time with Eve Carpe he would forget about any interest he ever had in me.

But why was Neil Burnham like this? Was it the war injury years ago that made him so cynical, so two-faced? I had felt so bitter about his apparent betrayal that I hadn't asked who had analyzed the contents of the preserve jar . . . if someone had. He could have told me anything—I had no reason to trust anyone but Tony Demos for such a task.

Polly and I rode clear out to Hyde Place in a taxicab, a luxury I might have found impressive at any other time. As it was, Polly must have found me a very dull, even a crabby companion during that interminable evening.

"It's so elegant, riding home with what you might call a

private chauffeur," Polly murmured, sinking back with a luxurious sigh.

I looked out at the world of rolling hills, each hill outlined by the dim lights of private houses, and I thought again of grandpa's lovely meadow and the lavender hill beyond. There were plenty of houses, plenty of ruined hillsides already. The city's contractors and builders didn't need mine. I decided I would sell the Hyde Place block eventually, but I would keep my beautiful, unimproved meadow for as long as I chose.

Polly studied me. "You do enjoy riding in a taxicab, don't you, dear?"

Almost without thinking, and certainly without tact, I blurted out, "I would if I were sure who was paying for it."

"But, dearie, aren't we all—"

"Don't call me dearie." It made me think of the sinister downtown streets the night I had arrived in San Francisco, and the poor woman who had called me "dearie" and claimed to be Polly Hyde.

"Mery, whatever is the matter with you? You were so gloomy during the movie. You didn't laugh once. And Jack Barrymore was so debonair, so witty."

Like Neil Burnham, I thought. I shook off the memory and got to the point. "Mother, you and Howard don't have much money yourselves, do you?"

"Why do you ask?"

As I might have expected, she was on the defensive, and afraid, too? If I could just get her out of this city, away from that schemer she was married to.

"Because, Polly, taxicabs cost money, and the new furniture in the house, and the food. Servants. All these clothes you and Miss Falassi had made for me . . . where is the money coming from?"

She twisted her lower lip just as I remember seeing her do when I was a child. "You know where it is coming from, dear. You made no protest. You have seen the lawyers and talked with them. You are a rich woman, thanks to Grandpa Hyde. I won't say I resented it when he made that will, but I was hurt."

I laughed. "How can you say you didn't resent it? Pa used to say you sulked for weeks."

"Hurt to the core," she added firmly.

I touched her gloved hand. "All the same, grandpa knew that what was mine was yours. And it is, mother. It's just that I don't like the way Howard and those lawyers are spending money that doesn't belong to any of us until the Hyde Place block is sold."

"And all that meadow property, don't forget, dear. What has been spent so far is nothing, just a bit to make up to you for all the years your daddy kept you so poor, without decent clothes or even food."

I said nothing. No need to agitate her by telling her the meadow was not going to be sold.

When we reached home and Polly had paid the taxi fare, she looked at her snap purse, and remarked as the taxi drove away down Hyde Place, "I guess all this is yours too. It came from those lawyers."

"Never mind. I'm sorry, I really didn't mean anything . . ."

We went up the stairs together but as we opened the front door we heard voices in the front room. Howard's was easily identified. The other I could not mistake in all the world. Had Neil arrived late by accident, or had he come out from town with Howard in Howard's (or my?) new Overland Touring Car?

"Ah!" Howard spread his arms wide as if to embrace the world. "Here are our two wandering ladies now. See who you missed by dashing off to see some paper-doll silhouette on the movie screen. It will never replace the live theater, I can tell you that."

He embraced Polly and would have drawn me into the embrace if Neil hadn't taken my hand and gotten me just beyond my stepfather's reach. Neil must have felt my reluctance, even if I couldn't bring myself to resist his touch with a physical gesture. For one thing, I found myself more or less hypnotized by the searching look in his eyes and though I tried to avoid his gaze, I could not.

"I'm sure the ladies are tired," he said, addressing Howard

while he kept his attention focused on me. "So I'll say good night . . . when Merideth has promised to make a Sunday outing with me."

"Impossible, I'm engaged to visit some friends," I said too quickly to conceal my lie.

"Dr. Demos, probably," Howard said.

I expected Neil's impatience or sarcasm but he appeared to ignore Howard's comment.

"How about Monday?"

With a cowardice I despised, I put him off. "I'll see. Why don't you call Monday morning?"

He didn't answer that. "Are you still routing sinister intruders out of your spacious garden?"

The memory was pleasant until I thought of tonight, of Neil on the long ride out to Hyde Place, telling Howard everything I had ever told him. . . .

"Back yard," I corrected him.

"It must be romantic by moonlight."

I was not too surprised when Howard nudged Polly, who chimed in as if paid to play the chorus, "It's so nice now, dear. Not muddy at all. I was out there this morning."

"Come along. Show me," Neil said.

Eve Carpe was in the dining-room doorway staring at us. Her presence reminded me of the danger.

"At this hour? Don't be ridiculous!" I hated the thought, yet I did wonder if his interest in getting me out into that darkness hidden from neighbors by the fence and empty lots wasn't less for romantic purposes than to set me up for an accident—courtesy of my adoring stepfather. If he had persisted, backed up by my stepfather, I think I might have suggested as much, but Neil did not persist. He seemed to know me uncomfortably well.

"All right, but at least see me on my way like a proper hostess."

Since it was the only way to get rid of him I went out on the porch with him and started down the steep flight of stairs. I heard someone open the door behind us, then my stepfather's footstep on the wooden floor of the porch. I shivered and Neil put an arm around me, but neither of us looked back. All the way down the steps I felt that presence behind us.

On the sidewalk, beyond Howard's hearing, I took a deep breath. With a sudden, and to me comprehensible anger, Neil said in a low voice, "If you had a little more faith in your fellow man, you would find life a good deal more rewarding."

"Faith in you and my loving stepfather, I suppose."

He withdrew his hand from my waist as if I had burned him, but said after a few steps: "Kindly don't equate me with Howard MacPherson."

Yet in a real sense they were equated in my mind and my suspicions. Ironically enough, though, I didn't want to hurt him by telling him that, and so I said nothing. I was completely unprepared when he said, "I hear you and some neighborhood children found a body in that park on Pompeii Street today."

"How did you know?"

"Jacopo is an old ally."

"They think it's the beginning of a Tong War."

"Out here? Preposterous. But I'd like to know about the young Chinese you and the children saw. What did he look like? Was he as sinister as the police seem to think?"

This must be for one of his columns. I thought about it as the cold starlight closed around us.

"The man I saw was attractive. Good manners. Polite. Not at all like a Tong warrior—whatever they call them."

He didn't smile. It was strange how I wanted him to joke now that he and I were so serious and I had made my mistrust plain.

"He is no Hatchet Man. He is the dead man's son."

"I felt sure he was telling the truth, but how can you be sure he's what he says he is?"

"Because I know him. His name is Gilbert Liu. We graduated from Berkeley together. The dead man you found is called Old Liu. He's been in some difficulties—smokes opium. He was sick. My friend has been looking for him for months. The other day Gilbert found the hole where the old man had been living in Chinatown, and on a copy of the *North China News* were scribbled the words, 'Hyde Place.'"

I remembered what the children said. "That was what this Gilbert Liu told the little girl. His father may have been looking for work when the Tong man killed him."

"But Old Liu did not die from a hatchet wound. That was made after his death."

I felt tension creep over me. "But why? Why put the hatchet there with the body, except . . . to make it look as if a Tong War had started?"

"Maybe. He may have been beaten to death. There were bruises and a bad blow to the head, but it seems to have been done with something blunt. . . . Would you like to help my, friend and me?"

"Help this Gilbert Liu?" But I don't even know him."

Here I was thinking about my own safety, trusting no one, and Neil Burnham was talking about two Chinese who may or may not have been involved in a Tong War. Was there, somehow, a connection? Was Neil the connecting link? I didn't know what to say, except simple decency forced me to say I would help him.

"Good, then I'll meet you tomorrow." He looked at me, smiled this time in that old way which had first attracted me. I told myself not to be swayed, but I also wanted to give him the benefit of every doubt. Every benefit . . .

I asked him directly, "Do you really believe I'm safe in going back to that house?"

He took my hands as if to examine the palms. He was behaving as tenderly as Tony Demos might have done.

"You are safe tonight, darling. Just don't—for God's sake—go around telling people how your stepfather persecutes or threatens you. Tell me, but no one else—not yet. You do understand?" He held my hands imprisoned while I agreed. I felt helpless to argue the matter, whatever my real thoughts and intentions. Anyway, he had called me "darling" once more, and even in this advanced day and age it was not a common expression that one threw about loosely. Unless your name was Neil Burnham? . . .

"Trust me." He kissed me over our four tightly scrambled hands. For me it was a valedictory kiss. I wished I hadn't enjoyed it so much. He walked back to the foot of the steps with me, and said, "Promise me?"

I wasn't quite sure to which of his various instructions he was referring, but I promised and he let me go. "Tomorrow, Mery."

"Where?"

He frowned. I think he found my question pretty unromantic. Too direct. I explained, "I'll meet you and your friend, this Gilbert person, but it must be somewhere with other people. Not alone." The starlight dimly showed me his face. His mouth tightened slightly. He looked as if I had slapped him. His reaction hurt and I quickly added, "I'm only being sensible."

But my attempt to soften my voice, my suspicions, didn't seem very persuasive. In that sardonic way I remembered from our first meeting on the streetcar, he said, "How about Golden Gate Park? On a Sunday afternoon that should be crowded enough even for you. I don't want Gil to be seen by the police until he's talked with you."

"Thank you, Neil. I'll meet you and your friend there. Say two o'clock?"

A reluctant smile lightened that chilly expression of his. "Golden Gate Park is rather a large place. Better make it more specific."

I had heard about a lake, a real lake in the middle of the park, so I promised to meet him and his friend there.

"Stow Lake," he said. We shook hands on it and he went away. He did not look back.

I went up the stairs, stopping on the tenth step because I knew, even before I looked up, that I was still being watched from inside the house. Sure enough, someone was at the bay windows in the front room—a slit of light gleamed on the garage driveway below. There was a movement behind the door as well, eyes looking out through one of the narrow glass panes.

"I won't stand for any more of it," I told myself. "This very week I'll go home to Nevada and stay there." Unfortunately, there was still tonight. I clenched my fists and went on up. The door opened as if by a ghostly hand. Sure enough, Eve was behind the door and flashed me her most sugary smile. I gave her the full benefit of my teeth. I found it disconcertingly easy to smile without feeling it.

I assumed therefore that my curious watcher in the front room was Howard MacPherson. I said nothing, pretending I didn't know anyone was there, and walked through the dining room and darkened hall to my room. I opened the door, expecting to find my way by the starlight glimmering through the windows, but the room was dark and as I moved across it to pull the cord of the overhead light, a pair of powerful hands closed on my shoulders.

I screamed. Seconds later the light came on, the globe swinging overhead under my desperate tug. Howard MacPherson was grinning down at me, his hands drawn back like a child being punished.

"Did I scare you? Sorry. Didn't mean to, just pulling down the blinds and all."

I pretended to believe him, but I suspected his intention had been to produce exactly the effect it had produced in me. I managed to look more calm than I felt as I thanked him for his thoughtfulness, said good night, and held the door open in a way he couldn't misunderstand. He went out, still smiling, and I closed the door.

NINETEEN

Once again I pulled the chair under the doorknob before I got into bed. Even after I had turned out the light and was trying to get to sleep, I puzzled over Howard's behavior. He was constantly doing things that aroused my suspicions and my dislike, yet he never carried on from these tentative attacks. It was as if he wanted me to accuse him, and afterward there was never any proof against him except "my own imaginings."

Hadn't Tony Demos believed precisely that about me, warning me not to think I was being persecuted by my stepfather? Maybe Neil was right. Maybe this really was what he meant when he warned me not to discuss Howard's attempts. I very much hoped it was so. But at the same time I was fully aware that there could be another interpretation of Neil's insistence that I not tell anyone about Howard's many suspicious acts.

I wanted so much to believe Neil, yet I tended to hold tight to my suspicion. I had been suspicious all my life, hearing my mother lie to my father about her drinking, her fame—all of which I knew were lies. Hearing my father tell about his stage opportunities, his past and future glory, and knowing all along that these stories, whatever the pity I felt at hearing them, were nothing but lies.

I awoke in the morning to find a warm, sunny spring day, almost like summer, pouring in through my windows. How beautiful it must be in Golden Gate Park on such a day.

No one at 379 Hyde Place went to church, although Polly apologized that she hadn't slept well or she would be glad to accompany me. I wondered if she had been drinking. The old memories died hard, but there were no signs of it in her manner or conduct.

It was such a nice day I got out the grass-green organdy dress I had been saving for summer. It was very feminine, very stylish, and would look just right in the park that afternoon. Meanwhile, since nothing wrinkled like organdy, I was particularly careful when I sat down at one of the long pews in the church on Geneva Avenue.

Beside me I felt someone stir, and squirm. My young friend Violet Thelma nudged me. "Wrinkles?" she whispered, referring to the care with which I was trying to preserve the smoothness of my dress.

"I hope not."

"I'm to go and identify that Chinaman tomorrow morning first thing. He's in jail."

That startled me. Was it Neil's friend Gilbert? He would be very upset. Or would he? Would it change our date for this afternoon?

"Did they say who he was?"

"Fellow that used to be a Hatchet Man. For the Hip-Sing Tong. Not any more though."

This didn't sound like Neil's friend Gilbert. I was relieved. On our way past Pompeii Street and along Hyde Place, Mr. and Mrs. Deutsch asked me innumerable questions, but curiously enough, none of them dealt with the dead man we had found in the pergola. They were avid for details about me, my grandfather, whom Mr. Deutsch had heard of, and about the columnist called the Passerby, who had written about me.

We separated in front of our houses. The garage doors were open and Eve was sweeping the basement floor. She called to me.

"Don't go up the front way, Miss Mery. It's locked. Come up the inside stairs."

I did so, but I was so uneasy in this house, with these people, that I even hesitated to go up those stairs which I had once climbed a dozen times in a single day.

Polly called down the stairs from the dining-room doorway, "Is that you, Mery? Mrs. Demos has been trying to reach you on the telephone for the last ten minutes."

I hurried up. Eve was right behind me. It made me so nervous I turned, snappishly asking her not to walk almost on my heels. As I swung around, she was so close that my elbow nearly struck her in the eye. She grabbed at the wall, her fingernails digging scratches in the wood.

I apologized with a single "Sorry!" that was as clipped and rude as her close pursuit of me. I was a little ashamed of myself. I might have knocked her clear down the stairs. All the same, I couldn't bear this close proximity and sense of being spied on all the time. I had grown up in so different an atmosphere, almost by my own volition, and always with privacy.

After a nervous fumble with the receiver, I managed to get the operator and ask for the number Mrs. Demos had left. The haughty housekeeper answered and condescended to get Mrs. Demos, who was her friendly volatile self.

"My dear, during Mass this morning I had the most splendid idea. Why shouldn't you come to Sunday dinner with us? Suppose we make it three o'clock? Then we can show you the gardens and statuary. And this time I promise not to cook for you."

I felt my own spirits rising because of her delightful manner. I laughed, protested and then told her I had a two o'clock engagement. Silence reigned behind me in the dining room. I looked around as Mrs. Demos reconsidered her time schedule at the other end of the line. Not a soul was in sight around me. I walked as far as the receiver cord would reach, looked into the front room, then the hall. Nobody in sight.

"Is it a long engagement?" Mrs. Demos asked. "I mean—Tony wants to know if he can pick you up later?" She laughed at something going on at her end of the line. "Dear, I'll let Tony speak for himself, but I wanted to add my persuasion to his."

She always made things easy. When Tony came on the line he appeared a trifle shy.

"I don't really have to ask my mother to make my dates for

me. Can I drive by after this engagement of yours? Or is it serious?"

"It is serious, and you can do me an enormous favor if you do drive by. Golden Gate Park isn't very far from Demos Heights, is it?"

"No. Matter of fact—then you are going to be in the park this afternoon? That's a sizable place."

"Stow Lake."

He said, "That's small enough. I can't miss you, Merideth, you are quite sure I won't be interrupting anything?"

Was there an answer to that? He wouldn't be interrupting a romantic date, if that was what he was afraid of, although I didn't know precisely what kind of a date I had with Neil and his Chinese friend. Or if I was even safe with them. It was unfair to use Tony Demos to protect me from Neil, but I was beyond being fair about whatever was happening in my life.

"Tony, could you come to the neighborhood of Stow Lake at two-thirty today?"

He sounded so pleased I was more than ever ashamed of myself for using him. "Wonderful! And you will come to dinner? Mother and father are counting on you too. Mama keeps saying you are the only real girl I've ever brought home. What do you suppose she means?" He paused. "You are real, aren't you?"

"Down-to-earth real," I assured him. "And I'd love to come to dinner. Could you be sure and meet me at two-thirty? I'd be so . . . grateful."

"I'll make it two o'clock if you say so."

"Two-thirty would be wonderful, Tony. And thank you so much. Thank your parents, too."

As I put the receiver back on its hook, I figured nothing very drastic could happen in a public park in the middle of a Sunday afternoon, with Tony Demos, a strong and powerful man about to arrive on the scene at any minute. I decided I wouldn't hesitate to tell Neil that I was expecting Tony.

I waited a minute or two, fooled around the dining-room buffet waiting to hear someone in another room close enough to have overheard my conversation. It wasn't until I gave up my sleuthing and went to my own room that I heard the door of the master bedroom open and close. I wondered if Polly had been in there. Would she betray even her daughter to Howard? But, sadly, I suspected she'd done something like that long ago.

I spent the next half-hour in my bedroom, walking back and forth and staring out the windows, wondering if I should just leave San Francisco tomorrow. Time passed so rapidly I couldn't believe it when Polly knocked on the door and asked me if I was going to be home for Sunday dinner at four o'clock.

"What time is it?" I called.

"One-thirty, dear. Are you all right? We've been wondering. You did act a little strange when you came back from church."

I opened the door. "Strange? Because I didn't stay around to gossip?"

She came in and looked around the room apprehensively. "It wasn't that. You seemed so—nervous."

I don't know why, but this infuriated me. "I wasn't nervous! I was sick to death of all this spying on me. I can't even answer a telephone without one of you listening."

She looked pale as she backed away briefly, then put a hand out, the short, sturdy fingers spread. "Mery, please don't do this to us. You mustn't let yourself go to pieces like this. Nobody wants to hurt you. Can't you see that?"

She apparently expected me to believe all this rigmarole. I snapped, "Don't be silly! And to answer your question, I won't be here for dinner."

She nodded. "I understand, dear. Have a good time. Don't forget to take a wrap. The fog comes in early there."

"Where?"

She swallowed, swiped her tongue over dry lips. "Where— wherever you are going."

A bad lie, I thought, unworthy of Howard MacPherson's supposedly well-coached little company of players. Or was I exaggerating again? Overinterpreting innocent chance remarks into grand conspiracies?

"I've had my plans changed by Mrs. Demos," I said, and carried on the lie with a twist of truth. "So many of us are meeting today we could form a parade." I would take her advice about the wrap, though, and I got out the new light mantle Eve Carpe (probably) had chosen for me. I stopped briefly by my stepfather, who was at the player piano in the front room.

"I'm afraid I'll need some money," I said. "That little chore seems to have been neglected."

He was so surprised he let the piano roll jump out of his fingers and the metal fastener kept lashing around and around, making irritating sounds. He managed an effusive grin. "Sure, how much?" He took a couple of dollars out of his pants' pocket. The sunlight glittered on them and I took both.

Then I said, with my best smile, "That'll take care of immediate needs, but I will need some gold, too—in case I want to buy some things."

There wasn't much gold around these days, but sure enough, he could oblige, though under protest. "But, honey, this is Sunday. What can you buy today? Couldn't you wait until tomorrow and see Brubick?"

"You never know"—I dismissed his objections airily—"Besides, I like to feel I have my own money in hand. . . . Otherwise, what's the point of selling any of my property? The market might be better in 1920 or 1921 anyway."

He nearly caressed a twenty-dollar goldpiece before parting with it. I blew him a kiss and left the house.

In order to save my money, which I never forgot was only an advance on a sale not yet consummated, I took streetcars across town and a taxicab for the final lap, since I wasn't sure where Stow Lake was. My driver proved to be obliging, however. He showed me the Japanese Tea Garden as a point of reference, and was about to give me directions toward the path that would take me to the lake when I saw Neil Burnham on the path, looking toward the street. Obviously I was late, though I had no watch and could not gauge my time. So in my present spirit of bravado I waved to him and said, "Am I early?"

He helped me out of the cab and paid the fare, surprised at the low rate. I explained and he found this amusing. I could tell that his body was tense as he took my arm. And then he kissed me and there was the excitement between us that he must have felt as much as I did and we remembered our surroundings only when we heard the titter of a child as his mother hustled him out on the sidewalk with a muttered "disgusting."

"Not to me," Neil called after her, and we both laughed. How easy it was in his presence to forget suspicions, his reputation, my own common sense!

With an anxious effort at straightening my hair I brought things back to reality. "Where is your friend Gilbert Liu? And why aren't you at Stow Lake?"

"He's waiting for us. To the left, down that path. Toward the west."

We turned off the path a few steps farther and went into what appeared to be an endless tangle of roots and dry, prickly branches. The strange, forbidding trees, all twisted eastward under the eternal blast of ocean wind and fog, hid us from all the park's strollers, many in what must have been elaborate Easter finery. When I could no longer see any of those Sunday strollers, I held back. "No, wait. I don't like this place." I fumbled for an excuse. "The branches catch on my hair."

"Sorry." Neil stopped, making no effort to force me on. "It's just that Gil is reporting to the police today and he wants to learn as much as he can about what you discovered. I can't get the whole story out of Jacopo." He left me there, took a few steps on into that thicket of roots, branches and thorny evergreen, with one hand raised to protect his eyes from the grasping claws of the cypress.

Just to be doubly careful, I called after him, "I'm meeting someone here at almost any time, so we'd better hurry."

He had been almost out of sight but he looked back, stopped and asked, "Who? Not your medical hero, I trust."

"The same."

He shook his head, but waved for his friend to come on. I watched them as they made their way back through the thicket to me. I looked over my shoulder, saw one of the park's many paths close enough to reach in a few seconds. I saw a policeman stroll by, casually flipping his nightstick at the cypress grove. I moved backward to make a sudden exit even easier, and then was being introduced to Gilbert Liu.

He was every bit the gentleman he seemed to be the day he spoke to the children. He explained to me in his quiet voice how he had tracked down his father, whom he hadn't seen since the older man had begun to smoke opium to the exclusion of every other interest in life.

"I heard you answer the children," I said. "You had been looking for him up and down the Hyde Place area. You don't believe it's a Tong War?"

He shook his head. It was difficult to tell how deep his feelings were. His face was unlined, his oblique eyes unreadable. "I have talked to several of the *Boo-How-Doys* who are known. They are all in other businesses now, of course. I have talked to the president of the Six Companies, and to individual Tong leaders. There has not been major trouble in several years. Differences between the Tongs are now settled by arbitration."

"But why else would your father have been killed? And why the hatchet?" Even as I asked the question I was reasonably sure of the answer. The crime's motive was quite different, and the murderer wanted to deflect attention. From the beginning it had seemed strange to find Gilbert or his father in that typical suburb populated by Anglo-Saxons on the west of Geneva Avenue and by Italians on the east.

A stern voice called to us through the cypress thicket from the path. It was the strolling policeman. "You in there! No shenanigans now. A little friendly handholding's as it should be, but don't you stay in there too—Holy Mary! It's a Chinaman! Now, see here! We're rounding up you fellers, what with your nasty Tong War starting up again and all."

I wondered why Neil and Gilbert didn't claim that Gilbert was Japanese. We were not far from the Japanese Tea Garden. But apparently the San Francisco police had a sharp eye for national differences. Neil got between us and the officer.

"Look, I'm Burnham, the Passerby. We met at the armistice celebration. I'm going downtown to the Hall of Justice with my friend here, Gilbert Liu. Meanwhile, I'd like to have a word with you." He stepped out into the path as a family of four passed. Not one of the parents or the children was wearing a flu mask. I hoped all these open faces I saw lately were a good omen.

Left alone with me in that thicket, with its peculiar pungent odor, Mr. Liu took out a slightly faded tintype and showed it to me. "That's how my father looked the day I graduated from Berkeley."

In order to see the picture better, I turned my back to the path and held up the metallic tintype. The picture showed a young man looking very much as Gilbert did now, in his cap and gown, beside a tall, thin man, much older, wearing a modern black overcoat but open to reveal his padded jacket beneath. He wore glasses.

"That's my father before the opium. He had nothing whatever to do with *Boo-How-Doys*. He belonged to a Tong, of course, like everyone else in Chinatown. Except the Foreign Devils."

"Foreign Devils," I repeated, unable to resist a little smile. "That's us whites."

"It's simply an accepted title. But, as you can see, my father was a quiet, studious man. What was he doing out there? Unless —it's my theory he was murdered and brought there from some other part of town. And his glasses were missing when he was found. He never went anywhere without his glasses. Did you see them around the little pergola where he was found? If not, the murderer must have kept them for some reason."

"I'm afraid we didn't find anything like that. I could look again, or ask—"

His immobile face was abruptly contorted. The next second I was flat on the ground, stuck with prickly underbrush, and a wind seemed to whistle over my head. Gilbert Liu had knocked me down. I heard the crack of dry underbrush and tree limbs under a heavy weight, and something fell across my feet.

It was Gilbert Liu. I instinctively drew my feet up, which turned his body a little, and then I saw his face, the staring open eyes, the gash across his smooth temple. I heard myself cry out. The *Boo-How-Doy* ax had fallen from his head to the brushwood, and there needles and small twigs were soaked with sticky blood.

I heard footsteps in the thicket from the direction from which the ax blow had come. Then a shadow blotted out the light from the open path. It was Neil Burnham.

He must have said something. I didn't hear it. He tried to lift me.

"Don't touch me! Look at him. At him!"

He turned from me, knelt beside the man I had supposed

to be his friend. I got to my feet, scrambled through the under-brush to the path. A man and woman stared at me. I probably looked a sight after my fall, with Gilbert Liu's blood on my stockings and shoes.

"Where is the policeman who was here?" I asked, then saw him coming along the path from one of the street entrances. His stocky form was overshadowed by the tall figure of Tony Demos. I ran to them.

"Told you that was the young lady you're looking for, sir," the policeman announced to Tony.

Tony hugged me to him. "What's happened?"

"Oh, Tony . . . Officer, how long ago did you leave Mr. Burnham?"

"Well, now, I just rang in and told Lieutenant Jacopo where to find one of them Chinamen they're raking in all over town. Wasn't more'n five, six minutes. Mr. Burnham had said it wasn't necessary. He was anxious to get back to you. But I thought I'd better, all the same."

Yes. Maybe Neil Burnham had been anxious to get back to me in that gloomy little thicket where I had presented so con-venient a back and where I would have taken that ax in my back if Gilbert Liu hadn't thrown me to the ground and been struck instead. I didn't believe he was the target. I remembered that last minute, and his shocked expression as he thrust me aside. I held even tighter to Tony's lean, solid arm while I directed the policeman.

"There's been an attempted murder in there. Please hurry! But be careful. The weapon is still there. And he—someone might use it again."

The policeman had been on his way, running. He stopped briefly, looked back at me. "Who might—what did you say?"

"Please . . . go on . . . I don't know. I can't be sure the man is dead but I think so. Just be very careful."

It was all I could say. I had to warn him. What else I would later confess to of my suspicions about Neil's arrival in that par-ticular spot at that particular moment, I couldn't bear to say aloud. Because I now suspected that Neil Burnham might be a murderer.

TWENTY

Teresa Demos made the decision about my immediate future, backed up by an equally indignant Tony.

"You cannot possibly go back home tonight, feeling as you do. I don't say I entirely share your suspicions—I do find Mr. MacPherson and the Passerby charming—but you could be right. . . . Besides, things get unbearably lonely here at the Heights. I need another female to talk to—especially one with spunk like you. Someone, if I may say so, of my own sort."

We had walked up the fabulous main staircase, through the hall with its impressive but rather ubiquitous statuary, and to the room I would occupy that night. Its windows faced the edge of the Heights, the highway below and the glass-domed barrier of the Demos Baths and the ocean beyond. Those domes, catching the sunset, appeared to be afire. It was almost impossible to stare at them with the naked eye, and the Demos family was endlessly proud of them, as of the great bathhouse itself.

In answer to her previous remark, I said, "You are kind, but I'm not afraid in most ways. I'm not like you. Father and I were always poor and—"

Mrs. Demos nodded vigorously. "Exactly. And do you think

my father was born mayor of San Francisco? He came to California over the High Sierras with nothing but a pack on his back. He sold the boots he stood in to get eating money when he got to Sutter's Fort . . . I think that should make him poorer than your father."

Tony laughed. He stood there in the beautiful if overly ornamented guest room with his arm around my shoulders, as if to shield me from the vigorous salt wind blowing in through the eternally open windows. "Mama, you act as if being poor were some kind of glory. It's not really. In fact, I can make out a case that it's much better to have money and use it."

"Now, Tony . . ." his mother began, but he went right on.

"Use it to help people. If I could get another ward fitted up, for instance—" he broke off, embarrassed, as we looked at him. "I know. That sounds pompous and—"

"No," I protested, "it's wonderful. You're a thousand times more decent a person than"—out of the corner of my eye I saw Mrs. Demos glance at me—"than lots of people."

Tony changed the subject by hastily indicating his father, who had climbed the road around the Heights and headed into the grounds toward the pillared front of the building.

"Father believes in patronizing his own properties—in this case the Baths."

We all waved to the stout, dark figure of Mr. Demos below us. He called up to us with gestures toward the great domes below the Heights and across the highway. "It's good for you, miss. You must be brave and visit the Baths again. Make the good health." He pummeled his own strong chest and laughed.

But he didn't succeed in enticing me. The old fear remained, and I avoided those blinding glass roofs, turning my attention to my own troubled conscience. When I made a statement to the police I had hedged in my recollection of the horror itself. I hardly mentioned the fact that I believed I was the object of that ax thrust. Everyone seemed to ignore the implication of Mr. Liu's pushing me aside, saving my life. I didn't know how long Neil Burnham had been gone before he appeared there in the thicket where the murderer must have stood as he threw that ax. To the policeman there seemed no doubt. He and Neil had argued for several minutes because Neil had wanted him to wait, to give his friend time to talk with me. Neil had said, "Gil would like to come in of his own volition, not as a result of your call."

Surely, I thought now, that conversation had lasted as long as my conversation with Gilbert Liu. In which case, Neil couldn't possibly have thrown that ax. Besides, even if he were deceiving me and working with Howard for a share of my estate, there were many times when he might more easily have killed me. He might have frightened me by apparent attempts on my life to provoke me into running off before my inheritance came through, leaving it to Polly and thereby Howard. They could get the same result if I did get the inheritance and forthwith turned it over to Polly out of fear for my life—with the same profit for Howard and any accomplice of Howard's. . . .

Maybe it was a Tong War, after all, as the police assumed. The evening papers were already out, several boys selling "extras" at the doors of the Demos Baths, a copy of which Mr. Demos waved at us as he disappeared into the house below us.

"Come along," Teresa Demos commanded her son and me. "Shall we have a glass of something before dinner?" She saw me anxiously smoothing the organdy skirt of my dress. "Now, Mery, you look charming. Don't fret."

In spite of the importance the newspapers gave to the murder of Gilbert Liu, with headlines proclaiming SECOND TONG MURDER, no one mentioned it at dinner, for which I was profoundly grateful. I had no idea what I ate, or even what this meal was. I tried hard to banish from my mind those minutes during the time in the park, but an image kept returning, flickering before my eyes, blurring the present: his face, smooth, unlined, the oblique eyes staring, the gash in his forehead . . . the frontal bone . . .

"Are you all right, Merideth?" Tony asked anxiously.

"Fine, just fine. I was thinking about—I just hope mother is all right."

Mrs. Demos was reassuring as always. "She will be all right. Howard MacPherson looks like a man who can take care of a woman. You know, Mery, all step-parents aren't necessarily villains. Remember how suspicious you were the night of the new play at the Giralda? And yet you were quite safe."

Had Neil lied about that medicine Howard fixed for me? True, I was feeling sick that night before I left Monte's. Howard couldn't very well have poisoned me at Monte's and who else present would have done so? Still, seeing an opportunity, he might have taken advantage of it. . . .

"I don't know," I said. "I don't know what to believe anymore."

They all tried to assure me that I was safe here on the Heights above the very edge of the continent, and I let them believe they had succeeded.

Later that evening at the door of that elegant guest room Tony kissed me good night. I summoned up every bit of excitement I could remember having felt in my life, and responded with a lively counterfeit of real feelings. "Dear Tony," I thought as he went away and I closed the door on the world, "I don't deserve you." I leaned against the door, shaking and cold.

I slept straight through the night, however. I had disturbing dreams but couldn't remember any of them. I was awakened by the housekeeper who announced, as if I were responsible, "The police are anxious to contact you, miss. Likewise a Mr. Burnham."

I sat straight up in bed. "Is he here?"

"Who would that be, miss?"

"Never mind. I'll get up immediately."

The housekeeper coughed. "The information was relayed by telephone." She retired politely but before she left the room I turned in time to catch her looking me up and down. I had no doubt of her opinion: Who is this nobody?

She went out, closing the door quietly.

I washed and dressed, relieved to find that something had happened to my green organdy overnight and it looked like new, no wrinkles, no stains. It cheered me some when I observed my reflection in the standing oval mirror as I combed and brushed my hair. Looking like this, I could meet anyone and be reasonably "prideful," as Grandpa Hyde used to say.

I hurried downstairs, almost losing myself in the labyrinthine rooms of the ground floor. I had forgotten to ask where the family ate breakfast. Somewhere I had read that rich people ate breakfast in their bedrooms, but thank heaven the Demos family was old-fashioned western. After making my way through halls, rooms and passages I found Mr. Demos walking ahead of me. I followed him to the breakfast-room door, where he escorted me in. The little room was done in canary yellow with old rustic furniture painted white, and had a foggy morning view of the incredible Demos grounds and the distant city. If one turned in the other direction the rolling gray Pacific spread out to what seemed infinity.

Teresa Demos had the marvelous ability to make all her acquaintances believe she loved them, but with that special charm went a quality which began to intimidate me. She was forever excusing me for faults I hoped would be overlooked or passed by.

"Mery, my dear girl, a good night's sleep has done wonders for you. Come and sit down here by me. You were very right to enjoy your bed as long as you could. The fog won't lift until after ten and there isn't much to see of the gardens. . . . As soon as you've finished breakfast, that fascinating Passerby fellow is waiting to talk to you in the conservatory."

The idea that he was here in the house, and expecting to see me, was too unnerving. "I don't want to see him, please."

"You don't mean that. Merideth, you must never run away from a confrontation. Meet it head on." She looked at me with fork raised on which a three-layer piece of flapjack dripped honey. "You owe it to my son."

I picked up my water glass to hide my embarrassment. I felt that I was being pushed into something, not only the confrontation with Neil but the rapid substitution of Tony Demos in his place. Almost at once I asked to be excused and hurried out of the room.

Neil Burnham stood at the far end of the semicircular conservatory. I saw his back first. I made my way between exotic, moist plants, a great deal of greenery and occasional rare white flowers called gardenias that scented the whole glass-roofed area and made me think of magic places like the Hawaiian Islands and what Violet Thelma had called the "Anti-podees."

He must have heard me long before I reached him but he didn't turn until we were separated by only about six feet. He looked tired, older than I remembered him, which tended to make him more endearing to me. His smile flickered, faded.

"Good morning, Mery. You ran away so quickly yesterday we didn't have time for explanations. . . . Let's see if you like butter."

It was absurdly like him. At a time such as this he had picked a small California poppy from the grass knoll below a luxuriant bush of magenta-colored Hawaiian blossoms. He held it under my chin and tickled me with it. Indifference was neither easy nor reasonable.

"I made my explanations to the police," I said. "I didn't get a chance to do much talking to Mr. Liu."

He took back the poppy slowly. His eyes looked hurt, quite different from the lively green eyes that had fascinated me.

"I told you I was arguing with that cop. He insisted on walking to a call box. Is it possible—*is it possible* . . . you think I am involved in the murder of my closest friend?" Before I could answer something happened to him. The cold, aloof quality returned; the man standing there in front of me was exactly that cynical, supercilious person I had met for the first time on the streetcar the night I arrived in San Francisco. He then said, "What you think of me is immaterial. Gil believed, as I do, that his father might have meant something particular when he wrote 'Hyde Place' on that newspaper. Had there been any connection between Gil's father and your house that you know of?"

I was intimidated by his tone, the abrupt freeze in his manner. I suppose I must have hoped for some explanation of his behavior, some persuasive words, almost anything that I could accept. But there was nothing—only his chilly assurance that what I thought of him was immaterial.

"I don't understand you," I said. "Your friend told me very little before he was murdered. He showed me a picture of his father. That's about all."

"Then you don't think there is any connection with your own house at 379 Hyde Place?"

I stared at him. Was he trying to find out how far my suspicions ran? And if so, was it because Howard MacPherson wanted to find out how much I knew? Was he perhaps again doing Howard's dirty work?

"I don't know why Gilbert Liu or his father should be connected with my house. Maybe you do. Surely you know my stepfather better than I do. Find out from him and you can help us all."

We heard a man behind us clear his throat. We were both startled to see Lieutenant Jacopo in the open doorway of the house entrance to the conservatory. I wondered how much he had overheard. After that first small movement of surprise, Neil answered my question as though he had not seen the detective.

"I think I told you that I've known MacPherson for less than a month. I had my own reasons for cultivating the fellow. But I can see that you aren't going to believe anything I tell you."

I started to say something, to remind him that I had been told he knew MacPherson in France during the war, but he brushed me off with a slight movement, as if he were dispatching flies.

"Never mind, I've a few ideas of my own," he continued. "I think the answer to nearly everything that's happened to you since you came to San Francisco lies in Chinatown. And when it's all over . . . I'll expect an apology from you. *Not that it matters.*"

This last flat statement, added in a voice icy with rage, startled both myself and Lieutenant Jacopo, who walked toward us. Neil started past me suddenly. I reached out without quite knowing what I intended except to touch and maybe detain him. But he went past me, past the lieutenant, who also put out a tentative, friendly hand. Neil left the conservatory by the small garden door.

Lieutenant Jacopo came over to me with an apologetic shrug. "He's usually very cool, unruffled. What happened?"

"Well, he's angry now. Anyway, angry with me." I started to walk with him along the brick-paved path that went around the semicircular glass-enclosed room.

"We may as well get down to essentials," the lieutenant said. "This new Tong outbreak seems even more mysterious than usual. Did Gilbert Liu mention anything about Chinatown problems to you during the time you talked?"

"He said a Tong War was very unlikely. He had talked with the heads of the Tongs. He showed me a picture of his father, too." I wondered what Mr. Liu had been getting to after that, and I said so aloud. "His glasses! Gilbert made such a point of their not being with the body. . . . He said his father was never without them."

"Obviously they were left where the murder took place. Anything else?"

"Not from Gilbert Liu, except that he probably saw whoever threw the ax, and he pushed me to the ground."

"You are absolutely certain he knocked you down deliberately?"

My voice rose as I tried to make him understand. "To protect me! Only to protect me. He saw that ax aimed at *me*, not at him."

He nodded, but I didn't think he believed me. He was so set on his Tong War theory.

"Yes. That is one theory." Seeing my expression he added hurriedly, "and we are taking it into consideration, believe me."

All the same, by the time he had finished his questioning I could see he was still holding to the idea that the intended victim had been Gilbert Liu and not Merideth Hyde—which made so much more dramatic a case, a Tong War over an assault on a teenage heiress-to-be. To be . . . ?

As he left, I asked him—casually, I hoped—to find out what my stepfather was doing on Sunday afternoon. He looked unsurprised and said, "Of course."

I wondered if he had gotten some information out of Neil Burnham after all.

With Tony Demos at the hospital I became more and more aware that a great house with many servants could become a boring if luxurious prison. Having showed me over the landscaped gardens, Mrs. Demos suggested I might like to go down and see the Baths.

"I should be getting back home."

"Well, anyway, you must stay through tomorrow. It's Tony's

birthday. You must be here for that, to help us with our plans. Otherwise, that Gerda person will interfere. She always wants to run things."

I explained that I would have to get some clothes from Hyde Place, and this finally satisfied her. She suggested I call first to let my family know I was coming, and cowardly as it might be, I did call in order to arrive after Howard MacPherson had gone to rehearsal. There was no answer. All three must be out. As for Polly herself, I had talked to her on the telephone last night. She was all in favor of my spending the night at Demos Heights, and in such spirits she had added, "The most wonderful thing! Miss Falassi called today after you left—on Sunday, mind you— to say you are set. The property is yours. You can sell it immediately, upon the approval of Mr. Cafferetto or Mr. Brubick."

Which hadn't delighted me at all. In spite of my determination to sell only enough property to pay off the debts incurred in my name, I dreaded the furor with those two at Hyde Place when I told them I was going to leave without receiving the hundred thousand dollars they expected. And planned on. . . .

Teresa said, "I'll have our chauffeur drive you across town and back."

I argued briefly and only to be polite. It would make my trip home much easier. As soon as I could I got ready and rode out of the Heights in the splendid isolation of the limousine's back seat.

. . . Wait until the children across Hyde Place see this car, I thought, and wished that Violet and her brothers could be driven around town in such elegant style. As the usual morning fog lifted and the city flashed and gleamed in the sunlight, we drove up Hyde Place, arriving just in time to see the Deutsch children coming down the hill from the new grammar school.

Seeing me get out of the car with my shawl and the ends of my sash flying in the wind, the children ran across the street and crowded around the car. Miles, the chauffeur, a good-looking, sleek young man who held the door open for me, wasn't much interested in children. I went up the long, wooden stairs and pressed the bell. Nobody came to the door, but then I hadn't expected anyone to be home. I got out my key and unlocked the door. It was the first time I had used my own key to the door of a house I owned. It gave me a good feeling.

I looked back down the stairs at the children bouncing around the chauffeur, asking him a thousand questions. I called to him and he looked up at me with considerable relief.

"Miles, would you mind giving the children a ride around the block? Ten minutes or so, just around here? I want to pack some clothes."

Violet and her brothers screamed with delight. She sent the youngest brother running home to tell their mother of their glorious adventure, and I went into the Hyde Place house.

It was rather stuffy. I raised one of the dining-room windows, then went to my room and packed a few more things into Father's carpetbag. How the old house now creaked and cracked, as I began to listen closely. A few minutes ago it had seemed deserted. Then there was a sudden metallic crash below me in the basement, followed by rattling noises. Large rodents down there? The wind howling the length of the high-ceilinged basement? I had no intention of being scared again, or worse, by Howard MacPherson. I carried the carpetbag to the front hall, letting my footsteps be heard on the bare floor of the hall. I opened and closed the front door. Then, quietly as possible, I went back to the inside flight of stairs opening off the dining room. The door was ajar. In my childhood I had discovered how to move silently down those stairs. I did so now.

TWENTY-ONE

I SAW THE LONG scratches on the wall as I went down and I remembered the time I turned abruptly and almost knocked Eve Carpe off her feet. There were other scratches. I wondered how many occurred when one of our tenants had slipped or had some other accident on the stairs. As usual on a sunny day, the basement was light and I could see its entire length to the back-yard door. A whisk broom was propped against the wall near the door, with a dust pan lying beside it. The touring car was gone and in its place was the usual oil stain. Because my life had been made up of practical considerations, wondering constantly how father and I would eat and be sheltered the next week, I looked at the oil stain and wondered how much of my inheritance had to pay for that car. I would let Howard keep it as a sop, so at least he wouldn't take his anger out on Polly when he found they weren't going to be rich, as he had doubtless schemed and hoped.

At any rate nothing mysterious seemed to be going on in the basement. The big, clean room was deserted. The noises had probably come from an ashcan evidently overturned by the draft from the open back window. Whatever had been in the can was now strewn around the basement—mostly garbage, vegetable peelings, old newspapers. I decided the garbage hadn't been put out because of the recent rains. I crossed the basement to the back door, picked up cabbage leaves and newspapers, potato peelings . . .

I came to the dust pan and noted that something in it sparkled, just where the handle joined the pan. It looked to be no more than pulverized glass, which meant nothing to me. I had swept up this sort of thing once before in the basement after Eve Carpe had her bad fall down the inside stairs. But a new idea came to me now.

I rolled the overturned garbage can, placed it upside down on the cement floor in order to scrutinize the inside of it carefully. I might have known nothing incriminating would be found. I didn't even know what I was looking for until I pricked my thumb on a piece of glass and examined the glass itself. Small and thin, but recognizably convex in shape—and I knew why I had been looking for glass . . . the missing eyeglasses that had belonged to Gilbert's father. I held the little piece of convex glass, which had apparently stuck to the bottom of the can when its contents had been thrown out earlier, in the palm of my hand, staring at it.

A piece of Mr. Liu's eyeglasses? How? . . . Mr. Liu . . . Mister—Lew! The man who had called on the telephone and asked to speak with Howard—"Lew" he had said his name was, and his voice had been peculiarly pitched, like an Oriental who did not speak English without accent.

The wind whistled through the basement, tossing a newspaper to my feet. I tore off a piece of the paper, wrapped it around the glass and any bits of pulverized particles I could find. I had the paper in my palm when a blast seemed to shake the entire building and the wind tore past me. I swung around.

The garage doors had been pulled open and I could see Howard MacPherson's huge silhouette against the sunlight in the street beyond. Had he seen me put away those bits of glass?

"Now, what in the world, Mery, are you doing down here all by yourself in the dark?" His stagey voice seemed to be close enough for me to feel his breath across my face, yet we were still separated by the entire length of the basement.

I tried to keep tight hold of myself and said, "You're just in time, I was looking for Polly's old wicker suitcase. I'm staying at the Demos place over Tony's birthday. . . ." He was coming toward me. "Polly mentioned it, said it was over here by the trash can but I've looked everywhere, can you—"

He kept on coming toward me, reached for my arm and caught it. In that sickening stage voice he murmured, "You are lying to me, Merideth. I wonder why."

I tried to avoid him, edging around to get a clear path toward the open garage doors. "Lying? What are you talking about?"

"Polly never told you about any wicker case."

"Why—why not?"

"Because she couldn't possibly know whether a wicker case existed. Now, then, tell me what you were really after."

He reached around for my other hand just as I heard the glorious sound of the Demos limousine's horn. The sound jarred Howard long enough for me to break away and start on a tearing run toward the open doors and the driveway. The Deutsch children had poured out of the car and down the driveway to thank me.

Behind me I heard Howard, breathing a trifle fast, slow to a walk as he also saw the children.

I rushed around Howard's car and into the limousine so fast I didn't use the chauffeur's help or even make a pretense of saying good-by to Howard. Recovering my breath, I asked Miles to go up and get my carpetbag, and when Howard handed it out to him with the utmost courtesy, I said good-by to the children and to that accursed house. The sooner it was sold, the better.

The children had been delighted with their ride and waved to me until the car reached Pompeii Street and turned out of their sight. I asked Miles to drive downtown to the Hall of Justice, where I took a few relieved breaths while explaining my suspicions and showing my evidence to Lieutenant Jacopo. He nodded, considered what I had told him, did not spurn what I offered in the piece of torn newspaper, but neither did he act as detectives had done in novels I had read. I rather expected to be thanked. Instead, I felt the gentle chiding by which he explained that I had diminished the importance of my evidence by not leaving it where I claimed to have found it.

"At any rate, we would need considerably more proof." He saw my expression, and hastily added, "Not that we may not find more proof when we go through the house, as we certainly will. But if the fellow saw you take this, then—you see? He would be a fool to allow evidence to remain for us to pick up. I wish you had left it where you saw it."

Exasperated, I pointed out, "It could still disappear!"

"Very true. But as it is, we have your word that you found it and that is all. Curiously enough, you found the body of the man who—as you suppose—lost the glasses and this little piece of them."

"You don't think I killed him, I hope."

He took this caustic remark as a joke, but I could see that I had done something stupid, even when I explained about the telephone call I took from "Lew" only a few days before Mr. Liu's body was found. Lieutenant Jacopo agreed that this certainly focused attention on the Hyde Place house.

"The man died sometime after this phone call you just mentioned. Probably the next morning." He settled back in his chair. "I can tell you this, Miss Hyde. We've had our eyes on that house for our own reasons. You have been of help to us and we appreciate it."

"But you won't arrest that man . . ."

He got up, which I knew was a signal for me to leave. I wasn't satisfied but felt we were at least a little further than we'd been before he saw the bit of glass and I had remembered the telephone call from "Lew." As I left the building, however, it occurred to me that the deaths of the Chinese father and son involved Neil Burnham almost as much as they involved Howard. But I didn't want to think about that.

I had been so shaken by the happenings at Hyde Place and the bits of evidence that convinced me if not Lieutenant Jacopo that I was relieved to be set to work that night at Demos

Heights. Mrs. Demos instructed and I, along with the servants and the gardener's staff, began to decorate the grounds for Tony's birthday party the next evening. Some of our work was done for nothing, however, as Gerda Edwards appeared on the morning of the party and began countermanding her hostess' decorative ideas.

The evening of the party I looked through my clothes, but there was no question of what I would wear. My other evening dress was the sapphire gown with georgette panels over satin, made in the new harem style with the skirt falling in slim lines to my ankles. It was quite sophisticated, with a low neckline and, of course, no sleeves. 1 was so stunned by the female I saw revealed in it that I couldn't believe in my own mirror image. I walked up and down my room for almost an hour trying to feel natural in it, but it wasn't until Mrs. Demos came in with Polly to see what had delayed me that 1 felt I must look like myself. Teresa Demos brought me an aigret, which she slipped into the sapphire ribbon that confined my hair. It was a style not so popular as formerly, and was, indeed, frowned on by the lovers of that beautiful bird, but it had been hers "at a happy moment," she said, and with that delicate plume rising out of my hair, I felt as though I were wearing a crown.

That was as far as the regal air went, however. The queen of this enterprise remained Teresa Demos, marvelously right in royal-crimson velvet which proved more practical under the onslaught of the Pacific breezes than did many of the transparent silks present. My gauze wrap was also handy, as I wore it around my shoulders, and Polly looked piquant and charming in the green and black she had worn to the opening night of Howard's new play.

"Poor Howard," she murmured, "he's just sick that he can't attend dear Tony's party. But the show must go on, and he is on tonight."

Since I had never been able to satisfy anyone that my suspicions of Howard MacPherson were really justified, I did my best to conceal the slight shiver his name produced in me when Polly and I descended the staircase on either side of our hostess. Several of the guests had already arrived, to be greeted by Mr. Demos in fine fettle, having taken "a sip or two of the fortifying beverage," as he put it.

"I only hope he won't drink the champagne bowls dry," his wife confided to me without, however, showing much disapproval. I smiled. Then I caught sight of Tony standing a little behind his father, looking dark and sturdy, and as if he were not quite at ease dressed in his formal evening clothes. The orchestra struck up a tango in the conservatory, which opened off the ballroom to allow more dancing space. Three couples were already swooping about the room to the applause of the party newcomers.

Word of Mrs. Demos' belated appearance had apparently spread among those standing in the ballroom doorways, at opposite ends of the long room, and most of the heads turned. With a slightly self-conscious pleasure I noticed the gradual focusing of attention on Polly and me. More whispers, especially when Tony left his station near the big front doors to greet the three of us.

"Ladies, I swear I've never seen three lovelier—"

"Never mind," his mother broke in her crisp way, "but Mrs. MacPherson and I can manage for ourselves. Anyway, here is the real belle of the evening." She gave me a little push, sending me down those last few stairs faster than I had intended to travel. Tony caught me. His slightly harassed look as he greeted guests had softened now and he told me, "You look . . . better than I've ever seen you. Radiant."

He went to get me a cup of champagne from the punchbowl. The champagne fascinated me as it had the time I drank it at Monte's Midnight Café, but I was even more impressed by the cut-glass cup itself. I was constantly afraid I would drop and break it until I found a long side table and set the glass down, much relieved.

More and more guests were arriving. Tony was called to greet them and took me with him. I didn't know any of these guests and found it difficult to make conversation with them. As it turned out, I needn't have been concerned about conversation. The gentlemen were jovial and complimentary. The ladies asked countless questions about my relationship to Tony. Had I named the day? Was it true I was the Hyde Place heiress? Had I actually fallen in love with him when he saved me from the flu epidemic?

Tony heard most of these questions and made no effort to correct them. I could only fumble for an answer that wouldn't embarrass him or commit me to anything irrevocable. Stout little Mr. Demos came along and saved me by insisting that I should dance with him. It was a one-step. I'd never had much practice in this rapid dance but I welcomed the interruption and we went into the ballroom, where the floor was now crowded.

As we danced I suddenly caught sight of Gerda Edwards in the far doorway surrounded by young men and looking her vampire-best in what I thought of jealously as "serpent-green," which seemed to swathe her from head to foot. She even wore a turban of a glittering green silk and her plume was much higher than mine. I wondered who had been her escort. Tony was talking to her now, but being interrupted by one or two of the other men.

Mr. Demos was scarcely winded by the time the dance ended and when the orchestra, perhaps influenced by the exotic blooms in the conservatory, struck up "Tales from the Vienna Woods." Mr. Demos grabbed me and started to swing me onto the floor again. As his head barely came up to my chin, I was able to see Neil Burnham step out onto the floor behind him, while I felt myself moving in a dream, saying nothing, making no protest as he tapped my partner on the shoulder. I hadn't seen him enter and I wondered if he could have been Gerda Edwards' escort.

Mr. Demos bowed to me, left me in Neil's arms and went directly to Gerda Edwards. It was one of those minutes both awkward and pleasurable, when I would have given years of my life to have said the right thing. I didn't, though. I said, "Where on earth did you come from?"

And he said, "From the arms of Gorgeous Gerda, of course," which was even less satisfying than my remark.

To waltz in his arms was a dizzying whirl and turn and dip and whirl, until I decided this was his revenge for our quarrel that morning. Like Neil himself, it was unorthodox, breathtaking. I knew during those moments what it must be like to go on loving someone who might be a criminal, a confidence man, perhaps even a murderer.

People had begun to watch us. Teresa Demos, dancing with one of the guests, smiled widely at us, but she kept looking our way until I was sure she still watched from the far end of the room.

Neil must have noticed also, because I found myself maneuvered out into the conservatory seconds before the music ended. Remarking on this maneuver, I said, "You must have been reading women's romances lately."

He didn't regard this as amusing. "I want to talk to you!" There was nothing romantic or forgiving in that voice. I thought we would stop here, wait for the next dance, or even that he would kiss me in spite of that angry voice. I was prepared to cooperate. Instead, he drew me along none too gently, out through that small door onto the Heights and the dark eucalyptus barrier above the cliffs.

"What are you doing? Why can't we talk in the house?"

His face was all light and shadow in the golden flickering of the distant, swinging lanterns. He appeared as cold and angry as he had looked that morning, but I had learned to love even that expression—the curve of his mouth, his eyes that nearly always looked as though he were secretly laughing at the world.

"What did you tell Jacopo today?"

I was so disappointed I jerked away from him, tried to pass him to make my way back to the house, but we were not far from the cliff's edge and he stopped me. "Mery, I've spent the day in Chinatown. I think I've located a friend of yours." It seemed to me his expression softened but his grip on me remained harsh. "Did you learn anything about our friend Gil and his father? Any connection with your stepfather?"

"Mr. Liu called Howard a couple of days before we found him. Neil, please don't—" I was about to say "Don't tell Howard," but I couldn't. If Neil was innocent he would never forgive me. Instead, I told him the rest of what I knew. "And I think it's possible Mr. Liu's glasses were broken in my house. Not that Lieutenant Jacopo agrees with me—or at least he feels that by removing the potential evidence from where I found it I damaged its usefulness and my credibility. What did you find in Chinatown?"

He smiled and his grip relaxed. "So I'm no longer Mac's supporting cast of assassins—"

I rubbed my arms to restore circulation but I was happy in spite of his rough treatment and the wisps of of fog coming in around us. "Let's go back and dance. I'm freezing."

He pulled me to him by one arm. His other hand stroked my hair, pulling out the plume I had been so proud of, and he kissed me. When I could get my breath, he said, "You are going to marry me, you know. In spite of the plans of the redoubtable Mrs. Demos. And the sooner the better." Before I could answer, he added, "That damned inheritance of yours has come between us long enough."

"What shall I do? Throw it away?" I nearly meant it.

"No, you are just going to keep it. I'll pay off the debts that family of yours has run up but you can keep your damned inheritance for our children."

I laughed and felt a pleasure so exquisite it was almost like a dream. "My children?"

"Ours."

Suddenly, lightning seemed to strike my shoulder and left side. Something dark brushed past me briefly and another violent shove sent me tumbling sideways over the cliff's edge. The force of my fall brought Neil to his knees, still holding me by one arm. He dug in among the roots of a huge eucalyptus tree and began to pull me back up over the edge. I scrambled up, heard dirt and pebbles roll past me to the highway thirty feet below.

In the seconds before he dragged me up beside him I had a glimpse of the great Baths across the highway, and through my brain flashed weird, distorted images from a long time ago, things I had long forgotten. . . . I was falling—falling not to the paved highway, but into endless depths of water. I was sinking, flailing my arms, my clothes dragging me down. I could not breathe. I swallowed a vile, strange-tasting water. And then hands pulled me up from that terrible, liquid grave, and the memory faded away.

As Neil dragged me into his arms and we knelt there trying to recover from our narrow escape, people came running from the house, drawn by a scream that I hadn't even known I'd uttered.

Neil looked at me. "What happened? What made you pull away from me like that?"

"I was struck by something. And somebody . . . pushed me."

He glanced over my head at the people who had gathered around us. I didn't need to hear their incredulous remarks to know my would-be murderer had dissolved into the darkness of the eucalyptus grove. Whoever he was, however, he had done me at least one enormous favor. In those seconds that I hung there in space, he had made me relive the horror that had haunted me since my infancy. I knew now why I was terrified of the Demos Baths.

TWENTY-TWO

THANKS TO THE common sense and practicality of Mrs. Demos, the party went on after what I imagine must have been some choice gossip about the Passerby and the Hyde Place heiress found kneeling in each other's arms in the eucalyptus grove. Whatever explanations she made seemed to satisfy everyone except Neil, who had gotten the chauffeur and searched the extensive grounds but found no intruders, which confirmed the crowd in their sly, whispered remarks that "Burnham and Tony Demos' fiancée had been doing a little smooching." Tony took me aside while Neil was brushing himself off and asked me directly if "that fellow" had tried anything.

Too much had happened for me to mince words. "No," I said. "If it hadn't been for Neil, I'd be lying dead on that highway right now. Excuse me, I've got to make a telephone call."

Neil, who was describing my fall to Mrs. Demos and Gerda, looked over at me. I mouthed the word "theater" and he nodded. At Mrs. Demos' advice, everyone began to filter back into the house. I hurried on ahead with Tony, who took me to his father's den where I looked up the telephone number of the Giralda Theatre. An elderly male voice answered, cross at being disturbed.

"Box office closed. Call tomorrow ten A.M."

I said, "I want to speak to Howard MacPherson. He's in the play tonight."

"I know who he is, lady. He's always getting phone calls from females. Four, five a day, but you can't talk to him tonight."

My heartbeat quickened. Studying several raw, scraped marks on my arms, I asked more calmly than I felt, "He isn't playing tonight?"

"Sure, he's playing. He's been on most of the show."

That set me back. There was never more than ten minutes in *The Pine Box* when Howard was offstage. "You are sure Mr. MacPherson's understudy didn't go on tonight?"

"Lady, I know old Mac when I see him. And I can see him right now from where I'm setting."

I thanked him and hung up.

"Satisfied?" Tony asked me lightly, hoping to change the trend of my thoughts, no doubt.

"Yes." I held onto the telephone and called the Hyde Place number. No one answered for eight or ten rings, then I heard a sleepy female voice. It was Eve Carpe. I couldn't even think of an excuse. "Wrong number," I said, and hung up.

I stood there by the telephone, considering all the possibilities while my gaze took in the contents of Mr. Demos' study without being much aware of them. In one corner, beneath a huge oil painting of the Con-Virginia Mine of Virginia City, I saw a little museum-type display on a velvet-covered side table: a sword, slightly tarnished and probably once used by a European, for its pummel was elaborate and nothing like grandpa's Civil War sword. In front of it were several pistols and a small derringer of the wholly impractical kind used by gamblers I had known in Goldfield. When they did fire, they often backfired, blowing the hand off the gambler who used them, usually under the faro table. The little derringer gave me an idea. I said to Tony, "Would you see if you can find out where my mother has gone?"

He hesitated, then went out to the hall. I dashed to the side table and took up the derringer. The short barrel was split and the pistol would never fire, but I didn't intend to fire it. I quickly replaced the six-shooter and the other guns so that a casual glance would not reveal anything missing. When Tony looked in at me again, I joined him in the hall.

"She's upstairs with mother," he told me. "By the way, that—fellow is waiting to see you."

I knew very well who "that fellow" was. Neil had been waiting by the newel post of the great staircase and he came to me now. Even though I knew Tony was watching, I returned Neil's tender good-night kiss with a tenderness of my own that brought back his light humor and put the sparkle back in his eyes, which now seemed to me irresistible. He told me he would meet me tomorrow and take me to Chinatown. "Don't go anywhere until I come for you. Don't trust—well, just don't go anywhere alone, even on the estate. Promise?"

I promised. "You do believe, finally, that someone threw something at me, and then pushed me tonight?"

"I couldn't miss the jolt you gave me when that tree limb hit you. Of course I believe you."

My recent telephone check had puzzled me, though, and I ran after him to keep Tony from hearing. "Howard was at the theater all evening."

"The shadow I saw was too small for Mac. I've been following him all over town lately, even to those infernal Baths. I think he was trying to rig up something there."

"He did! He made me look like a clumsy fool, complaining about him. Tony thought I was imagining things."

"Exactly. That's one of the reasons I didn't want you to turn that perfectly innocent headache remedy over to Demos. He would have reacted just the way Mac intended."

I shivered. Neil shook my shoulders in a friendly way and I saw Tony at the end of the hall bristle, start forward, then stop. Neil said, "Don't worry. I'll see to Mac. I'll tell you how I think it all fits if I get a little cooperation in Chinatown. Promise not to leave the Heights until I get here tomorrow."

"I told you I wouldn't. I won't go anywhere except to the Baths across the road. I must go there. And I'll take Mr. Demos for protection."

"All right. But be ready by noon." He kissed me again, and left.

Tony came along the hall to join me as I went upstairs. The rest of the party was going in to ten o'clock supper. Obviously, the excitement of the "accident" was all over and they could get back to the enjoyment at hand. I only wished I could. Tony said, "I still don't trust that fellow. Are you sure you do?" He knew from my expression what my answer would be, and held up one hand. "Never mind, I know. You're obviously taken with him. God knows why."

And I certainly couldn't explain why to Dr. Tony. After all, my reasons were highly unscientific.

We met Polly and Mrs. Demos in the room I was assigned upstairs. Mrs. Demos had brought Polly a pretty outing-flannel nightgown with pink ribbons. Somehow, in the excitement, I had forgotten that Polly would share this room with me tonight, and I wanted to laugh, with a slight touch of hysteria, when Mrs. Demos said, "You'll feel better with your mother tonight, dear. Sleep well, both of you. Tomorrow all these nasty accidents will have become a thing of the past."

Polly was twittering a bit at the idea of sleeping in this beautiful room, and worse, borrowing her hostess' lovely nightgown, but when the door closed and we were alone, she smiled and hugged herself with joy. "Isn't it wonderful? I've dreamed of living in a place like this."

Although I was still badly shaken by my second near-miss in forty-eight hours, I felt a twinge of regret, knowing now how much her dream of this life must have influenced her to join Howard in his schemes. The question remained: How far had she gone with him? As for my own taste for the luxuries of Demos Heights, I couldn't seem to feel comfortable with all this wealth. The beautiful clothes, the splendor tonight meant little to me. It wasn't the background I loved, but a man named Neil Burnham. And as for Tony, it was impossible to think of him without this rich background, his remarkable if formidable mother, and all the elegance of the Heights. Neil was the man I loved, and I thanked God I'd cleared away my suspicions of him.

I wished I could as easily have swept away my suspicions of Polly Hyde. I slept badly that night, without even a dream of Neil. Nor was I frightened as I had been earlier after the ghastly business in the eucalyptus grove. Or the uncertainty of my suspicions at Hyde Place. Now I felt I knew the answer to the deepest mystery that had troubled me so long. I wasn't wandering in the dark. I felt I knew at last the truth about Polly Hyde.

What really troubled me now was Polly's presence when I wanted to think, and though she carefully kept to her side of the bed, and breathed lightly, there were so many questions I wanted to ask her that I dared not ask yet out of fear she'd warn Howard . . .

Each time I woke up that night I looked over and saw her face against her pillow, and more than once I saw her eyes wide open, as though studying me, reading my mind?

In the morning after that long night Tony went early to a clinic, Mrs. Demos was sleeping late, and I had to dress rapidly to head off Mr. Demos before he went down from the Heights to the Baths. He was on his way out the front door when I caught him.

"Ah, my dear Merideth, you are feeling better after that terrible misstep last night?"

"Much better. I know everyone had a wonderful time, except for—my misstep, but I wondered if my mother and I could visit the Baths with you this morning, perhaps wander about and get our bearings before the customers come in." I was sure he was going to tell me he would be busy and unable to escort us, which suited me admirably. "While you're at your work, we could just get an idea of how grand the place is. Walk around the tanks. Look at all your wonderful exhibits, and the swimming medals . . ." He was becoming more enthusiastic by the minute and it didn't take him long to become the willing host for Polly and myself, though he reminded me, "I must make out the monthly payroll this morning. You understand, young lady, you will be—as they say—on your own behavior."

Nothing could have been better. I ran upstairs and got Polly out of bed. She was too sleepy to understand and I had to help her dress, but we showed up at the front door in ten minutes and Mr. Demos proudly escorted us out along the estate drive to the big open redwood gates. As we strolled around the curve in the Great Highway, I looked up at the place where I had nearly fallen last night. The roots of a eucalyptus crawled over the edge of the cliff, holding the ground together. But for that,

I had little doubt that the earth itself would have given way and I would have fallen, perhaps dragging Neil with me.

Polly tripped a couple of times over the hem of one of my long dresses that she was forced to wear in place of the gorgeous black-and-green evening gown she'd worn the previous evening. Mr. Demos unlocked the doors of the Baths, which were at the top of a long, plunging flight of steps that led past the offices on the first landing and past long tiers of seats to the first of the tanks below.

The fog had cleared away from the ocean, and sunlight filtered through the glass roof. With none of those screaming, laughing voices that I'd heard on my night visit with Tony, I was conscious now of the many echoes produced in the silence of the great empty building. Water was pouring into the far tanks, probably filtered sea water, and I wondered how many workmen and cleaning men were within sight of the high springboard.

I remarked to Mr. Demos, "You must feel very lonely here at this hour of the morning, or is this huge place full of unseen workmen?"

As Polly shivered and huddled closer to me, Mr. Demos said proudly, "No workmen this early, only me." As we came opposite the offices, the sound of running water stopped abruptly and Mr. Demos went on in triumphant proof of his boast, "That was Guido. He has finished his night's work. He goes home now, this minute. Always from the tidal pools to his car beside the carbarns, and then home. The cleaners left an hour ago." He teased Polly with a ferocious face. "We are alone. Are you frightened, ladies?"

We laughed obediently. Polly managed to control the uneasiness that I felt in her and counted on, and Mr. Demos pointed out the whereabouts of such choice items as a miniature California mission, and a mummy complete with sarcophagus.

"Moths have done some damage," he confessed.

But he was anxious to get to his payroll reports and we left him in his room behind the locked box office. As Polly and I moved down the steps toward the first of the pools the tension began to grow in me. My only consolation was that Polly was even more nervous.

"Really, dear, I don't know why you've changed your mind about this place. You always said it frightened you."

I shrugged. "I thought you would like to see the museum. It is really quite remarkable—photographs and relics of the fire, for instance. Up here. Aren't those glass roofs wonderful? Just look up there."

With her mind on the huge girders and curving roof overhead, she went with me up another tier, becoming genuinely interested in the spacious interior. She had gotten her mind off my own peculiar behavior and now forgot to wonder why I wanted her so high above the tanks, whose blue-green waters shifted gently as I glanced down at them below the high diving board and the upper tiers. It was easy to picture how these tiers must have looked during those world-championship meets held here during the last few years, when every tier was full of eager, cheering spectators.

But before we got to that height, there was the diving board. It was reached by its regular flight of steps, but it could also be reached if one took a very long step from the rail of the middle tier of seats to the base of the springboard. We had now come to this spot. Aside from the echo of the waters below, there was no real sound in the great interior.

I waited until Polly was exactly opposite the springboard and still looking up at the girders. Then I said abruptly, *"Who are you?"*

She opened her mouth, started to say something, and looked about in sudden confusion. I felt sorry for her but I would not let her know that. She managed, "You are pushing me, dear. Please, let me by."

I crowded her against the salt-sticky railing. Her back arched over it in her effort to avoid me as I forced her. "I know you are not Polly Hyde."

"But I am!"

All the uncertainties, the doubts and terrors and near-misses I had gone through since I'd met this woman had coalesced into my coldly deliberate actions now. I said, "Duck your head under the rail."

"Merideth, are you crazy?"

I slipped the derringer into the palm of my hand. I don't think she had ever seen a gun before. It was clear that, unlike my mother and me, she had not been brought up in mining country. She was so terrified she could hardly carry out my order. With my free hand I pushed her shoulder a little and she fell to her knees. She ducked under the rail, staring back at me. Far below her was the nearest swimming tank, its waters seething with a mysterious motion of their own. I could well understand a part of her fear. I had once almost died from this height. I knew the danger.

"Mery, please . . . I'll lose my balance. You know I can't swim."

"My mother swam very well." She shook her head, but I went on, just as I'd planned all during the night. "She brought me out here long ago, probably when I was just learning to walk. She'd been drinking and sat down along here somewhere. Maybe she was sleepy. I don't know. Someone had been working on the diving board. There was a plank from this floor to the board and I crawled out on it. And I fell into that tank."

She looked down, shivery. "Is— That's why you're afraid of swimming tanks and pools. Mery, please put that thing away."

I hadn't needed the broken derringer, after all. I was convinced now that she would tell me what I wanted to know— she was on the verge of hysteria. "When I tumbled off that board, my mother screamed for help. I think I remember that sound. Then she dove from that board, clothes and all, and brought me up from the tank." I remembered only snatches of this, but she would have no way of knowing. I pushed her. "Go on, prove you are Polly Hyde. Walk out on that diving board. There isn't the handy plank we had in my day, but you can reach it from here."

"No! I'm not . . . I'd drown . . . she said they wouldn't hurt you, she said you'd never miss the share you gave us."

"She? You mean Eve Carpe, don't you? And just who is Howard MacPherson? Or rather *what* is he to you and Miss Carpe?"

She looked down, then away quickly. "Mery, I'll scream—"

"Scream away."

She believed my bluff. "I didn't want to do anything to harm you at Monte's restaurant, but Eve said you prowled around too much at night and if I put a few grains of a sleeping powder in your food you'd get a good night's sleep. I hated it, I was afraid but it *was* only a few grains . . ."

Whatever it had been, I thought, it wasn't sleeping powder. Probably a very minute amount of a common rat poison, just enough to make me sick briefly.

"Mery, I found out later that they *wanted* you to complain about that stomach remedy Howard made for you at home. They weren't worried that anybody would trace the restaurant food, even if you left any to be traced. If right after you got home Howard gave you a stomach remedy and you were feeling increasingly bad, they decided, it was a good gamble that you'd blame how you felt on the powders Howard gave you and not the restaurant food. When you complained about the powders, even if you had them analyzed, you'd be proved wrong because there was nothing wrong with them."

So this was why Howard had made his behavior so obvious that night. He *wanted* me to be suspicious that something was wrong with the powders. And when Mery with her poor over-active imagination began to accuse him, he'd quickly be shown to be innocent and I'd be even more certifiably unreliable in my suspicions of him—which cleared the way for him to get away with what he wanted. No amount of incriminating evidence would be very persuasive against him in the face of my endless false accusations . . . It was really very clever, and very frightening.

And if it hadn't been for Neil, it would have worked out that way. I would have browbeaten Tony, insisting that Howard was trying to kill me, and Tony would have been sadly doubtful and unintentionally played into their hands. I said, "You look very much the way my mother looked years ago. Where did they find you?"

"Mery, let me get up . . ." I made no move to help her and, still kneeling on the floor, she held tight to the rail. "It was because I looked like a picture Howard had that gave them the idea. Eve is my daughter. I am Esther Carpe. I was once

233

an actress myself, in stock companies. Eve was with me. Very good, too, but not many jobs. We came to San Francisco and she met Howard."

Well, that explained much about how they must have involved this essentially decent woman. I wondered if she knew about Mr. Liu's connection with Howard, or that Eve or Howard, probably Howard, had tried to kill me with that ax in Golden Gate Park. And last night, in the eucalyptus grove? I put the derringer away but waited to give her a hand until I'd asked, "Why did they try to kill me? They can't get my property until I've made out a will to you—to Polly Hyde as my mother, and I haven't. Of course, as my mother, you would be the next of kin, and Howard as your husband—"

"Tried to kill you? Oh no, please don't say that . . . all the same, you shouldn't have signed that paper that gave Howard and me the right to handle all your legal affairs."

It was my turn to be shocked. "I didn't. I've never signed any papers." But I had! Something about a few dollars refunded to previous tenants. I had examined the papers, read them carefully, and then the pen fell, *thanks to Eve Carpe*. I remembered searching around on the floor, picking it up and then signing the papers *without rechecking them*. There must have been a switch and I must have signed an agreement giving them my power of attorney, or whatever they needed, at that time. No wonder I saw Howard so soon afterward at my lawyers' offices with the sheaf of blue-backed legal papers! He couldn't wait to get them into Brubick's hands.

Whatever else she told the police would not interest me so much as the all-important matter: She was not Polly Hyde. The realization was painful. I felt lost again. I began to help her up. Her knees buckled and it was an effort. "Mrs. Carpe, how did your daughter and her—and Howard know so many things about my mother?"

She shook her head. "They never told me," and I believed her. "We couldn't get jobs. The flu epidemic was on. Everyone was in a panic. We were desperate. And then Eve met Howard . . both actors . . . they'd met overseas . . . and saw that picture of your mother. I don't know how he got it."

I tried to lift her up so she could stand on her delicate high heels, but as she began to rise I heard a footfall on the boardwalk at the end of the tier. I didn't want Mr. Demos to find me browbeating my "mother" and looked around quickly.

Howard MacPherson was running toward us. There was no mistaking the look on his face. He had heard at least a part of Mrs. Carpe's confession and undoubtedly guessed the rest. I pushed Mrs. Carpe aside and ran, calling to Mr. Demos for help and hearing the weird echo of my voice like a rondeau sung and repeated from all parts of the Baths. Mr. Demos would surely come out of his office at any minute, and a man with his collection of weapons at home should certainly have a gun in his office, handy to the cashier's cage.

It was unlucky, though, that Howard was between me and the staircase going up past the offices, but the echo of my voice, my shouts would certainly carry through to Mr. Demos. I scrambled over a row of seats, got onto the tier opposite Howard, separated from him by one of the smaller tanks.

"It's no use, Howard," I called to him across the rippling blue-green depths below. "Mr. Demos will hear me."

"Try a loud scream, Merideth. He's on his way to a small accident down the highway. I'm afraid Eve ran into the corner of the Cliff House."

And I did scream, calling Mr. Demos again, but by now, with my throat raw, I knew it was true that Dr. Demos had been enticed away. I edged along the tier, hoping to find a way to the water level where I might reach the entrance staircase. There were intricate catwalks all over the Baths between the tanks. I had only to reach the right one. At the end of the tier I took the steep steps downward at a run, trying to give out a call for help that would raise ghosts in the deserted Cliff House half a block beyond the window of Mr. Demos' office.

Across two tanks Mrs. Carpe stood where I had left her, leaning against the rail and wavering.

"Run," I called to her. "Get help." It was no use. She was staring as if hypnotized, awaiting her orders from Howard.

I had just reached the narrow walkway between tanks and started across in a breathless run when I saw his long arm pass in front of me and I was picked up like a toy and hurled through the air, over the rail, into the waters of the tank. I struggled blindly, seeing and understanding nothing for a second or two except a world of water, an infinity of space overhead up to the girders and the roof. And, always, the waters in my mouth, my eyes, my ears, my clothing pulling me down, gradually becoming saturated and heavy. The shock and suddenness of it made me a panicky drowning child again.

I heard muffled noises, came to conscious awareness of what had happened, and saw that Howard was trying to shove my head under as I sputtered and strangled.

Mrs. Carpe had finally come out of her trance and was calling out, "No! Someone will come, leave her, they will never believe it . . ."

Above my struggles, Howard said, "But they'll believe you, her mother. The clumsy girl fell just once too often—"

I tried to rise under his hand, to bite him, but he sent me under again. My throat seemed bursting.

The whole of the enormous Baths roared with what appeared to be two explosions. The pressure on my head was eased. A heavy weight crashed into the water, striking my shoulder, though I scarcely felt it. There was so much noise I thought my head would burst. . . . Then a great splash as Howard MacPherson sank below the surface, Mrs. Carpe's hysterical screams, and Mr. Demos, far below, shouting, "What is it? What is happening?"

Now I was being drawn out of the water, and looking down at me, very pale, totally unlike his urbane self, was Neil Burnham. He had never looked better to me.

TWENTY-THREE

❧

"THE STAGE LOST A fine, old-time matinée idol when Howard MacPherson died," Mrs. Demos said. She sighed. "I wish you had confided in me," and offered me a glass of her husband's best vintage wine. Her heart wasn't on my reply. She was trying to eavesdrop on Neil and Mr. Demos, who were discussing the whole terrible business with Lieutenant Jacopo.

I said, "I'm sorry, but I had no proof against Howard and nobody would believe me."

"Ghastly business," she agreed. When the conversation at the other end of the room had gotten down to technicalities, she looked at me again. "I suppose there is no chance of our having you in the family. . . . I have an awful premonition I'll end up with Gorgeous Gerda."

Lieutenant Jacopo looked around at us. "Miss Hyde, are you ready for our drive into Chinatown?"

I got up and set my wine glass back on the table. I was anxious to find out what Neil had discovered in Chinatown, and also what the lieutenant had learned from questioning Eve Carpe and her mother—the woman I had known as "Polly Hyde." But I also knew this was the end of a pleasant, comfortable relationship with the Demos family, and so I was sad when we reached the front door, where Mrs. Demos with tears in her eyes hugged me, and her husband kissed me on the forehead.

"I'm sorry about the derringer," I told him again. "I shouldn't have taken it without telling you."

He shrugged. "It should have been a loaded pistol. Then you could have shot that unspeakable fellow."

As Neil and I were getting into Lieutenant Jacopo's car, Mrs. Demos called to me, "Tony will be down to that Chinatown address with the ambulance crew."

I didn't know what she meant, but Neil and the lieutenant nodded and we started off, this time up around the Heights and into town. I sat between the lieutenant and Neil, squeezed warmly, protectively in the front seat as the two men continued what must have been a discussion begun after the detective returned to the Demos house from questioning the Carpe women.

"Burnham, the only thing that keeps you out of jail is Mrs. Carpe's testimony that you yelled at MacPherson from those steps before you fired. You had no legal authority to kill MacPherson, and you know it. You're lucky Mrs. Carpe agrees you saved Miss Hyde's life. Otherwise you might well be brought up on murder charges. Two bullets in his back . . ."

"I did call to him, warned him," Neil put in. "I heard Merideth call out before I even entered the Baths. I was too far away to jump onto him and save the day with proper heroics. Besides"—he grinned—"I might have lost."

With Neil's arm around me, I said, "A second or two later and I'd have gone down for the last time, I can tell you." I felt the muscles in Neil's arm tighten behind my neck and I looked at him. Even some five hours after the horror of my encounter with Howard MacPherson he looked tense, though his grin was again his own, thank heaven! As for me, my throat was sore from yelling, my nose pained from the water I'd breathed in, and I still found my legs shaky after all that running up and down stairs.

As for Eve Carpe, whose presence outside the Cliff House with Mr. Demos had warned Neil of my danger, she apparently was proving as talkative as her mother. Lieutenant Jacopo told us now that according to Eve, currently in the city jail, everything was Howard's idea, and that she and Mrs. Carpe were innocent lambs who had fallen under the wicked man's spell. I didn't believe it and told the lieutenant so. He agreed.

"No doubt about two things. It was Eve Carpe who tried to kill you last night on the Heights. She had to work fast, and it certainly was accepted by everyone except you and Burnham as one more of those clumsy accidents you seemed prone to."

"I called her afterward . . ." I thought about that and now realized over half an hour had gone by since the "accident" when I had made the telephone call—time enough for her to get home and pretend to have been wakened when I called . . . It would have been awkward for her, though, if she had been stopped for speeding or had had an accident. "What was the second thing you mentioned?"

The lieutenant said, "The old Chinese's fingerprints are all over the inside staircase at your Hyde Place house. Miss Carpe claims he had come to see MacPherson on business—"

"What business?" I asked.

"That's what you are going to find out in Chinatown," Neil said.

The lieutenant went on, "Old Liu saw the Carpe girl in the garage, about to close the doors. He followed her in and persisted in his complaints and demands to see MacPherson. When she ordered him to leave, he followed her up the inside stairs. The way we figure it, she swung around to order him out again, hit him with her arm or hand and the old man lost his balance, scratched at the wall trying to get a hold on something, then tumbled down the stairs, cracking his head."

"I know when it happened," I cut in, suddenly remembering that series of tumbles followed by Eve Carpe's claim that she had fallen. "I always thought she was more frightened than hurt. She'd disguised his fall by a contrived one of her own."

"There's a scene like that in MacPherson's play," Neil put in. "The murderer's victim is thrown over a balcony and to disguise the noise, the murderer pretends to have fallen. How appropriate."

I added, "She must have hidden the body in the cellar somewhere until Howard came home and got rid of it after dark with all that Tong rigmarole to make it look like another

Chinese had killed him. I thought Howard and Eve were awfully nervous that afternoon."

Neil nodded. "Mac would have had to move pretty fast. You or Mrs. Carpe might have gone down to the basement at any time. Mrs. Carpe has proved a pretty unreliable ally for them, I'm glad to say."

"I'm sorry for her," I told him. "I believe she didn't know about the murders, or what they planned for me. Howard boasted to me in the Baths—he was sure I'd never survive to tell it—that he had tried to kill me in Golden Gate Park. He said throwing that Tong ax was at least one thing he'd learned in Chinatown . . . Is that why we're going there in all this hurry?"

Both men told me to take it easy, that they would handle everything. In view of my own record, I was pleased to hear it.

For the last ten minutes of our ride the men stopped talking. They seemed to become increasingly subdued, and I caught Lieutenant Jacopo glancing at me now and then in the rear-view mirror.

"I haven't turned into a pumpkin," I said at last, a caustic edge to my voice.

The smile I expected from the lieutenant was forced. He parked on old Dupont Street, lately a continuation of down-town's elegant Grand Avenue which split Chinatown in two. I looked around. It seemed to me that more Occidentals had poured onto these narrow sidewalks, shopping, peering into the dark, shadowed windows of small stores. Yet behind all this trimming was the real life of the district, the saffron-smooth faces immobile to white outsiders only. Shopkeepers were in their dark shops, ignoring us as we passed them, reading their Chinese newspapers or working accounts on a beaded abacus.

I said, "I remember I came here the night I arrived in town. A funny old lady took me up that alley to rent a room. I wonder if Mr. Liu could have seen me that night."

Neil and Lieutenant Jacopo exchanged glances. This time I couldn't be mistaken. "Is that what this is all about? Mr. Liu saw me that night? Or Howard—Howard saw me?"

"Probably," the lieutenant said, which only added to my curiosity.

We turned off Dupont and started into a crowded, picturesquely squalid alley. We were about three blocks from Mrs. Angel Ybarra's rooming house, where I had gone that first night. I thought a great deal about the woman who had tried to get money from me and then stolen a little in her masquerade as my mother.

"Funny," I remarked aloud, "she wasn't half the fraud the other Polly Hyde—Mrs. Carpe—turned out to be."

Neil said nothing but looked abruptly at Lieutenant Jacopo, and I began to have a premonition . . . I was hurrying now, Neil holding my hand. I turned my fingers and closed them nervously around his knuckles.

"Neil! You've found Polly Hyde? You've found my mother?"

He raised our locked hands to my cheek, rubbed his knuckles along my jaw. There was a gentleness about all this which warned me.

"She's ill?"

"Dying," said the lieutenant quietly.

Neil cut in, "For God's sake, Jock, couldn't you put it a little less bluntly?" But I understood the lieutenant. It was better to know and be prepared. It hurt like a dull, deep ache. Regret, mostly, for the lost years when I could have known her and maybe taken care of her. I could have loved her, anyway.

Lieutenant Jacopo, walking ahead of us, started into a little hole, dark as a coal cellar, on the ground floor. The door was made of slats and many of these were cracked or broken out entirely. The interior smelled of something sickly sweet, a kind of smoky air that made me look for a handkerchief to breathe through.

Then I forgot the awful squalor and the smells. I saw the woman in the bed, her small face seamed and pugnacious as it had been that first night in San Francisco when she accosted me, a face strong and mean and lively, but only the watery hazel eyes were lively now. A thin Chinese girl in a crisp nurse's uniform stood behind the bed up against a wall on whose ancient paper everything in the world seemed to have accumulated.

Polly Hyde drew a long, painful breath. "Didn't believe I was your ma, did you? Dumb, like your pa." Her fingers groped for me. They were skeletal. "But you're not weak, Mery . . . stronger'n Jeff. Stronger'n me. Thought you were going to die that night. You were sick, kid . . . Now, stronger'n me, by a damn long shot."

I took her fingers and kissed them. "*You* saved my life that night, mother. Nobody else knew I had the flu, including myself."

She closed her eyes briefly. "Nice feller you sent me last night. He got the nurse. Fed, took care of me. Pret' near starved after Old Liu never come back. He got scared, you know. Give me too much of the smoke. Went off to Egon to get help . . . never back."

I looked up at Neil. "You brought the nurse? Thank you." He nodded. I said, "What happened to make her like this? She was all right when we met a month ago."

Lieutenant Jacopo sounded angry—at the world, at himself, at the man who had been the final instrument in the destruction of the woman who had once been called "pert, pretty Polly Hyde." He said so aloud. "She's been under opiates since you arrived in the city. Since she got out that night and met you, apparently. It was her pimp—I beg your pardon, Miss Hyde, but what else can you call a man who lives off a woman?— Well, he kept her here full of liquor and opium, with Old Liu as hired watchdog, while he played out his part to rob and murder her daughter."

Neil cut in with the calm that I knew from experience covered his deepest feelings. "And you were concerned when I shot that rotten—"

I was looking at each of them in turn. "You mean her—friend—was Howard? But the night I met her she called her boyfriend Egon. She said Egon didn't like her working south of Market. And for this Egon, or Howard, to find a woman who looked like mother!" "What luck!"

"Not according to Mrs. Carpe. Remember, they'd met before. And she says he planned at first to use your mother, force her to make a claim on you. She told him at some point you'd probably come into some money. This was even before you put the ad in the paper. Then Egon took up with Eve again, a shrewd girl who saw the similarity between her mother and the old album pictures of the real Polly. After that, it was simple. He would get the facts from the real Polly and pump them into